Praise for Violet and Boy's

PERFECT ADVENTURES

"A creepy, magical tale of bravery and self-belief."
Sunday Express

"Full of the adventure, mystery and sinister goings on…"
Rachael, Waterstones bookseller

"This is one of those books that you think about when you're
not reading it and can't wait to find out what happens next."
Tom Fletcher

"Brimming with humour, intrigue, danger and thrilling
adventures…"
Lancashire Evening Post

"Helena Duggan builds an intriguing world
and tells a gripping story…"
The Scotsman

"A quirky, intriguing novel…"
Through the Looking Glass (blogger review)

"A creepy adventure story full of twists and turns…"
Scoop magazine

D0280640

For Robbie, my Boy

First published in the UK in 2019 by Usborne Publishing Ltd., Usborne House, 83-85 Saffron Hill, London EC1N 8RT, England. usborne.com

Copyright © Helena Duggan, 2019

The right of Helena Duggan to be identified as the author of this work has been asserted by her in accordance with the Copyright, Designs and Patents Act, 1988.

Cover illustration by Karl James Mountford © Usborne Publishing, 2019

Map and "The Story so Far" illustrations by David Shephard © Usborne Publishing, 2019

The name Usborne and the devices ♀ ⊕ are Trade Marks of Usborne Publishing Ltd.

A CIP catalogue record for this book is available from the British Library.

ISBN 9781474964371 05324/1 JFMAMJ ASOND/19

Printed in the UK.

THE BATTLE FOR PERFECT

HELENA DUGGAN

USBORNE

CONTENTS

THE STORY SO FAR

IN CASE YOU'VE FORGOTTEN

1. DR EUGENE BROWN ARRIVES IN PERFECT WITH VIOLET.

2. THE ARCHER BROTHERS ARE HIDING A BIG SECRET.

3. VIOLET RECEIVES A PAIR OF ROUND-RIMMED GLASSES THAT REVEAL BOY AND NO-MAN'S-LAND.

4. BOY AND OTHER ORPHANS IN NO-MAN'S-LAND HELP VIOLET UNCOVER WHAT'S GOING ON.

5. THE ARCHER BROTHERS USE TEA AND THEIR GLASSES TO CONTROL THE PEOPLE OF PERFECT.

6. THE WATCHERS WORK FOR THE ARCHER BROTHERS, GUARDING PERFECT AND STEALING IMAGINATIONS.

7.

IMAGINATIONS ARE STORED IN JARS AND HIDDEN AWAY IN THE ARCHERS' EMPORIUM.

8.

VIOLET DISCOVERS THE GHOST ESTATE WHERE THE ARCHER BROTHERS GROW THEIR EYE PLANTS.

9.

BOY'S MAM, MACULA ARCHER, IS A PRISONER IN A ROOM IN THE GHOST ESTATE.

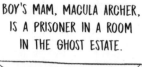

10.

WILLIAM ARCHER DEVELOPS THE REIMAGINATOR — A MACHINE TO GIVE PEOPLE BACK THEIR IMAGINATIONS.

11.

PERFECTIONISTS AND NO-MAN'S-LANDERS UNITE TO DEFEAT THE ARCHER BROTHERS AND THE WATCHERS.

12.

THE GATE BETWEEN PERFECT AND NO-MAN'S-LAND IS KNOCKED DOWN.

≥ WELCOME TO TOWN! ≤

PLEASE TURN OVER...

13.

GEORGE ARCHER AND THE WATCHERS ARE IMPRISONED IN THE TOWN HALL. EDWARD HAS DISAPPEARED.

14.

AS STORM CLOUDS GATHER ROBBERIES BEGIN TO HAPPEN IN TOWN.

15.

CONOR CROOKED AND BEATRICE PRIM GO MISSING. BOY IS BLAMED FOR ALL THE BAD THINGS HAPPENING IN TOWN.

16. VIOLET IS ATTACKED BY A MONSTER.

17. BOY SAYS THINGS THAT MAKE NO SENSE AND IS ACTING VERY STRANGELY.

18. VIOLET IS CAPTURED BY NURSE POWICK AND THE CHILD SNATCHER, AND IMPRISONED WITH BEATRICE AND CONOR.

19. EDWARD ARCHER SEEMS TO RESCUE THE CHILDREN AND RETURNS TO TOWN A HERO. GEORGE IS RELEASED.

20. THE ARCHER BROTHERS PLOT TO RETURN TO POWER BY DIVIDING THE TOWNSFOLK. BOY APPEARS TO BE WORKING WITH THEM.

21. JACK NOTICES TWO BOYS IN A PHOTO VIOLET FOUND IN THE ORPHANAGE. BOY HAS A TWIN BROTHER.

22. VIOLET AND JACK DISCOVER THE OUTSKIRTS AND RESCUE THE REAL BOY.

23. THE ARCHER BROTHERS REVEAL THEIR SINISTER PLOT TO TAKE BACK TOWN AND ARE ARRESTED.

TOWN TRIBUNE
THE ARCHER GEEZERS BACK IN THE SNEEZER

24. MACULA ARCHER DIES IN A TUSSLE WITH NURSE POWICK AS SHE TRIES TO RESCUE BOTH HER SONS.

MACULA

AND SO OUR STORY CONTINUES...

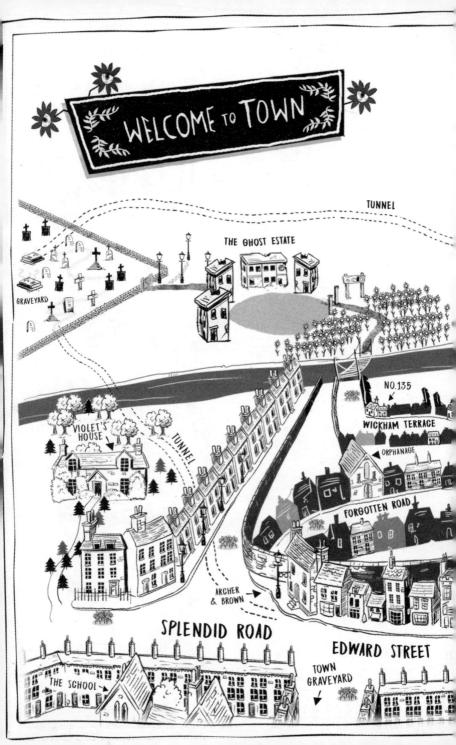

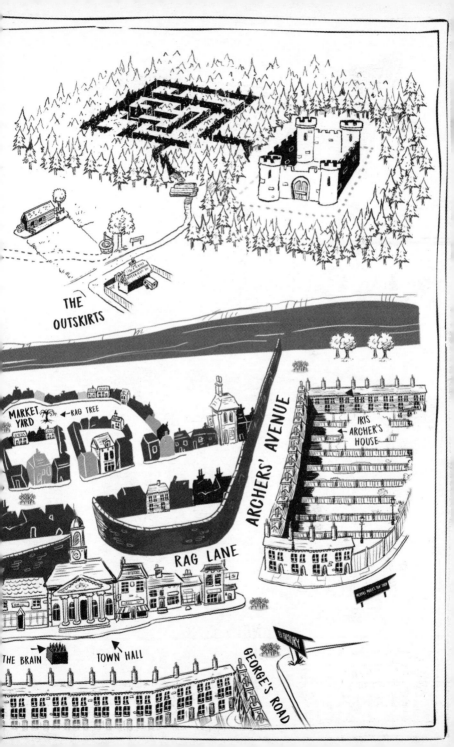

CHAPTER 1

BOY'S BIRTHDAY

Violet stared at the miniature eye plant blinking inside a small glass box. She shivered as the creature turned and looked straight at her, its translucent skin-like petals flapping slowly as its thin red stem pulsed with the blood that fed it.

Eugene Brown, Violet's dad, clad in his white lab coat, was busy scribbling some sort of complicated maths equations on a blackboard across the room to her left, a cloud of chalk dust surrounding him. Her best friend, Boy, was scratching his head, sitting at the large steel table in the middle of the room as he tried to tackle the homework Mrs Moody had set them. The summer holidays had only just finished and Boy was finding it hard to get back into the swing of school. His struggles hadn't been helped by Mrs Moody's workload.

They were in the cellar of Archer and Brown, the town optician's. It was a much nicer place now than when it had been owned by Boy's evil uncles, Edward and George, and known as the Archer Brothers' Spectacle Makers' Emporium. The cellar used to be where the Watchers, Edward and George's vicious army of thugs, had hung out and it had been a cold, unwelcoming room. Rough hammocks had hung from the bare stone ceiling on large metal hooks and old wooden crates were used as tables and storage around the space. It had smelled too, of large, sweaty, hairy men. Now, since Eugene had started using it as his new lab, coloured rugs dotted the flagstone floor, paintings hung from the walls and a large old fireplace, which had been uncovered behind some of the Watchers' stinking mess, blazed heat from its hearth, warming the grey walls. And there were eye plants everywhere, encased in glass boxes on steel lab benches.

It was because of the eye plants that Violet's family had first come to the town formerly known as Perfect, when Edward and George had read about Eugene's research in *Eye Spy* magazine and sought him out. First the Archer brothers had tried to use the plants to do terrible things, then William Archer had installed them as a security system around Town, but now Eugene had decided he wanted to use his eye plants the way he'd originally intended. He'd recently been given money from a university to do so, and was working diligently on developing the eye plants to help the blind see.

Violet's mam, Rose, had been a successful accountant before Perfect but after her imagination was stolen by the Archer Brothers she'd given all of that up. When Eugene got his funding she stepped in to run the optician's shop above with Boy's dad, William. Violet hadn't seen her mother as happy in a long time.

"I still think they're creepy," Violet whispered, looking through the glass box at a distorted Boy, who was busy biting the end of his pencil. She'd finished her homework ages ago and was getting bored as she waited for her friend to finish his.

"They're not creepy, Violet," her dad corrected, looking round at her through a veil of chalk dust. "These little beauties are going to help so many people! Won't that be amazing?"

Violet knew he was right – the plants would help people. After all her dad was a great scientist, everyone told her that. But it didn't mean the things weren't disgusting. Even after everything, the sight of them still gave her shivers.

"I know," she said, looking across at Eugene, "but why can't you experiment with something less disgusting, like hair transplants or ears or anything else?"

"Oh yeah, that sounds lovely, Violet – imagine a field of ear plants!" Boy smirked, distracted.

Boy was talking about the field on the far side of the river just over the footbridge. Eugene Brown needed space to sow and mature his eye plants and so, with agreement from the Town Committee, he'd begun growing them in the wasteland separating Town and the Ghost Estate.

"Why are you two talking?" Rose Brown rounded the bottom of the spiral stone staircase reaching down to the cellar from the shop above, and marched into the room. "Aren't you meant to be doing your homework and not disturbing your father, Violet?"

"I'm finished!" she announced as her mam dropped a copy of the *Town Tribune* on the table where Boy was working.

"That's great, pet," Rose said as she pulled Violet's opened copybook over to her and peered down at the text. "Maybe you'll get a smile from Mrs Moody this time!"

Mrs Moody was their teacher and she never smiled.

"That'd be a miracle, Mam," Violet snorted, plonking down into a yellow armchair beside the fire.

Violet and Boy had been coming to Archer and Brown to do their homework ever since classes started back. The building was just at the bottom of the road from school, it was an easy place to get their work done quickly and meant Violet and Boy didn't have to go home alone. Violet had never liked being on her own – she'd always imagine all sorts of wild scenarios for every sound – but Boy normally didn't mind his own company. Ever since his mam had died though, Violet noticed her friend didn't want to return to Wickham Terrace unless William was there, and William was working so much lately that Boy had practically spent the whole summer at the Browns'. Violet had overheard her mam whisper that Boy's dad was burying himself in his work.

The pair normally stayed in the basement, using the large steel desk to finish their school stuff. Then, if they got everything done, sometimes Eugene gave them money and they'd race to Sweet Patisserie on George's Road for buns before the baker's shop closed for the evening.

"Seems Marjory Blot has the same nose for a story as Robert. It must run in the family," Eugene said, staring at the *Tribune* now opened on the table.

Robert Blot, Marjory's brother, had once run the local paper but had given up his position when he was offered a place on the Town Committee. His sister now wrote the news and Violet had often seen her sneaking through the streets wearing sunglasses as if she were some sort of undercover detective. It was kind of funny since the woman's mass of white frizzy hair meant she could never be mistaken for anyone else.

"What's the story?" Rose asked, looking up from Violet's copybook.

"The missing scientist, the one I was telling you about, Dr Joseph Bohr. Marjory has written an article on him. The whole thing is very strange really – it says he was taken in the middle of the night, straight from his home."

"Oh! Iris knew him!" Boy said excitedly, clearly looking for more distraction. "She told Dad about it the other day. I think she worked with him or something, like a million years ago."

"Your granny's not that old, Boy!" Rose laughed.

"Iris must have had important friends. Dr Bohr is one of the world's greatest minds, though he's long retired now. I must pick your granny's brain – it'd be interesting to hear all about him. Fascinating man, fascinating mind!" Eugene shook his head.

"You've skipped a few questions, Violet." Rose gestured to the page in front of her.

"No I haven't," Violet said, walking over to the table. Her cheeks flushed as her mother silently pointed to the book. "It's this place, Mam, the eyes creep me out. I can't concentrate with them watching me the whole time!" she snapped defensively.

"That's a silly excuse, pet," Rose said. "You'd better

do them or Mrs Moody will be writing more notes in your diary."

Violet huffed and sat back down at the table beside Boy, pulling over her book to read the first missing question.

"The eyes made me do it!" Boy teased quietly as Rose disappeared back up the stairwell.

"Very funny." Violet swiped a look at her friend.

"I thought you weren't scared of anything?" he continued.

"What do you mean? I'm not!" she replied, trying to write her answer.

"What about the eye plants then?" he smirked.

"I'm not scared of them, Boy, they just freak me out. They're disgusting!"

"You seem pretty scared to me!"

"I'm not!" she snapped, flustered, as she picked up an eraser to rub out a mistake.

"Well, if you're not scared then prove it! I dare you to stay in the eye-plant field tonight!" Boy whispered.

Violet stopped what she was doing, looking up to make sure her dad hadn't heard. "The whole night?"

"No, just maybe…fifteen minutes. I dare you to spend fifteen minutes alone in the eye-plant field tonight." Boy grinned. "You can call it an early birthday present to me! You keep asking me what I want!"

"So for your birthday you'd like me to stay in a field? That's not a present!" Violet said, her cheeks glowing red.

"It's not any field, Violet." He put on a scary voice and stared straight at her as his dark eyes grew large. "It's an EYE-PLANT FIELD. Anyway," his voice changed back to normal, "the look on your face will be the best birthday present ever!"

Boy's thirteenth birthday was approaching in a few days and Violet had racked her brains for something to get him. It was the first since his mam had died and she wanted to make it nice so he wouldn't be sad. She'd thought of baking a cake but the last time she'd tried that she almost burned down the kitchen. Then she'd considered a football or boots or even a skateboard, but nothing felt right, nothing seemed special enough.

"That's a stupid present – it's just a dare, and anyway I won't be scared!"

"Then it'll be easy." Boy laughed, turning back to his book. "And it's my birthday – you're meant to do whatever I want!"

Violet fumed into her book. Saying no to a dare, especially one from Boy, was almost impossible.

"Okay," she sighed, rubbing a frustrated fluff-filled hole in her page.

Spending fifteen minutes in the field wasn't that long

– surely she could manage that. And it would wipe the smirk from Boy's face – something she couldn't wait to do, even if it was his birthday soon.

CHAPTER 2

THE DARE

Violet stayed deadly still as hundreds of eye plants slept around her. Their see-through petals cocooned rapidly moving pupils. She sat stiff on the damp soil, hugging her knees, afraid to breathe too deeply in case she woke the creatures. The shrill cries they let out when they were disturbed still haunted many of her dreams.

She was meant to be at a Committee meeting but had told her dad she was going to Boy's house to finish a school project. Boy had told William the same thing and the pair had met on the footbridge just as night was closing in.

Her friend had handed her a walkie-talkie and pointed across the river.

"I'll be watching." He looked serious. "You've to stay fifteen minutes otherwise I win!"

"Win? This isn't a competition, Boy, it's a dare!"

"Exactly, if you break the dare I win!"

She willed herself not to respond. Her mam said she was the easiest person on earth to wind up. Violet knew it was true because, if it wasn't, she wouldn't be sitting in an eye-plant field right now, her best friend's birthday or not.

"Boy...Boy!" she hissed into the walkie-talkie. "Time has to be up now? I've definitely been here fifteen minutes!"

The handset crackled, breaking the quiet. Violet jumped and shunted it under her jumper to dampen the sound.

"No, not yet!" her friend's voice filtered out through the wool.

"How long's left then?"

"You've only been there, erm..." He hesitated. "Six minutes."

"No way, I've been here loads longer than that!" she whispered angrily.

"Are you chickening out already?"

She was sure Boy sniggered before the line went dead.

"No I'm not!" she snapped, stabbing the call button.

The plant beside her jerked. Violet froze. The creature

23

fussed a little then settled back to sleep. She shifted uncomfortably, frustrated over Boy's timekeeping. She was sure he was cheating.

A sudden noise startled her. She turned towards it and spotted someone sneaking along the potholed road that cut through the middle of the plants. She craned her head to look.

The hooded figure wore black and moved quickly through the field. She was sure it was Boy, obviously trying to play a trick on her. She shifted carefully onto all fours and crawled across the soil, between rows of sleeping plants, towards the road, determined to catch him in the act.

She'd just reached the road when a large raven swooped down from the dark sky above and landed on what she had thought to be her friend's shoulder.

"Tom?" Violet gasped, her whisper loud in the quiet night.

Boy's identical twin brother turned and spotted her, his ice-blue eyes startling, their cold colour the only physical difference between him and his dark-eyed brother. Tom tripped as he scrambled forward and sprinted for the Ghost Estate. Violet climbed onto her feet and raced after him.

She hadn't seen Tom since just after Edward and George Archer were caught, having tried to take over

Town for the second time. Edward, with the aid of Tom, plus a strange zombie creature called the Child Snatcher and a crazy nurse named Priscilla Powick, had captured two of Town's children and pointed the blame towards Boy and William. Then, staging the children's rescue, Edward had returned to Town a hero and released his brother George. The pair worked on setting the Townsfolk against each other in order to win back control, until Violet, Boy and the others stopped them, tragically losing Boy and Tom's mam, Macula Archer, in the process as she tried to save her sons.

Violet had last seen Tom secretly visiting his mother's grave. He'd run away and she'd felt guilty since. Before Macula died she'd asked Violet to help bring her twins together so they could be a proper family, but so far Violet hadn't done anything about that promise.

Boy and Tom didn't grow up together. Way back at the beginning of Perfect, after William Archer had disappeared, Macula stumbled across Edward and George's terrifying plans for their town. They aimed to control everyone, using their rose-tinted glasses to steal people's imaginations. Anyone who didn't conform would be thrown into No-Man's-Land, a place cut off from the rest of the town by a huge wall. Petrified, Macula gave birth to her twin sons in secret and, to protect them from their uncles, left her babies outside the orphanage in

No-Man's-Land to be brought up there without anyone knowing who they were.

Tom had been taken from the orphanage as a child by Nurse Powick, who'd worked there. She'd reared him and forced him to do terrible things, so people thought Tom was bad. But, just like Boy's mother, Macula, Violet believed Tom was a good person who'd never been given the chance to show it. Firstly, Tom had a pet raven that he really seemed to love and Violet didn't think a bad person could be nice to animals. And secondly, when Edward and George had tried to take back Town, Tom had saved Violet – once from the Child Snatcher as it attacked her outside her home, and then from the same monster in the graveyard, with Nurse Powick standing just metres away.

On the night Macula died, Tom had saved Boy too, ordering the Child Snatcher to give his brother over to their friend Jack. Violet was sure he must have gotten into huge trouble when Nurse Powick found out. Tom had said something strange as he handed Boy over, he told Jack to "tell Mam I do feel it sometimes". Jack was confused by the message but Violet understood it.

Standing in the Market Yard that same night Macula had pleaded with Tom to come back to her, telling him she loved him. She'd said that a mother's love was strong and that she knew he felt it too, even though they had lived apart for so many years. Violet had been excited to pass Tom's message to his mother, but Macula had died before she could.

"Tom, please stop," she called now as he raced ahead through the pillars of the Ghost Estate.

Violet hesitated.

The Ghost Estate had once been a place full of fear. Every bad thought imaginable had crowded the mind of anyone who stepped inside its crumbling entrance. Then Violet discovered the mind-altering mist that Edward Archer had concocted in his cloud-making room and released to create this terror. After the Archers had been arrested and locked in the Town Hall, the Committee had destroyed the white room, stopping the gas. Now, she reminded herself, though the Ghost Estate was still derelict and looked eerie, it at least felt normal.

"Tom, please," Violet called as she walked up the cracked path surrounded by half-built houses. "I need to talk to you. I think you've been told awful things about your family. I know you're not bad, not really…"

Wind rustled black plastic sheeting in a cavity window, startling her.

"Please, Tom." A quiver rattled her voice. "I saw you visit Macula's grave. I know you think about your mam…"

Silence hung heavy in the night air. A door creaked and Tom stepped out onto an overgrown lawn to her left. He stared straight at her.

CHAPTER 3

ABOUT TOM

The walkie-talkie crackled to life.

"Violet, Violet, where are you?"

She fumbled in her pocket, trying to switch the device off. When she looked back up, Tom was disappearing over the hill at the back of the estate, heading towards the graveyard. She wouldn't chase after him up there, not alone.

"Violet, stop messing! Where are you?" Boy shouted. This time the sound came from the eye-plant field.

"I'm here," she called, turning to walk back out between the pillars.

The beam of a small headlight bounced along the road as Boy hurtled forward on his bike, skidding to a halt just in front of her.

"What are you doing up here?" he panted, a balancing foot touching the ground.

"I was definitely in that field longer than fifteen minutes!" she snapped, annoyed at her friend for making Tom run off.

"Someone was scared!" Boy laughed.

"I wasn't scared! It was a stupid dare!" she replied, walking back towards Town. She wasn't sure she should tell him about his brother.

"You'll have to get me another present now," he joked, pedalling slowly behind her.

Another present? An idea suddenly popped right into her head. She wanted to get Boy a present that was special, something that'd mean a lot. What if she got Tom back, reuniting Boy's family for his birthday? It was so perfect, and she was sure William would be really happy too.

"Did one of the eye plants bite you or something, so you ran away?" her friend teased again.

She ignored him, lost in thought. Macula would have wanted it – Violet would be fulfilling her promise to Boy's mam. She'd also be getting her best friend a gift money couldn't buy, and that was how adults described all the best presents. She'd have to do it carefully though. Ever since Macula died, the slightest mention of Tom made her friend clam up.

The last time there was any talk of Boy's twin brother was back in spring. A search party, led by Violet's dad, had combed the Outskirts, looking for signs of Tom or Nurse Powick. They found nothing. Powick's small thatched cottage was empty. So were the attached caravan and the stables across the field where she'd kept Hugo the zombie, who they'd nicknamed the Child Snatcher, and two other similar creatures named Denis and Denise.

After she'd heard the outcome of the search, Violet had begged Boy to come looking with her again. She was sure the adults had missed something – they usually did. When he refused, she told him about her promise to Macula to bring him and Tom together, to make them a proper family. Her friend got really angry, angrier than she'd ever seen him – in fact he'd told her never to mention it again.

But a few months had passed since then, so maybe Boy would be okay now? And even if he was a little angry at first, he'd get used to it and surely he'd be so happy to have a brother in the end. Violet had always wanted a sister or brother herself. It was lonely sometimes being the only kid stuck between two adults. Parents were usually boring – all they ever wanted to do was sit around and drink tea. What if she could find Tom and bring him back to his family? A brother. What a birthday present that'd be – Boy would never be bored again! And Macula would definitely be smiling down if she saw all her family together for the first time ever.

Now Violet knew that Tom was around again, it might not even be too hard to find him. He'd run towards the graveyard and that was the way into the Outskirts. Maybe she was right, maybe the adults had missed something when they searched there?

"Have you calmed down yet?" Boy interrupted her thoughts.

"I wasn't *not* calm!" she snapped, walking across the footbridge back into Town, the black waters resting still beneath her.

"Yeah, right!" he laughed, his bike rattling over the wooden planks behind her.

Violet turned up Wickham Terrace, stopping at number 135, Boy's home.

"Dad wants me to meet him at the Town Hall after the Committee meeting, so I'd better go," she said.

"You still haven't told me what you were doing in the estate!" Boy sounded a little frustrated now as he dismounted his bike.

"I did – I told you I wasn't doing anything!" she replied.

"Girls never make sense," he sighed, bewildered, as he pulled his keys from his jeans pocket.

"And boys do?" Violet mocked. "Now hurry up – I need to get my bag so Dad believes I was doing a project!"

Boy pushed open his front door, which led straight into the kitchen. The small space was still the colourful place Macula had left but somehow it felt less cosy without her. There were dirty dishes on the table from the morning's breakfast; some even looked to be from the previous night's dinner, though an opened *Town Tribune* had half hidden them and Violet didn't want to stare. Mounds of clothes hung off the back of a chair and piles of paper tumbled from the worktop onto the tiled floor. William wasn't the neatest person. Boy said his dad's head was so full of ideas he didn't have space for stupid things like dishes or washing.

Violet grabbed her khaki-green school bag from the beaten wood table as Boy pulled out a chair and sat down, studying the *Town Tribune*.

"Do you ever think about Tom?" she asked, stopping at the doorway.

Boy looked up, his dark eyes unblinking.

"Why'd you say that?"

"I just..." She struggled for a reason. "I don't know, I just wondered!"

Boy stared back down at the paper, pretending to be engrossed in an article. Silence filled the space between them. Violet shifted awkwardly.

"So...do you?" she asked again, still hovering by the door.

"No, Violet, I don't!" His reply was sharp.

She reddened and was about to step outside when her frustration caught hold. "Don't you at least want—?"

Boy glared at her, cutting the sentence short.

Her face more than a little rosy, Violet stepped silently out onto Wickham Terrace, closing the door behind her.

She picked up her bike from round the side of the house and cycled back through the Market Yard and onto Forgotten Road, heading for Edward Street.

At least Boy hadn't gotten really angry. That was progress. If she could just prove to him that Macula was right and Tom was good, then Boy's thirteenth birthday could be the best one ever.

The Committee were already filing out of the Town Hall when she pulled her brakes. Her dad sat patiently on the steps.

"Get your project done, pet?" He smiled, standing up and dusting down his trousers.

"Almost, Dad," she lied, slowly pedalling off ahead. She hated lying to him, but Violet knew he wouldn't approve of her upsetting the eye plants.

The pair continued down Edward Street towards Splendid Road in silence. It was an easy quiet.

"Dad?" she asked, slowing down as they passed Archer and Brown.

"Yes, pet?"

"What would you do if you had the best idea for a birthday present ever and you knew that the person you were...ahem...buying it for would really, really love it, even though they think right now that they don't want that present at all. Would you still buy it?"

Eugene Brown ruffled his hair, something he did whenever he was confused.

"Are you buying me a present?" he asked, furrowing his brow.

"No, Dad, it's just a hypotechnical question..."

"So you're not buying me a present? Because you know I do like presents!"

"No, Dad! Pleeeeaase, just answer!"

Eugene laughed. "Okay, pet, but your *hypothetical* question is a little hard to follow..."

"So you wouldn't...buy it...the present?" she urged.

"Violet, I didn't say that. You do whatever you think is right. You're a good judge, pet. My advice is to trust yourself. If this friend is a good friend then they'll know you got them something for the right reasons, no matter what it is. It's the thought that counts, pet... Anyway, everybody loves presents!"

"Thanks, Dad." Violet smiled, pedalling ahead again.

She climbed the stairs to bed that night, her mind made up.

Her mam believed in signs like feathers and robins

and, though her dad didn't think that was at all scientific, part of Violet believed in them too. Seeing Tom tonight after all this time, and so close to the twins' birthday, had to be a sign. Macula wanted Violet to bring her family back together.

And anyway, just like her dad said, everybody loves presents!

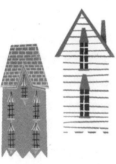

CHAPTER 4

PROMISES

Violet raced excitedly down the stairs the next morning. It might have been because it was Friday – after today she wouldn't see Mrs Moody for a whole weekend – but it might also have been because she'd made a decision and was going to act on it.

Boy's birthday was on the twenty-third, only a few days away. It'd be tight but she would do her best to find Tom before then.

"You're in a good mood, pet." Rose smiled as she looked up from scraping char off her burned toast. "Happy it's Friday?"

"Something like that, Mam."

Violet wasn't going to tell her parents anything, not yet

anyway. Her dad always told her off for poking around in other people's business and she was pretty sure he'd think Boy's business wasn't hers to interfere with.

She opened the fridge, looking for milk. Her dad was at the kitchen table engrossed in reading the paper again.

"He's been like that since I got up. Your father is great company at times, pet! Something about that missing scientist again." Her mam sighed, sitting down across from him.

"It's not just one scientist, Rose," Eugene announced, taking a bite from his toast. "More are missing now. These are some of the world's greatest minds."

"I thought you said they're retired, Eugene? So they *were* some of the world's greatest minds!"

"Once a great mind, always a great mind, Rose! It's a very odd story really. There's four of them now. And they've all been taken from their homes in the middle of the night."

Eugene pointed to the blotted black and grey pictures in the paper. Two men and two women stared out from the page. They looked granny-old – one man's nose hair almost touched his top lip.

"They've each contributed hugely to society and our understanding of the world!" her dad continued.

"A great mind," Rose muttered. "I'm not sure I'd like to be remembered that way! Wouldn't it be nicer to be remembered for your kindness or caring or something like that?"

"But why would anyone want to kidnap those scientists, Dad? They all look ancient!" Violet stabbed her finger at the pictures.

"Age is just a number, pet. The scientists were old friends – it says they met in Hegel University, where they all worked in their heyday. They were celebrities in their time. What I wouldn't give to have studied under any of them!"

"Celebrity scientists! Well, I've heard it all now." Rose laughed, buttering the toast she'd half scraped away. "Anyway, did you get your project done last night, pet?"

"Yes, I did it at Boy's. It took a while – he hates maths!" Violet avoided her mother's eyes and looked down at her bowl.

"Maths is everywhere, pet." Eugene glanced up from the *Tribune*. "Tell Boy to look for it outside his books, he might find it interesting then. Maths is in nature. Take a sunflower or the way trees branch out – they use a type of numerical symmetry called the Fibonacci sequence. Each number in the sequence is determined..."

"I'm going to be late for school." Violet jumped up before Eugene could properly launch into his lesson. "But I'll tell him. It sounds...ahem...really interesting!"

She grabbed her bag from the floor and headed into

the hall. The front door banged behind her as she crunched across the gravel and round the side of the house, pulling her bike from the pebble-dashed wall to pedal towards school.

Violet arrived earlier than normal, hoping to finish the project she was meant to have done last night. Boy was already perched on the bench that hugged the yard wall, crouching over his books in serious concentration. He clearly hadn't done it either.

"I meant to do my project when I got home last night but completely forgot," she fussed, pulling out her exercise book.

"Oh brilliant." He smiled. "We can do it together!"

"No, Boy! You have to do it yourself! Mrs Moody will know if we helped each other."

"Come on, Violet, you know I'm useless at maths."

"Well you won't get any better if you don't do it yourself! Dad says you should look at nature and you might enjoy maths more. Something about sunflowers and a Fibber sequence—"

"The Fibonacci sequence." Jack suddenly loomed above them. "Are you learning about that with Mrs Moody? I think it's amazing. The world is so weird in a cool kind of way! I mean, it all follows patterns, you know, nature, everything. I bet humans do too – I must look into that, I'm sure there has to be a book on it somewhere."

Jack was an ex-orphan too and had been one of Boy's best friends in No-Man's-Land. When Perfect fell he'd been reunited with his family and since their adventures saving Town, he was now Violet's friend too. Unlike Boy, Jack loved books and studying and school and seemed to know everything there was to know about everything.

"Jack, just the right person!" Boy smiled. "Can you do my project?"

"No!" Violet scolded. "Don't, Jack – he needs to do it by himself!"

"Thanks!" Boy replied. "I'll remember that next time you need help!"

"I like doing other people's homework," Jack said, taking the offered copybook as he sat down on the bench.

"See, I'm doing him a favour!" Boy smirked.

"Anyone want to do my homework?" Anna Nunn asked, joining the threesome. "I didn't get time to do it last night 'cause I was—"

"Sneaking out again?" Boy smiled.

Anna was a few years younger than Violet and had been an orphan in No-Man's-Land too, where Boy and Jack had protected her like older brothers. Violet often thought Anna didn't need protection – the little girl was one of the most daring people she knew. Anna was always sneaking out of her house and exploring Town at night, a habit she'd picked up in No-Man's-Land. After Perfect fell, Anna had been reunited with her family too. Her mam Madeleine was a Town Committee member.

"You can't tease me, Boy," Anna replied defensively. "I saw you sneaking up Forgotten Road last night!"

"No I wasn't," Boy replied, confused.

"Yes, you were. You ignored me when I called you!"

"That wasn't me. Are you sure, Anna?"

"Yeah." The blonde girl nodded.

"Maybe it was…ahem…maybe it was Tom?" Violet said, careful how she broached the subject.

If she'd seen Boy's twin last night then it was possible Anna had too. Maybe he was visiting Macula's grave again – she was buried in the Town cemetery up past the school and he'd have to go by Forgotten Road to get there.

"Don't tell me he's back?" Jack looked up from writing in Boy's copybook.

"He's not!" Boy stated, standing.

"But if it wasn't you," Anna replied, "then it had to be Tom. It was dark so I didn't see his eyes. You— I mean, *Tom* went into one of the old, falling-down houses at the bottom of Forgotten Road. I knocked on the door and said it was me, but you— I mean, *he* didn't answer. I was a bit annoyed at you but now I know it was him, I forgive you, Boy!"

"Which house? What time was this, Anna?" Violet questioned.

41

"Around seven I think, 'cause I sneak out when Mam goes to Committee meetings – she leaves early to prepare. She'd get cross if she caught me, so I only do it when she's not home. It was the house we used to use to get onto the roof and over to the wall down into Perfect, I think, or maybe it was the one beside it – one of them ones anyway!"

"Why would he be back?" Jack looked concerned and had even stopped writing. "Maybe we should look into it a bit. What if he's trying to help Edward and George escape? I don't like the sound of this!"

Edward and George Archer had been held in the clock tower of the Town Hall ever since their last attempt to take over. In the basement cells of the same old stone building were their Watchers, a band of cruel and brawny criminals who'd helped the twins to control Perfect.

Violet didn't share Jack's concern. Edward and George were locked up. Nurse Powick was still free but nobody thought she could get up to much on her own. The eye-plant beds, used as a security system throughout Town, were still in operation and William Archer checked the small screens in their control centre, the Brain, daily. The Brain was a small black box about the size of a garden shed, situated just by the Town Hall on Edward Street. It was filled with tiny monitors connected to every single eye plant in the town, recording everything they saw.

For the first time in ages Town felt truly safe and Violet's old nightmares had all but disappeared.

"He couldn't help them escape even if he tried. Dad says nobody can get in or out of the Town Hall without being caught," Boy stated.

"Well Tom got through Town before. The eyes didn't see him then," Anna replied. "He messed with their signals, remember?"

"Dad's fixed that glitch!" Boy snapped, taking his copybook from Jack.

"Maybe Tom was visiting your mam, Boy," Violet half whispered, careful again. "Maybe he wants his real family back?"

Boy glared straight at her as he shoved his book into his bag.

"I don't think so," he replied coldly. Without another word, he turned towards the school door and disappeared inside.

"I don't think he wants to talk about his brother!" Anna was red-faced as she looked at the others.

"But shouldn't we find out what Tom's doing back here?" Violet asked the others. "Maybe he wants to be friends this time?"

"Why would he want to be friends? And anyway, even if he did, he doesn't deserve it. Have you forgotten Macula died because of him?" Jack was angry.

"She didn't. I was there, I saw it. Powick pushed Macula and she hit her head. Tom was really upset. He gave Boy back to you, Jack. Don't you remember that?"

The older boy sighed. "Look, maybe we should just leave it alone. He's Boy's brother after all – it's none of our business."

"Unless he starts trouble again?" Anna insisted. "Shouldn't we at least tell William that I saw him, just in case?"

"No," Violet said, shaking her head. She didn't want anybody to scare Tom off. She needed to talk to him first.

"Violet's right," Jack said as the bell for lessons rang. "We shouldn't upset Boy or William if we don't have to. If Tom appears again and starts to cause trouble, we'll tell him then, but not before. Promise, Anna?"

The little girl nodded slowly as Jack stood up and brushed off his trousers before heading inside. The two girls followed behind in silence.

Violet had just settled at her desk when Mrs Moody stormed in, her red cardigan, crisp white shirt and blue skirt pristine. She pointed to the homework questions already chalked on the board and began calling people up to answer them. As Beatrice Prim, the most annoying girl in class, demonstrated her genius, Boy leaned across on his elbow and whispered.

"I know you, Violet. You'd better not be planning

anything. Whatever Tom is doing here, just leave it alone. He'll probably disappear again soon anyway."

"I wasn't planning anything!"

"You promise?" Boy stared straight at her.

She crossed her fingers behind her back and nodded. She'd seen Beatrice do the same thing before when a friend asked her to make a promise. Beatrice later said that crossing her fingers cancelled the agreement.

Violet didn't like lying to Boy but was it really a lie when it was for his own good? She knew he needed his brother even if he didn't know it yet. After all, family was everything – at least that's what her mother said.

CHAPTER 5

MISSING SCIENTISTS

Violet was already packing her bag behind Mrs Moody's back as the bell rang to signal the end of school; she was in a hurry. She told Boy she'd see him at Archer and Brown later as she'd forgotten something she needed to pick up at home.

She waited round the back of the school for the rush to die down, giving Boy enough time to get to the optician's. When the bike shed was almost empty, she took her bicycle from its stand and pedalled carefully towards Forgotten Road.

Anna said she thought Tom went to the house they had used to get onto the rooftops, the one that gave them access to the wall they climbed down into Perfect so they could avoid the Watchers during the Archers' reign. Violet wasn't entirely sure she remembered exactly which house that was, but Anna had described it as "falling down" and since Town was slowly being renovated there weren't many like that left.

She raced down Forgotten Road to where she thought the young girl meant. Checking that nobody was watching her, she slipped inside the run-down home.

The hallway was dark and full of rubbish which she had to trudge through to enter the room on her left. It looked like it might have been a sitting room once. Morsels of ornate floral wallpaper clung to walls that were also decorated with sweeping strokes of graffiti. A broken chandelier hung at an awkward angle from the ceiling, its bulbs either smashed or missing.

Violet didn't recognize the place as somewhere she'd been before.

She climbed back across the hall over a tattered purple couch into what appeared to be a kitchen. The light-blue cupboards were missing handles and one of the doors hung off a single hinge; the stainless steel washboard was stained by a spill of white paint and the lino was ripped away in sections, revealing the grey concrete floor beneath. She stepped back out and mounted the first step of the stairs. The wood cracked under the flower-patterned, frayed and filthy carpet and her foot fell through, scraping the skin of her ankle. A little shaken and unsure what she was doing, Violet left the house without going upstairs.

"I knew you'd be here!" Anna laughed, swinging her legs from a bench on the other side of the street.

"What do you mean…?" Violet flushed, embarrassed. "Mam just asked me to…"

"It wasn't that house anyway," the little girl stated, jumping to her feet.

The small blonde figure marched ahead down the street, stopping at another derelict home. The three wonky storeys of this building looked more familiar, though the door was now replaced and a large sign reading DANGER, KEEP OUT was nailed to it.

Violet watched Anna disappear inside before following.

Anna closed the door behind them, blocking out most of the light. The place was dusky dark as if night were falling, the windows too caked in dirt to allow in the day. It took a few moments for Violet's eyes to adjust.

"I knew you'd go looking for Tom!" Anna whispered. "Jack said we shouldn't, you know."

Violet ignored her as she took in the coarse brown carpet that covered the stairs. It brought her back to the first time she'd been here – the time Boy brought her onto the rooftops of Perfect. She walked into the sitting room on her left. An old armchair rested by the far wall.

She collapsed back onto it and yelped as a stray spring dug into her back and a world of dust flooded her nostrils.

"Bet someone really old lived here," the little girl said, poking her head in from the hall. "It's really smelly. My friend lives with her granny and says that old people are smelly because they never wash!"

"No they're not, Anna!" Violet corrected, struggling out of the sunken chair.

"Well that's what my friend says and I believe her 'cause she lives with her granny who's really, really old, like more than sixty, I think!"

Anna kept rambling as Violet picked her way through the room. The floor was covered with old cups and cutlery, bits of torn carpet, a bed head, a broken rusty wheelbarrow… She even kicked away a burst football as she pushed through the mess, still unsure what she was looking for.

"See, I told you an old person lived here!" Anna exclaimed, holding something aloft.

Violet squinted through the darkness. The little girl had something long and thin in her grasp that she began to twirl round her head. It looked like a walking stick.

"Stop swinging it, Anna!" Violet ducked, just avoiding a slap as she tried to get near.

"It's an old person's stick!" She held the object out to Violet, who took hold of it. The stick was long and made mostly of highly polished wood. There was a silver cap at the bottom where it met the ground and the top was milky white, smooth and carved in the shape of a bulldog's head. Just under the handle was a small gold engraved plaque: *Dr Joseph Bohr.*

Violet recognized the name from somewhere.

"A doctor," Anna whispered. "I didn't think they were smelly! I don't know that name and Mam and me know nearly everyone in Town."

"I don't think he's from Town..." Violet said absently, trying to place the name.

"I'll ask Mam," Anna announced. "She definitely knows everyone here!"

"It looks new" – Violet was thinking aloud – "not like the rest of the house. This can't have been here that long. It's still polished and shiny."

"Well, nobody has lived here in ages," Anna replied.

"Maybe it's nothing," Violet sighed, setting it down.

She continued her search, the name still tickling her memory.

Violet was looking for signs that Tom had been here, she realized. She didn't know how it would help her, but maybe it'd point to something that might tell her where he was hiding. If she was going to bring his family back together, she'd have to talk to him first.

"Aren't you going to take this? It's evidence," Anna

said, picking the walking stick back up as Violet moved towards the stairs.

"Evidence of what? Anyway, it's not ours, I don't think we should. It looks valuable – maybe the man who lost it might come looking."

"Or maybe he's dead and the stick is haunted!" The little girl laughed, poking Violet with the metal end. "And it attacks everyone who enters this place!"

Violet laughed too. She knew why Anna had been an orphan in No-Man's-Land – she had so much imagination the Watchers would never have been able to steal the whole thing.

She checked the rest of the house, Anna sticking tight to her heels. Increasing street sounds filtered inside as they walked back down the creaking stairs; people were leaving work.

"I better get home. Mam will be worried if she gets back before me."

"Are you going to tell Boy?" Anna asked back out on the street.

"There's nothing to tell!"

"So we weren't looking for Tom?" The young girl smirked.

Violet blushed, the heat reddening her cheeks.

"No, definitely not." She shook her head. "But don't tell Boy anyway!"

"Okay, but only if you bring me on any more adventures where you're not looking for Tom. You have to promise! I wasn't allowed do anything when Edward Archer came back last time so you can't leave me out of stuff any more. I'm not a little girl, I'm big now!"

"I'm not going on any adventures!" Violet turned back towards Rag Lane and her bike.

"Okay, but if you are you have to promise..." Anna panted, trotting behind her.

"I'm not!" Violet crossed her fingers again.

Why did everyone want her to promise things all of a sudden?

She pushed her bike up the lane to Archers' Avenue, with Anna chattering all the while. Violet tuned in and out; the name on the walking stick was haunting her. She glanced up at the clock tower as they rounded onto Edward Street – the hands were almost at six. The pair waved goodbye and Violet pedalled furiously towards home, determined to pass Archer and Brown before her parents closed for the night.

❄   ❄   ❄

She crunched up the gravel drive to their house just as the sun was setting. Dismounting her bike, she was parking it round the side when movement high up in a tree caught her eye.

A coal-black raven flapped its wings. A shiver danced across her shoulders.

"Tom," she whispered, "are you here?"

Maybe she was going mad – there were loads of black birds about.

"I want to talk to you, Tom. I want to help you…"

Her words hung in the still air. Her heart thumped. There was a rustle in the bushes nearby and Violet jumped. Suddenly the bird launched from the branch above, disappearing into the fading blue sky.

Violet raced to the front door, sure someone was watching her.

If Tom was hanging around, what was he after? Did he just want his family, like she hoped and wanted to help him with? Or what if everything she and Macula thought was wrong? What if Boy's twin really was bad?

What if, like Jack said, Tom was back to help the Archers escape? She sat down at the kitchen table, lost in thought. She wanted to tell her mam and dad, but something told her not to.

A key sounded in the door. As her parents walked inside Violet frantically pulled out her books so it didn't look like she'd just gotten home.

"Where were you?" Rose asked, poking her head into the kitchen. "You didn't come back to the shop!"

"I was here. I couldn't find this and I needed it for my

homework." Violet grabbed a random book from the table and waved it around. "By the time I found it, it was too late to go back to the shop. I told Boy to tell you."

"I'll be expecting great reports from Mrs Moody with all the work you're putting in." Rose smiled, opening the fridge door to take out a bottle of milk.

Eugene switched on the kettle and sat down heavily at the kitchen table, pulling out the *Tribune* as was his habit.

"I thought once Robert Blot had stepped away from that paper, we'd see your father's face again!" her mother teased as she sat down, placing a heap of files on the table in front of her.

"What's that, Mam?" Violet indicated the pile.

"Just work, pet. There's not enough hours in the day and I couldn't stay on late when everyone had gone home. That building gives me the shivers sometimes. I know those Archers are locked up but I still feel their presence there," Rose replied.

"It's called Archer and Brown now, Rose, and that's a lot of nonsense – you can't feel a person in a building after they're gone."

"How come Boy says he can still feel his mam then, Dad?" Violet interrupted.

"That's different, pet," her father replied.

"Science can't explain everything," Rose continued. "Most of what science knows is based on theory, meaning

questions are more important than anything. [...]
opens the mind, Eugene – as a scientist you [...]
that! Violet had a valid question. Who says [...]
someone after they've left a place?"

"Well maybe somebody should investigate that question, Rose." Eugene frowned. "Might help find some of the world's greatest minds! This all feels a little ominous to me…"

"What do you mean, Dad?" Violet asked, uneasy.

"Another scientist has been taken, pet. These are some of the greatest living men and women in the history of science. If somebody has kidnapped them, why? What do they want them for? The world feels just a little unsettled right now."

"You've an imagination just like your daughter. I bet they'll all turn up on holiday somewhere. They probably just forgot to tell anyone. Age does that to you!"

Violet's dad set down the paper and poured himself a cup of *UniTea*.

The tea had been a creation of Edward and George Archer, though they'd called it Archers' Tea. They developed their concoction using the Chameleon plant, which meant the tea tasted like anything the drinker wanted it to. This property had made it hugely popular in Perfect. Then the Archers had added a potion to the mixture, turning everyone in the town blind, allowing the twins to begin their plans to control the place. After Perfect fell, William Archer had twisted something bad into something good – the blinding potion was removed, the product renamed and *UniTea* became a staple in everyone's diet.

Violet leaned over the paper, her eyes drawn to a fuzzy picture of a young man in a white jacket. The photo was captioned *"Dr Joseph Bohr, Hegel University, 1956."*

She gasped. That's where she'd heard the name before!

"Is he one of the scientists, Dad?" she asked, a tingle shooting down her spine.

"Yes, pet. He was the first to go missing." Eugene blew on his tea. "It's a very confusing case. The missing scientists specialize in different areas of study – there is no link in their work! It seems to me all they have in common is that they worked at Hegel University at the same time and, of course, their friendship!"

"Exactly, they're friends, Eugene! So maybe they're all off enjoying a sunshine cruise together," Rose interrupted with a giggle.

Violet's parents continued to debate as she slipped quietly from the table and out into the hall, her heart pounding. She had to get away. She raced up the stairs and into her room.

Dr Joseph Bohr – the very name that was on the walking stick in the house on Forgotten Road! Did it belong to the scientist? Surely there couldn't be many people with the exact same name? Could it just be chance? But if Joseph Bohr had been in Town recently, then why was he here and where had he gone?

Another thought struck her. Anna had seen Tom go into the same house – was he involved somehow?

Her head swam as she sat in her window seat looking out on the night.

Should she do something? Tell someone? But what and who, and did she really know anything? Maybe she could tell Boy – not about the birthday bit and reuniting his family, but about the missing scientist Joseph Bohr and the walking stick with his name on it and how it was found in the same house Anna had seen Tom go into.

Maybe it was all just one big coincidence…but what if it was something more and she did nothing?

CHAPTER 6

THE NOTE

Violet rose early the next morning. Her mind had come to a million conclusions overnight, meaning she'd hardly slept. Quietly, she dressed then slipped down the stairs and out the front door. The air was cold, a mist hanging low and thick over the dew-dropped grass.

She shivered and hugged her elbows close as she walked to her bike. Using the sleeve of her fluffy fleece top, she dried the saddle, and had already climbed onboard before noticing the piece of paper wrapped round her handlebars.

It was soggy from the damp morning, the blue copybook lines heavier in places. Gently she unrolled the paper, not wanting to tear it.

A message was written in red pen; the letters leaked a little on the page.

Town is in immense trouble and this time you won't win! They've been devising this for years. Nothing will stop the pair. If you really want to help me, please, you must all leave before the 23rd.

Violet shivered; both the note and the cold rattled her bones. She reread the words over and over again, trying to make some sense of them. *Town is in immense trouble and this time you won't win.*

The words played round her mind as she cycled through the quiet morning streets towards Wickham Terrace. *If you really want to help me, please, you must all leave.*

She gasped, remembering the last words she'd said before entering her house last night after she'd seen the raven: she'd told Tom she wanted to help him. Could the note be from him? From Tom? It was written in the same way he spoke, using big words she'd never be able to put into a sentence.

Violet pulled on her brakes outside Boy's front door. The screech of rubber shattered the peaceful morning and a cat scurried away from her.

She climbed off her bike and picked a few pebbles from the road, launching them at Boy's window. Her aim wasn't great and it took some minutes of frustration before a few reached their target, ricocheting off the glass. Moments later the curtains shook and Boy rubbed his eyes as he peered out.

Violet pointed to the door and was standing impatiently on the threshold of number 135 as it opened. She swept past him inside, the note still in her fist.

"What are you doing here so early?" Boy croaked, plonking himself down at the kitchen table.

"I thought you loved early mornings!" Violet said, sitting on the chair opposite.

"That was the old me! I'm getting used to lie-ins now, especially on Saturdays. There better be a good reason for this," he grumbled.

Violet passed Boy the handwritten note.

"It was on my bike this morning." She nodded as he read.

"This is what you woke me up for?" Boy sounded annoyed.

"No, there's more…" She grabbed the *Tribune*, folded at the edge of the table, and opened it on the photo of Dr Joseph Bohr. "Remember Anna saw Tom the night before last… Well I went back to the house where she'd seen him—"

"Violet…" Boy sighed, rubbing his eyes. "I told you to leave things alone!"

"I haven't finished yet," she pleaded, willing him to hear her out. "Anna was with me. We found a walking stick with Dr Bohr's name on it – he's one of the missing scientists." She pointed to the picture. "It has to mean something!"

Boy looked confused.

"He's been kidnapped! Five of them are missing now. Dad says they are some of the greatest minds in the world, and someone has taken them and we don't know why and then I find that stick, Boy! I think something really bad might be happening in Town!"

"Like what, Violet?"

"How do I know, Boy? Like something bad!"

Boy raised his eyebrows.

"Okay, well maybe…some crazy person is forcing the scientists to make a bomb or a machine that sucks all the oxygen out of the air, or something that makes everyone's skin itch for ever so people have no other choice but to scratch it all off!" She threw her hands into the air. "It could be anything, Boy – how do I know?"

"You're the one sounding like a crazy person now." He smiled.

"Very funny!"

"Seriously, Violet, you think whoever kidnapped the scientists brought them here, to Town? Why would they do that when they could take them anywhere in the whole world?"

"Well I don't know that either, Boy, but I do know we found evidence that Joseph Bohr was in the same house that Anna saw Tom go into only the other day…"

"So you think Tom kidnapped the scientists? Really, Violet!" Boy sneered, shaking his head.

"I know it sounds crazy but how else do you explain the walking stick? And then last night I thought Tom was in our yard so I told him I wanted to help him, and then this morning I get a note on my bike, one that says, 'If you really want to *help* me…'" She pointed to the curled piece of paper. "It can't all be a coincidence. I've been up all night…I think…"

She stopped rambling, falling quiet as her mind caught up with her mouth. Her dad's words ran round her head: *Think before you speak, pet.*

"You think what, Violet?" Boy urged, his forehead creased.

"If I say it, you won't be mad?"

"Well I don't know what you're about to say!"

"Just don't be mad…promise," she pleaded.

Boy crossed his fingers, waving them around in front of her. "I promise," he smirked.

"Hey, that's not fair," she argued.

"Why not? I've seen you do it loads. You're not exactly good at hiding things, Violet!"

She blushed.

"Just tell me," he sighed, impatient now.

"I think Tom left me the note. I think he's trying to warn us to get out of Town. I don't think he's bad, I think he's good, Boy!"

"But if you think he's good, tell me why he would kidnap those scientists? You're making no sense!"

"Because someone is forcing him to do it!"

"Forcing him? Like who? Edward and George are locked up! This is sounding very far-fetched, Violet!"

"I don't know, maybe Powick, or maybe Edward and George are behind it all somehow even though they're locked up! If Tom was bad and doing all this on his own, he wouldn't leave a note, would he?"

"You don't know Tom left that note or that those scientists are even in Town! You've just made all this up in your head!" Boy sounded frustrated. "There could be lots of explanations for the walking stick being in that house. Iris was a friend of that doctor's – maybe he gave her the stick years ago and she lost it or something. Think about it – how could Tom kidnap five scientists on his own? And if he was planning something, why would he warn you about it? He knows you'd tell me and all he's ever wanted to do is hurt my family…"

"But don't you see, that's what I mean, Boy. He's good, just like Macula said. He warned me because he knew

I'd tell you and William and he doesn't want you both to get hurt…"

"If he was good he wouldn't have killed Mam!" Boy half shouted, his voice cracked.

Violet fell silent for a moment. She could almost touch his pain. She looked down at her hands, then back up at her friend.

"But he didn't," she whispered gently. "I was there. It was Powick."

Boy fell silent now too, his face flushed as he fidgeted with the note she'd handed him.

"Who's 'the pair'?" he asked after a little while.

"What do you mean 'the pair'?"

"In the note. It says, 'you won't stop the pair'. If Tom wrote the letter then he can't mean himself, unless he's even weirder than I thought. So who are the pair?"

"Oh, um—" Violet hadn't thought about that.

"Anyway, I don't believe Tom would help us," Boy interrupted before she could come up with something. "I think it's a trick. I bet Conor Crooked or someone put that note on your bike and they're probably laughing at you right now!"

Conor was the school bully. He'd calmed down a bit since his kidnapping a few months previously, but this was still the type of thing he might do. Boy was right – even Violet had to admit her mind had really run away with itself this time. The note could be from anyone.

Boy passed the paper back over and Violet huffed as she folded it into her pocket.

"Anyway," he mocked, "isn't it all a bit obvious? It's like the plot of a really bad film. Town's in trouble, you won't save it. Oh and by the way...leave before the twenty-third!"

"What do you mean?" Violet asked.

"Oh you've forgotten already, have you? The twenty-third's my birthday!"

CHAPTER 7

BACK TO THE OUTSKIRTS

The twenty-third *was* Boy's birthday, and Tom's too – how could she have missed that detail in the note? Surely the date was just a coincidence though. She couldn't imagine the twins' birthday could have anything to do with Town being in trouble!

The twenty-third was two days away. Was something really awful going to happen to Town then, or was it all just a stupid trick?

A niggling feeling ate away at her.

"I think we should go to the Outskirts!" she blurted out. "That's where Tom lived before and it'd be a good hiding place to keep a scientist."

"Not this again, Violet!"

"But we need to find out if anything is going on. What if we do nothing and then something bad happens? It's just a trip to the Outskirts, and if we find nothing then that's great, isn't it?"

"I don't want to, Violet." Boy looked upset and wouldn't meet her eyes. "I don't want to remember that nurse or Tom or what they did. I don't want to go back there!"

"I know, Boy, and I've tried not to talk to you about Tom or Powick for ages. But maybe you can't ignore those memories for ever. My mam says if you push things to the back of your mind, they normally come out somewhere else. She said it's better to feel the pain, as feeling it helps it to go away. And what if…what if your mam was right, Boy, what if Tom is good?"

"You never give up." He sighed.

"You don't usually either."

They both went quiet. Violet stood and walked to the window, easing back the net curtain. The street was quiet, morning only just beginning to wake the Townsfolk.

"People are still asleep," she whispered. "We could be back before anyone even notices we're gone."

"You want to go now?" Boy asked.

"Well I didn't come over just to talk about it. We only have a few days!"

"I'm telling you, this is just your imagination.

Sometimes I wish I had the Archers' glasses to steal some of it from you!"

"Okay, well prove it's just my imagination then." Violet turned and planted her hands on her hips, staring straight at him. "I dare you!"

Boy's face softened and a small smirk played round his lips.

"That's not fair," he replied.

"You owe me a dare," she stated, "so this is it. I dare you to come to the Outskirts with me. Prove that this is all in my mind!"

Boy didn't respond for a minute. Then he quickly stood up and slipped into the hallway. Violet listened as his feet crept up the stairs and across the floor of his room above.

She walked to the cupboard and had taken out two blue, chipped, cereal bowls and two equally battered silver spoons when he arrived back, changed out of his green-checked pyjamas.

"We'd better eat breakfast. Can't have an adventure on an empty stomach." She smiled, grabbing the cereal packet and a pint of milk.

"This is not an adventure, Violet, this is just you being bored or something. I'm only going so I can prove you wrong! The Committee searched the Outskirts already. There's nothing there!"

"Yeah, but you know they're adults and adults miss everything, even when it's right under their toes!"

"Under their noses!" Boy snorted, swallowing a spoonful of cereal.

"Well, under their toes makes more sense," Violet said, huffing over her bowl of freshly poured cornflakes.

The pair ate quickly and quietly, then headed outside. Boy grabbed his bicycle and was already near the footbridge before Violet managed to mount her saddle. Boys! She gave chase and had almost caught up to him by the time they reached the Ghost Estate and pedalled inside. Both slowed their pace as they rattled over the potholed road towards the grassy hill.

They dropped their bikes at the bottom and began the climb, a little breathless. They passed the lone lamp post at the top and arrived at the graveyard wall without uttering a single word between them.

"I'm sure I put him there!" A voice carried through the early morning mist.

The pair stopped. Violet glanced at Boy; he shrugged and ducked down a little behind the wall.

A short, stout figure was hunched over a tomb as though trying to get a glimpse inside. Iris Archer muttered as the edges of her black knitted shawl caught the breeze.

What was she doing here?

Iris was William's mam and Boy's granny. She was old, white-haired and known for being a bit odd. It wasn't the first time she'd been caught talking to herself.

Violet grabbed Boy's elbow as he moved to push open the metal turnstile.

"No, please." She shook her head. "Iris will stop us going to the Outskirts."

The old woman's ramblings grew louder as she walked up and down the path dividing the cemetery in two. She seemed to be growing frustrated and kept hitting her forehead with the heel of her hand.

"But if you put him there, why isn't he there now, Iris? Think, woman, think!" she scolded herself.

"What's she doing?" Boy whispered.

Violet ducked further down behind the wall, tugging Boy with her as his grandmother turned in their direction.

"You put him in that tomb, Iris! An animal maybe... yes, maybe an animal ate him. But surely there'd be bones? All his friends from Hegel, all of them gone. He vowed revenge. Oh, what have you done?"

Violet froze, her fingers pinching Boy's forearm. The old woman was talking about Hegel, the same university the missing scientists had worked at. What was she so worried about and what was she looking for?

Iris's long, frizzy hair fell over her eyes as she stopped and peered through a large crack in the lid of another tomb. She pointed a torch through the gap to light the darkness inside. Then she shook her head and mumbled something else before moving on to continue her search.

"Looks like she's lost something." Boy seemed concerned.

Violet held firm to his elbow, willing him not to move. She didn't want anyone to stop them going to the Outskirts – it had been hard enough getting Boy this far.

A while later, looking a little defeated, Iris weaved her way through the gravestones towards the back wall where Violet and Boy knew there was an entrance to a tunnel that led underground to Archer and Brown – they had used it themselves back when they were trying to stop the Archer Brothers. Iris eased down stiffly onto her knees before lowering herself feet first into the hole in the earth, disappearing bit by bit.

"Iris said Hegel!" Violet turned to Boy as they entered the graveyard a few minutes after his granny had left. "That's the university those scientists went to. The ones that are missing! She must be searching for something to do with them."

"I already told you she knew the doctor," Boy replied. "Maybe she was looking for his walking stick, the one you found at that house. I knew there'd be an explanation! Maybe that scientist gave her the stick as a present years ago and now he's missing, she's afraid she's lost it! Old people get sentimental like that."

"And you give out to me for jumping to conclusions!" Violet smirked. "Even if that was true, why would Iris be looking for the stick in a graveyard, and this early in the morning?"

"Because she's old and old people forget where they put things all the time!"

"But she kept saying '*him*', Boy, and she talked about bones. I don't think she was looking for a walking stick! And why wouldn't she go back to Town the normal way through the Ghost Estate? I haven't heard of anyone using that tunnel since Perfect."

"Going through the tunnel is probably quicker and she's an early riser. See, everything explained!" Boy smiled as he meandered through the gravestones, looking for the tomb that led to the Outskirts. "Let's just get this dare over with and be back for lunch. I'm starving already."

"You're always hungry!" Violet whispered, following behind.

Goose pimples peppered her skin as she imagined all the dead people that lay under her feet right now, their forgotten lives marked by broken crosses and unkept gravestones.

Boy stopped at the old stone tomb that marked the

tunnel to the Outskirts. Violet shivered, remembering the fear she'd felt months before as she hid with Anna, watching Powick, Tom and Hugo descend down the steps into the ancient underground passage.

The rectangular tomb was about hip high, a large stone slab lid concealing the secrets inside. A quote from Quintus Horatius Flaccus, who Violet now knew to be a really old poet, was engraved on the side.

"O FORTUNE, CRUELLEST OF
HEAVENLY POWERS,
WHY MAKE SUCH GAME OF THIS
CRUEL LIFE OF OURS?"

She remembered standing in almost the same spot with Jack, trying to figure out how to open the entrance. It was Jack who spotted that the word "game" in the quote was raised out from the rest of the text.

Violet hunkered down on her heels and pushed on the four protruding letters. The ground rumbled and shook as a loud scraping sound filled the air. The narrow front panel of the tomb disappeared slowly into the earth, revealing steps leading underground.

She ventured inside, looking back at Boy as he hesitated.

"I'm really not sure about this, Violet. Can't we just leave it alone?" he whispered.

"Please, Boy, I promise we won't stay long. If there's nothing to find, we'll come straight back. Anyway, it's a dare – you can't back out!"

Her friend sighed before ducking inside. He pushed past her on the steps and stopped on the flagstone floor below, waiting.

Quickly Violet closed the tomb, plunging the tunnel into total darkness. She reached for the rough earth wall and used it to guide herself down the remaining steps to her friend.

Suddenly the brown clay walls of the tunnel lit up. Violet jumped.

"I came prepared." Boy smiled, waving around a small torch.

She breathed a sigh of relief. Just like Boy, part of her didn't want to come back here either. The memories were haunting. She'd first spoken to Powick down in this place, when the nurse had ordered Hugo the zombie Child Snatcher to capture her. She shuddered as they passed the entrance to the cell she'd been held captive in with Conor and Beatrice.

A way down the tunnel, natural light cast a circle on the ground and Violet stepped into it, onto an unusual stone-tiled floor. She looked up; a circular patch of sky hung a long distance above her head. She bent down and rubbed dirt from the stones, revealing a small letter in the corner of each tile. Together the floor tiles amounted to a full alphabet.

"It's U then P, isn't it?" Boy said.

Violet nodded as she remembered figuring out the code with Jack.

Boy pressed on the square marked with a U. The tile gave way under his pressure. Then he reached for the P and pushed it too. The platform they stood on shook and Violet braced herself quickly as the floor shot upwards towards the sky.

"I can't believe we're back," she whispered as they broke out into the Outskirts.

She scooted nervously across the platform and there was a dull thud as she jumped off onto the grass. Boy followed behind and the pair raced for the cover of the old twisted tree nearby.

As Violet settled her back against the knotted wood, she shivered. Everything was quiet – eerily so. Not even birdsong filled the morning sky. She remembered Powick and Hugo and the awful things that had happened here before. Her stomach churned, and for the first time, she wasn't sure they were doing the right thing.

CHAPTER 8

THE FOREST

Boy and Violet crouched by the base of the old twisted tree, which stood tall and bleak by the side of an overgrown road. To their left was Nurse Powick's cottage and to their right a barren field. Two stables stood lonely at the other side of the field, once home to Powick's three zombies Hugo, Denis and Denise.

The first time Violet had seen the zombies, they'd been strapped to the back wall of one of the stables. She remembered with horror the deep purple and green marks that mottled the creatures' skin, so decayed in parts she could see bare bone beneath. She remembered the metal bars that traced their legs and arms like an outer-skeleton, enabling them to move, and the battery packs that powered the undead. She also remembered the smell of rot.

Violet shuddered. "Maybe we should check the cottage first?"

Boy nodded, standing up.

"Let's get this over with!" he sighed, crossing the road, Violet a few paces behind.

Unlike the first time she'd seen it, Powick's cottage now showed slight signs of neglect. The tidy yellow fence needed some repairs, the surrounding garden, once neat, had an overgrown lawn and the rose bushes were a little wilder than Violet remembered.

Boy pushed open the squeaky wooden gate and walked down the red brick path dotted with weeds.

"Looks like nobody's been here for a while," Violet whispered.

The yellow front door was open, leaves and dirt holding it ajar. Red and black tiles chequered the hall floor just as Violet remembered and the same stained glass lantern hung from the low ceiling. She stepped into the first room on their right, following Boy.

Just inside the door was a stubby table, its mahogany legs sawn off. It had once been laid with miniature cutlery, and tattered stuffed toys sat round it as though waiting for dinner, but now only a single tiny teaspoon rested on its surface. A cream stove stood unlit on the far side of the room, a solitary, bandaged bear resting against it as though forgotten.

They stepped back into the hallway and entered a room a little ahead on their left.

The space was empty except for a single bed squashed into the far corner. All of the tiny hospital beds and battered children's toys that had once filled the floor had vanished. The ice-cream cone patterned curtains still hung in the window, though now a little greyed by dust.

Violet returned to the hallway and looked at the steel double doors ahead, a complete contrast to the warm decor in the rest of the house. Part of her didn't want to go through them, as she remembered what they had concealed.

"Come on." She faked confidence and walked forward – the doors swung open easily when she pushed them.

As they closed behind, the smell hit first. She coughed and pinched her nose. Boy gagged beside her. It smelled like the fridge in her house did once when some meat lay forgotten at the back – but this was so much worse. Violet wondered if a zombie's loose finger had rolled into hiding and festered there.

The huge steel sheets that clad the walls were bare, no longer covered in gruesome images of wounded bodies on the battlefield, and only one metal wheeled table remained, a selection of sharp utensils left to rust on its shiny surface.

"Can we leave?" Boy was pale. "I don't like it here!"

"I forgot you didn't see this place before," Violet replied. "This is where Powick made her zombies. There was a body on one of those tables when..."

Boy's face went a sickly shade of green and he dashed through the second set of steel double doors at the far side of the room. Violet raced after him, afraid he was going to puke. Boy stopped on the frayed orange carpet, bent over as though catching his breath.

"It's okay, we're in the caravan now," she felt the urge to whisper, "where Tom had you hidden—"

"I remember!" he snapped.

She fell quiet. When Tom had kidnapped Boy and hidden him there, the run-down caravan had been packed to the brim with boxes full of teddy bears and dolls, but now everything was gone. The small space was empty.

"Powick and Tom can't just have vanished, can they?" she said, confused. "I mean, they have to be somewhere!"

"You never listen, Violet." Boy sidled past the narrow kitchen work counter towards the door. "Everyone told you the Outskirts was empty!"

"But Tom's got to be close. I saw him and so did Anna! Where's he living then?"

"You saw him?" Boy stopped, his hand on the white plastic door handle.

Violet froze. She hadn't meant to let that slip. Her

friend stared at her, waiting for an answer.

"I...yes, I saw him. The same night Anna did. That's why I was in the Ghost Estate – I followed him there."

Boy looked annoyed. "Why didn't you tell me?"

"Because I didn't want you to..." She stopped. She couldn't tell him about her plan, not now anyway. "...To be upset."

"But you brought me here, Violet. Didn't you think this would make me upset?"

Boy grunted, shouldering open the stiff caravan door, and raced down the steel steps onto the lawn.

"I'm sorry, Boy," she said, catching up to him.

He didn't reply as he walked round to the front of the cottage and stared over at the stables.

"If they're empty," he nodded across the field, "we're going home."

She guessed that the stables would be just as empty as the cottage. But they couldn't go home, not yet. Her gut told her there had to be some clue to Tom's whereabouts out here.

Violet trotted ahead of her friend, crossing over the road to the well that gave access to the tunnel they had come through earlier. She jumped up onto its platform, needing to think. She could see the whole of the Outskirts from this central position. Apart from the stables and the cottage there weren't any places to hide here.

So where could Tom be? He'd run towards the graveyard the night she'd seen him. He had to have come back to the Outskirts.

She looked ahead. In the distance, a little down the overgrown lane, was a forest. She'd seen it before, but it was the only place in the Outskirts she'd never been.

Boy pulled himself up onto the platform beside her.

"They checked the forest too," he said, stealing her thoughts, "and found nothing. Dad said it was like a maze in there."

The grass grew thick and heavy on the lane, covering over most of what must once have been a proper road. Her eyes fell on a small worn path meandering through the grass where the blades had been stamped down or broken through regular use. It wound its way from the well towards the forest.

"Look, Boy!" She pointed. "There's a trail worn on the roadway as if someone walks there all the time!"

"That could be from the Committee search!"

"No it couldn't! They only searched here once or twice. I'm sure it'd take more than that to wear a path in grass. Can we just follow it, please?"

He shook his head. "No, I said just the stables and if there's nothing, the dare's over! You said we were just checking the Outskirts!"

"That's still the Outskirts," she argued. "I don't see

new signs anywhere, so the forest is included in the dare! And anyway, it's not for me, Boy, it's for Town. What if everyone's in trouble just like the note said?"

"Town is perfectly fine, Violet, and you can't just make up the rules!"

"You do it all the time," she said, stubbornly jumping off and following the trail. "They're my rules anyway, Boy. A dare is a dare – if you go home now I'll tell Jack and everyone how you backed out!"

She didn't look around but could hear his feet stomping through the grass behind her.

"The dare is over when this track stops. Okay."

"Deal." She smiled.

Boy brushed straight past her and strode towards the forest. Violet trotted to keep up with his pace.

Soon the worn grass trail took them under the thick forest canopy. The morning light almost totally disappeared above them, blocked out by branches.

Violet tensed.

"You're the one who wanted to come here." Boy shrugged, sensing her unease.

"I'm grand," she lied.

After a while they reached a pile of felled trees, blocking their path, and the worn grass trail came to an end.

"Dare over!" Boy smirked, turning around.

Violet rushed forward, trying to rescue the search, and clambered onto the log pile. "I bet the path continues on the other side of this lot!"

She panted, struggling upwards until she lay flat on her belly at the top. She looked down and wobbled, grabbing the sides of the trunk beneath her for balance. Boy seemed a lot smaller from this height.

"Well?" he called.

Violet shuffled around slowly so she was facing away from Boy and pushed off her stomach onto her knees. She trembled, trying to stand up for a better look.

Suddenly the tree trunk twisted under her footing. She gasped, stumbled and fell, tumbling head first towards the ground.

Everything slowed as if time had lost its hold. The tree trunks parted, unleashing a large mass of rope from within their depths to engulf her.

Time resumed and Violet was catapulted skywards, caught like a fish in a net.

CHAPTER 9

NURSE POWICK

Violet was curled tight in a ball, constrained in the rope net, her knees almost touching her nose. She tried to unfold her legs but her small prison twirled round and round, making the world below her spin. She looked up. The rope holding the net was looped over the thin branch of a nearby tree, which was now straining under her weight.

"Violet!"

She looked down, struggling for breath as her head spun. She couldn't see Boy anywhere. The ground looked miles away as it zipped past below.

"Boy?" she called.

"Down here!"

The net began to slow its cycle and she could just see Boy waving up from the path.

"What happened? How did I get here?" Everything seemed a blur.

"I don't know," he called. "I heard a click and saw you fall. It happened so fast. I thought you were a goner, then the net sprang out of nowhere! It was pretty cool!"

"Not exactly what I'd call it!" she replied as the branch creaked above. "What if the tree won't hold my weight, Boy? I need to get out!"

Her heart pounded as panic robbed her of air. She wriggled to free herself, sending the net into another wild spin.

"Calm down!" Boy shouted. "Don't move. I'll figure something out!"

"Calm down?" she wheezed. "I'm caught in a net up a tree!"

"Just breathe, Violet. I'll get you out."

He began to search around him as she closed her eyes and slowly forced breath in and out of her flaring nostrils. Soon the rhythm steadied her rapidly beating heart and the gentle swaying began to soothe her.

"What are you looking for?" she called, her eyes still firmly shut.

"Not sure," he replied from what sounded a distance away. "I thought maybe I'd find a sharp stone to cut through the rope but there's—"

"Powick's house!" she blurted, her sudden movement rocking the net once more. "The rusty knives in her operation room!"

"It might take a while?" He seemed unsure.

"Just go!" she insisted.

"Okay, I'll be as quick as I can… Oh, and if I'm late back you don't need to hang around!"

Her friend burst into laughter as he sprinted off along the path, his footsteps pounding the forest track. Violet might have laughed too had she not been caught up in the clutches of a tree.

As Boy's steps faded into the distance, the silence seemed huge.

A breeze blew through the trees; the leaves rustled. As Violet swung above the ground, her mind spun. Why was the net trap here? And who had set it?

Suddenly, heavy footsteps stomped through the undergrowth below her. Someone was mumbling.

It couldn't be Boy, he'd never be that quick, and anyway the sound came from the opposite direction. She froze. Whoever it was had just stopped beneath her.

A familiar smell of rot snaked up Violet's nose. Goosebumps pimpled her skin. Terrified, she forced her eyes open a sliver. Two large zombies stood on the forest floor below, glaring up.

She squealed as one of them made a lunge upwards for her, its fingers just grazing the rope. The net swayed across the path away from them.

Thinking quickly, she reached over her head and grabbed the knot at the top of the net, pulling herself up and away from the creatures. Her arms shook, shivering in pain, as she clung on tight.

Both zombies were fitted with the same steel frames as Nurse Powick's creations. Familiar stitch marks and patches of teddy bear fur traced their features. Terrified, Violet looked around for something that might help her.

The taller zombie jumped again, his grunt animal-like. He narrowly missed the bottom of the netting. She shifted her weight in one direction hoping to make the net sway. It worked and slowly she got into a rhythm, flying forwards and backwards in a large arc across the path as the zombies clawed for her.

One of the creatures wore ragged black pinstriped trousers and a once-white shirt; both items hung loosely from his bruised figure. He was missing a large chunk of grimy grey hair, which had left a deep crevice in his scalp.

The other zombie appeared to be female. A string of dirt-caked pearls decorated her sinewed, purple neck. Her skirt was frayed, and her once-cream lace blouse was missing an arm, torn off at the shoulder.

Strange eyes bulged from their gaunt faces. Violet was sure they were eye plants, just like Hugo and the others had been given in place of their own eyes. The translucent skin-like petals flapped in anticipation every time she swung near them.

These had to be Priscilla Powick's creations too.

From experience, she thought the creatures weren't all that intelligent. Hugo had never appeared to be able to think for himself and only ever did what he was instructed. She reassured herself she was safe. They would never figure out how to get her down.

Then she felt sick. She remembered the stable in the Outskirts and its three screens, connected wirelessly to the eyes of each of Powick's zombies, enabling the woman to see whatever her creations did. What if the nurse was watching now?

Violet's lungs contracted, her breath a wheeze. Her mind began to race. Where was Boy?

She closed her eyes and willed the zombies to disappear, repeating over and over in her head that this was all just a bad dream, one that she'd wake from any moment now.

After what felt like ages, the thud of their continuous jumping stopped, the smell cleared and Violet opened her eyes.

They were gone.

Her relief only lasted moments – she was sure they'd come back. She had to get out. Searching for solutions, she spotted a small dot on the horizon. Boy. She jumped around in the net, trying to get his attention. He needed to hurry up.

"How you hanging?" he shouted getting closer.

"Shush!" She tried to signal him to be quiet.

He grinned, waving back. There was something in his hand. "I got a knife," he called, wielding it about.

Violet looked over her shoulder and listened, sure the zombies would hear them. Boy had reached the pile of tree trunks and already climbed to the top by the time she turned back.

He strained onto his toes, grabbing the bottom of the net in his fingers.

"Don't move," he ordered.

"Quick, Boy!" Violet pleaded, checking over her shoulder again.

"Thanks for the thanks!" he panted, red-faced. "I've just run the whole way to Powick's and back for you!"

"There were zombies here! Two of them," she blurted.

Boy stopped cutting. His eyes locked with hers. "But…what…who…how?"

"Keep cutting," she insisted, checking round again. "They were just like Hugo, metal frames, eye-plant eyes, everything! They came out of the forest! They have to be Powick's too!"

"Is this just another way to keep me out here, Violet?" Her friend grunted as he sawed at the net.

"What? No...just hurry!" she insisted, too scared to be annoyed.

He hacked a hole big enough for Violet to squeeze through. She dropped onto the logs, then scrambled to the ground and raced for cover in the forest. Her clothes and skin were ripped by the gorse bushes that traced barrier-like along both sides of the path. Beyond the gorse, the forest floor was soft and mossy, muting their footsteps.

Violet darted behind a group of tightly packed trees. Boy dived in beside her. His face and hands were scratched raw too.

"What happened?" he wheezed.

She was about to speak when three large figures passed through the trees a little way away.

The two zombies Violet had seen earlier grumbled as they headed towards the net. They were leading a third figure – a tall woman, dressed in a stiff navy cloak tied high at the neck over a starched white blouse.

"Nurse Powick!" Boy gasped.

CHAPTER 10

THE MAZE

"It's empty!" Nurse Powick cried, frustrated, as she hit the frayed net with a large stick. "The alarm sounded, so there must have been something in the trap. You're meant to be keeping watch! Why didn't I check the monitors before coming out here? As if I'm not busy enough right now! The sooner you things can think for yourselves the better!"

The zombies groaned, looking up at the net.

"Useless mush-for-brains!" she snarled, examining the rope further. "Seems it was cut. Who's been sneaking around? We don't need trouble. Not now. There's only a few days left. He's worked too hard for this!"

The nurse walloped the net again. Violet crouched down further into the mossy earth, while Boy gripped the sides of a tree in front of him, peering round it.

"Nevertheless, they can't have gone far. Search the area!" Powick ordered. "I'll check your screens at home. Where's Tom? Isn't he meant to be in charge of you idiots? Do I have to do all of this ungodly work myself?"

Sour-faced, she pushed past the zombies and disappeared back into the forest in the opposite direction to the Outskirts.

Her creatures didn't move.

"Search now!" she screamed, her sharp voice shattering the quiet of the forest.

The zombies groaned again then both stomped off the path, ripping through the gorse as though oblivious to its thorny fingers. Boy snuck quietly backwards then turned and crept away, beckoning Violet to follow him.

"What are we doing?" she hissed once they were a safe distance from the creatures.

"Getting away from them," Boy whispered, climbing under a fallen tree trunk.

"But we need a plan! What is Powick doing here? She said something about *him* working too hard for this and there only being a few days left. That note on my bike was right – something is up. I bet Town *really* is in trouble!"

"She said she's going to check the screens, Violet." Boy stopped and stared straight at her. "The zombie's eyes are the eye plants, remember? She'll see you in the net. She'll come looking for us. We have to get out of here."

"Well then, we have to go home. Tell Dad and William and the others…"

"Exactly!"

"Then why are we going this way? The Outskirts is behind us."

"Because I'm trying to sneak past the zombies, Violet. If we go wide enough, we should be able to circle round them!"

"Okay." She nodded uncertainly.

❉   ❉   ❉

The forest was dense. Every tree looked the same and Violet couldn't make out what direction they were heading in. Her gut told her to stop but she followed behind her friend – he was usually better than her at these things.

As the pair travelled in silence, the thick foliage dampened sounds until all they heard was the cracking of twigs in the undergrowth and each other's breath.

Everything grew darker. Violet lost track of time, unsure if the sun was dropping in the sky or if the forest had thickened even further. Her heart pounded. Surely they were lost? It couldn't take this long to get back to the Outskirts?

"We've been here before," she whispered as she climbed over a thick tree trunk. "I'm sure we have, Boy!

This is the third time I've done this."

"Maybe it just looks the same – all trees are alike!" Boy said, picking up a stick. He scraped his initials into the mossy bark. "If we pass here again, we'll know for definite."

She nodded and continued onwards. Boy seemed wary now too. Violet gulped a while later as they stopped in front of the initialled tree.

"We're going in circles!" she stuttered.

Boy looked around as though trying to make some sense of it all. The trees loomed large above them.

Suddenly he ran forward, disappearing around a corner ahead. Violet felt nervous – she was about to follow when her friend raced back towards her, his face etched in frustration.

"I know it sounds crazy, but I think we're in a maze," Boy panted, stopping short. "It's definitely not a normal forest – the trees are growing in lines. They're not normal trees either, not like the ones you usually see."

Violet looked at the tree beside her. Boy was right. The trunk was short but the greenery was tall, full and pointy at the top like a rocket. She'd seen pictures of ones just like it in her nature book at school. The trees were packed so tightly to their neighbours that together they created a dense wall of foliage either side of a narrow walkway.

"You're right," she said, looking around. "It's like we're standing in a passage."

The pair inched forward and round the next corner – it was the same there – another narrow walkway lined with foliage. In their panic to get far away from the zombies, Violet hadn't noticed this before.

"I was in a maze once," Violet remembered, steadying her racing thoughts, "when I was younger. I was scared 'cause I couldn't get out. Dad was with me. He said to touch the hedge with my fingers and keep walking, and never remove my hand from the hedge. It worked, we eventually got out!"

"That doesn't sound right. It can't be that easy to escape a maze, Violet!"

"Well it was, Boy, it worked!" she argued.

Her friend stepped back. "Since you're the maze expert then, lead us out." He gestured, not sounding convinced.

Violet stepped over to the line of trees on her left, reaching her hand until she touched its pine-scented greenery. Then she began walking.

"Mam and Dad will be worried," she whispered. "We've been gone ages now!"

"And whose fault is that?"

"Boy!" Violet snapped. "You can't blame me for—"

Suddenly her friend pulled her into the trees so fast

she almost swallowed a mouthful of prickly pine needles.

"What are you—?"

He shoved a hand over her mouth and pointed. On the corner ahead, hidden beside the base of a trunk, was a small clear-petalled plant, its eyeball centre scanning the area.

"Why would there be an eye plant out here?" Violet shuddered.

"I don't know," he whispered, not looking away from the creature, "but we have to sneak past. When its head moves left again, run."

The eye scanned slowly across the forest floor. Violet's heart pounded.

"Now," Boy said, tapping her shoulder.

He sprang up and sprinted round the corner, skidding into hiding by the base of another tree. Violet dived in beside him, her head almost colliding with the thick trunk.

"We have to be more careful," her friend whispered, "there might be more of them – they're well hidden. If I hadn't caught its movement, I wouldn't have spotted that one!"

"Boy, we're lost. I'm worried," Violet said, a little overwhelmed.

"I know." He sounded anxious too.

"But what is all this? First the trap, then the zombies,

Powick, the maze and the eye plants! What's going on?" She quivered.

"Let's just try to get home, Violet! We can think about all that later, after we tell our parents."

He pulled her up from their hiding spot. The pair continued forward, slower now as they checked round every corner for an eye plant. With each step Violet grew more nervous. They'd been walking ages and seemed no closer to home. Her tummy grumbled, but she was too scared to think about food.

The air grew cooler; it seemed like late evening. Violet shivered with the rising cold but didn't once remove her hand from the line of trees. They turned another corner and suddenly her fingers slipped into thin air.

"We've done it!" she almost shouted with relief as she turned to hug her friend. "We've escaped the maze, Boy!"

He didn't seem as excited and, confused, she swung back around, fully expecting to see the Outskirts in the distance, but they were standing at the edge of a vast empty field.

"Where…where are we?" she whispered.

CHAPTER 11
SEEING THINGS

"There's nothing here, it's just an empty field." Violet stepped further into the open.

They were standing at the edge of a huge circular meadow wrapped on all sides by thick forest. The sky had grown a little darker as though preparing for the night.

"I thought we'd be back at the start of the forest. I thought we'd be able to get home after we got out of the maze, Boy!" Panic gripped her throat. "Where are we, what is this place?"

"I don't know." Boy walked a little out from the trees. "But wherever we are, I think we're not meant to be here. I bet the trap, the maze, the eye plants, all of it was designed to keep people away."

"But away from what? A big empty field…? That doesn't make sense!"

Boy began to walk the edges, stopping regularly to peer into the forest. Violet sat down by the base of a tree, exhausted, hungry and confused. A thick lump formed in her throat.

She raised her knees and wrapped her arms round them, suddenly aware again of the cold. Now that she'd stopped, the air felt frigid and the sweat that dampened the back of her shirt made her shiver.

Across the expanse of grass, Boy was still walking the perimeter. She wasn't sure what he was hoping to find. She was continuing to follow his progress when movement caught her attention in the middle of the field. Violet sat forward and stared. There was nothing there.

She rubbed her eyes and checked again. Still the place was empty. Was she so tired, hungry and lost that she was seeing things now? She was forever being told she'd a vivid imagination. Still uneasy, Violet shuffled back further under cover of the trees.

Then something moved again, in the same place as before. At first a foot hovered in mid-air, followed quickly by an arm, until eventually a figure appeared in the middle of the field.

What was going on? This person seemed to have come from nowhere. But that was impossible. Maybe she was just overtired. She rubbed her eyes again – the figure was still there, standing still, as though waiting for something. At this distance and in the fading evening light she could just make out small details: a crooked leg, torn grey T-shirt and a missing hand. She quivered. It was a zombie but a different one to earlier.

Boy was over to her right now, having nearly finished his round. He seemed oblivious to this creature's existence. She needed to warn him somehow and was racking her brain for some way to do it, when the thing disappeared again. Like magic.

Violet was speechless when Boy reached her side.

"The field's empty." He shuffled down beside her. "And there's no other entrance into the maze except the one we came through. It's really weird, there's nothing here!"

Violet still stared ahead, trying to make sense of what she'd seen.

"Is everything all right?" he asked, glancing over at her. "You're acting weird. I don't think I've ever been able to speak for that long without you interrupting me."

"There was a zombie there," she stuttered, pointing forward. "They just appeared from nowhere and then disappeared again!" It sounded mad, even as she said it.

"What do you mean? Where?" he asked, squinting across the grass.

"In the middle of the field. It was like magic!"

"Magic?" he snorted. "There's no such thing!"

"I'm not crazy!"

"People don't just appear and disappear, Violet!"

"I know they don't usually but they did this time. Just there." She pointed again.

"Maybe it's your eyes. It's getting dark. Dad says our eyes play tricks on us at night. That's why some people think they see ghosts."

"I didn't say it was a ghost, I said it was a zombie!" she replied sharply. "And it's not night yet!"

Boy suddenly sat forward. "Look! In the middle of the field," he hissed, pointing.

The zombie was standing in the same spot as before. It now carried a flaming torch, casting a ghostly yellow light across the field.

"I told you," Violet whispered as another zombie appeared behind the first.

They were followed quickly by two more figures, each carrying a torch. A strong yellow glow now filled the centre of the field. The group then set off, moving rapidly towards Violet and Boy.

The pair scurried back to the cover of the trees and curled into the undergrowth.

Violet held her breath and gripped her friend's hand.

As the zombies got closer she could clearly make out

the limping step and imposing frame of Hugo, the Child Snatcher, one of Powick's original zombies. He was leading two more of the nurse's creatures, and behind them was a smaller figure, slight-framed and pale-skinned – he was like Boy in every way except for his cold ice-blue eyes.

"Tom!" Violet whispered.

The foursome passed dangerously near to Violet and Boy as they entered the maze. The zombies stared straight ahead, their mouths set in a permanent drooling grimace. A low growl slipped out from the lips of the grey T-shirted one with each pounding step. Tom looked tense. His eyes darted after every sound. He was dressed all in black, just like his brother.

"Tom's with those zombies – and you think he's good!" Boy whispered as the flaming torches disappeared into the distance.

"But…" Violet was breathless. "Why would he warn me about Town if he wasn't?"

Boy shook his head. "You don't know the note was from him. Anyway, we can't worry about that now. Those zombies were different to the ones in the forest earlier. How many more zombies do you think Powick has made?"

"I don't know" – Violet was shaking now – "and where are they coming from, Boy? They just appeared out of nowhere."

She climbed unsteadily to her feet and walked into the field. Boy passed her, jogging towards the middle of the open space. He was at the spot where the figures appeared when he fell suddenly backwards, landing with a dull thud on the grass.

Violet rushed forward.

"Are you okay…? What happened?"

"I…I walked into something," he groaned, rubbing his head before pushing up onto his elbows. "But there's… there's nothing there."

Violet looked round. Just as before, the field was completely empty.

A shiver ran down her spine and the hair on her arms shot up. She stood, put her hands out and crept forward. Almost immediately, the tips of her fingers hit a solid object.

There was definitely something right in front of her – she could feel it, but she couldn't see it. She fanned her hands out and placed her palms on it. The thing was big, solid and felt weirdly like the material in one of her mam's old dresses. Her heart pounded.

Then Boy was at her side. He held his arms out and moved them around the invisible object. He looked like one of those men with white faces and black clothes who she'd seen once in a circus.

"Can you feel that too?" he whispered.

Violet nodded. She placed her right hand on the thing and walked left, just as she'd done in the maze. She'd paced a good distance from Boy when her fingers slipped off into thin air.

She put her hand back on the invisible object and gently felt round to see if a corner existed. It did. She followed it and walked along again until her fingers slipped off once more. She turned another corner and continued to trace what she realized now was a large square shape. Weirdly, on every step of her journey round she could still see Boy. It was as though nothing existed between him and her but a field of grass, though Violet's sense of touch said otherwise.

She had just returned to her friend's side when something clicked nearby. Oddly it sounded like a lock. The pair were ready to sprint away when suddenly a dark-cloaked figure stepped out from the invisible structure just metres from them. They froze, statue still, afraid even a twitch would alert the person to their presence.

Priscilla Powick stood square-shouldered and stern on the grass, a large flaming torch in her solid grip. She fiddled with the high collar of her long navy cloak before striding across the field into the maze.

Boy raced to where the woman had appeared and began to feel around in the air.

"Got it!" he said, cupping an invisible object in his

palm. There was the same click as a moment before and Boy strained, pulling back on something.

"Quickly, Violet, come here!" he hissed. "It's a door!"

She raced round him, then stopped, suddenly disorientated. In front of her, hovering in the middle of the field, was what looked like a cobbled path and part of a distant stone wall. She hesitated.

"Step through!" he insisted. "Quickly, we need to find out what's going on!"

Boy, who had at first been the hesitant one, had suddenly changed his tune.

CHAPTER 12

A ZOMBIE ARMY

Violet stepped through the invisible doorway onto a cobblestone path which cut through grass on either side and Boy followed. Her mind spun as she tried to make sense of her new surroundings: behind her was the empty field and now straight in front of her, at the end of the path, was a huge arched wooden door set into the wall of a gigantic stone castle.

The castle was like something from a faerie tale. Its high walls connected four large towers, forming a square shape. Violet imagined a courtyard rested inside. The towers were topped with teeth-like battlements.

How could something this large be hidden right in the middle of an open field?

"Do you think it's some sort of magic?" Violet

whispered, breaking their shocked silence.

Boy shook his head. "Magic doesn't exist, it has to be science of some sort," he replied, turning to look back the way they'd come.

He gasped and stumbled sideways, knocking against her.

"What is it?" She looked around.

Violet choked, spluttering air as she tried to take in what she was seeing.

Where the field and the tree maze beyond should have been, now stood a huge metal wall. It stretched right to the sky and Violet had to strain to see the top, making herself dizzy. Along the wall were join lines, like scars, where sheets of metal had been welded together to form the enormous structure. It was propped up at regular intervals by thick steel bars dug into the soil and seemed to create a boundary round the whole castle.

"Do you think that's what we were feeling in the field, the invisible thing, what you walked into?" she asked breathlessly.

"It must be," Boy said, shaking his head.

"But it's not invisible and it's metal – the thing I touched felt soft and smooth. It reminded me of a dress Mam used to wear."

"Well, whatever it is, it works. It's able to hide the castle."

"Do you think Powick built it?" Violet shivered.

Boy looked nervous. "I don't know, but if she didn't, then who did? We'd better get off the path. She and the others could be back at any time."

As they crept along the cobbles, Violet noticed odd stone carvings – wolves with human bodies, two-faced men, and roaring lions – all standing guard round the ornate window frames of the castle, as if watching for intruders.

The arched door facing them was dotted with dark metal rivets and an enormous wrought-iron handle rested over the biggest keyhole Violet had ever seen. Above the door, set into the stone, was a carved coat of arms depicting a castle and two men holding bows and arrows. On either side of the entrance, mounted to the walls, were large wooden torches, both aflame, their light casting sinister shapes across the grass.

"I'm not sure I want to go in there," Violet stuttered nervously as they stood in the shadow of the huge doorway. "Do you think Powick lives here now? But why did she stay in the cottage in the Outskirts if this castle was here all along? And what's she planning, Boy? It must be something really bad – that note said we won't win this time…"

"Stop it, Violet." Boy grabbed her shoulders. "We can't panic, not here – we have to stay calm. We don't know what's going on or how Powick's involved. We just need to find out what's happening and get back home so we can all come up with a plan together…"

Violet steadied herself. He was right, she had to be calm. But she was finding it very hard with a stone gargoyle glaring down at her from the top of the arch above.

Boy tried to heave open the heavy door. His face burned with the effort but he couldn't shift the solid wood.

"There has to be another entrance somewhere," Violet whispered, regaining her cool. "I was at a castle once when I was on holiday with Mam and Dad. There were loads of doors into it."

Quickly the pair slipped off the path and onto the grass, heading round the side of the castle. Five flaming torches riveted onto the high stone wall lit the night here and they crept through the shadows, keeping out of their glare. They came across two smaller wooden doors, but both of them were locked.

Boy was just ahead of Violet as they rounded the tower at the far end of the wall when suddenly he vanished.

"Violet. In here!" he hissed.

An open iron gate led into the tower. Violet peered through the darkness. She could just see Boy waiting for her on the steps of a spiral stone staircase that wound upwards. Quickly she followed him, her breath heavy with the effort as she climbed.

A strange buzzing sound grew louder with each step. Close to the top, a sharp wind whipped round the narrow space, chilling her bones. She turned a corner and could see the starry sky above her as she stepped up and out onto a stone landing. Night had completely fallen.

The wind tore at her clothing. A battlement wall traced the top of the round tower and she barely spotted Boy's shadowed figure leaning against it.

He turned to face her.

"I know why the note said we won't save Town this time." There was a wobble in his voice and his face was ghostly pale.

"What is it?"

He didn't reply but gestured below.

Violet braced against the wind as she edged across the platform. What did Boy mean? The buzzing sound was really loud now. She reached the wall and peered through a gap in the battlements.

At first her mind couldn't understand what her eyes were seeing, then her stomach heaved. She wretched but nothing came out.

"Shush." Boy panicked. "They'll hear you!"

Standing in the torchlit cobbled courtyard below, like hundreds of soldiers on parade, were rows and rows of zombies.

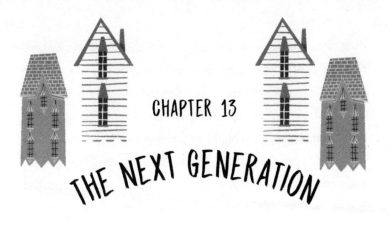

CHAPTER 13

THE NEXT GENERATION

"What…what's going on?" Violet stuttered, staring down into the courtyard.

"I don't know," Boy whispered.

The zombies were lined up from one end of the cobbled yard to the other, like an army ready to march to war. The thought made Violet quiver.

Flickering torches cast deep shadows across the creatures' gruesome features. Each of the zombies stood still, their eyes closed and heads hanging down, facing towards the main castle entrance.

They all looked similar to Hugo. Nurse Powick's handiwork was evident in the rough lines of stitching and patches of fur that traced their bodies. Their clothes were ragged and caked in dirt as if they'd been pulled from their graves; deep purple bruises covered their green- and yellow-tinged skin, and pus oozed from open wounds. Some of the creatures were missing limbs, while bones protruded at awkward angles from others. One particular monster's head was cocked at an impossible angle, as though its neck was broken.

These zombies had metal outer-skeletons too, like the others they'd seen in the forest. Thick bars of steel traced their limbs and spine, attached to wires that cut deep into the skin. The left foot of each creature was securely cuffed by a wide metal band, attached to a short sturdy chain that was anchored to the ground.

Beside each cuff was a small black box dug into the earth. Each box had a red wire that snaked up to the middle of the metal bar which traced the spine of every creature. The black box had to be the battery that charged the zombies.

Violet turned around unsteadily and sat down with her back against the battlements. Boy copied and they rested side by side in stunned silence. The buzz that she'd heard while she climbed the tower now seemed to engulf her.

"What's that sound?" Violet asked.

"It must be the batteries," Boy replied. "I think the zombies are being charged up."

"For battle…" The words were out before she could stop them.

Boy didn't reply, which made it worse.

Hugo was strong – his steel frame made him more powerful than anyone Violet had ever met. So what if hundreds of Hugos marched onto the streets of Town? Boy was right, maybe the note was beginning to make sense – if Powick had some kind of zombie invasion planned, they'd never be able to win, not this time.

"What does Powick have against Town? I can understand George and Edward's actions, at least a little – they hated William and how he was Iris's favourite, so they wanted to hurt him," Violet said, chasing her thoughts. "But Powick? She doesn't have any reason to hurt us, or Town, does she? An army this size must have taken her years to sew together. She must have been working on her plan for ages – but why?"

"I don't know, Violet." Boy shook his head in disbelief. "Maybe she doesn't need a good reason, maybe she's just crazy?"

"It just doesn't add up! Unless she's doing it for Edward and George…or maybe even for Tom? But she doesn't treat Tom as if she likes him. And the note said *they*…"

A loud bang rocketed off the walls. The pair scrambled up, peering back through the gaps in the turreted stone.

Powick, Tom, Hugo and the two other zombies from earlier stood at the top of the courtyard, just inside the huge arched door.

"They're back," Violet whispered. "We need to get out of here now! We need to get help."

"Shush," Boy hissed.

"They can't hear me from up here," she snapped.

Suddenly Powick marched through the rows of zombies towards the back wall of the castle. Tom followed like a shadow.

"She's here somewhere! Bring her to me!" the woman screeched, her voice echoing off the walls as she stopped in a doorway.

Boy's twin nodded feebly.

"Everything we've been working for has led to this moment. All those years of sacrifice! I won't have that cursed girl ruin it all! He's waited too long!"

"I think she's talking about me…" Violet trembled.

"But who's *he*?" Boy asked, his dark eyes large. "Who's waited too long?"

Violet shook her head, unable to speak.

"You're right though, we have to get help, now!" Boy continued. "Whatever is going on, it's too big for us this time! Let's get back to the maze – if we can find our way to the other side we should come out near the Outskirts."

The pair darted across the landing and down the spiral staircase onto the grass outside the castle walls.

Nervously, they snuck back the way they had come. Boy had already passed the first tower and was out of sight, heading for the door in the huge metal sheeting, when someone laughed behind Violet.

She froze.

"That's the spirit, dear, give up now! There's no use in running," a woman chuckled.

Violet turned slowly around and shuddered. Nurse Powick's big features were shadowed heavily by the flaming torchlight, making her look like a witch.

"Certainly makes my job easier when you submit," she cackled. "You really ought to be more careful though and not wander around on your own – didn't anyone ever tell you the world is a dangerous place? You were spotted by my creatures in the forest, you see, cornered like a rat in my trap. And then seen by those beauties."

Violet followed Powick's pointed finger and suddenly noticed tiny eye plants growing at the base of the metal sheeting. She groaned – why hadn't she paid more attention?

"My zombies are like dogs, you know, except much easier to train. Turns out that, unlike dogs, the dead can't think for themselves, so they do my bidding always!"

Violet was confused by what Powick meant until two

large zombies appeared from the shadows behind the nurse. Their bloodshot eyes locked on her while drool dripped from their cracked lips.

"Get her!" the woman cried.

Violet darted towards the exit. She needed to get to the maze, where she'd at least have a chance of hiding. The zombies pounded the earth behind her; the mechanical zoom-and-click sound of their metal frames followed them as they moved. A hand clawed at her shoulder…she ducked but it snagged her jumper and she flew backwards into the monster's arms.

"Do you like the improvements I've made to my creatures?" Powick smiled as Violet squirmed in the zombie's grip.

The nurse ran her fingers through the monster's dirt-caked hair, pulling away a tangled chunk.

"Hugo was my first experiment," she continued, "but these beauties are my latest – the next generation, if you will. Years of work makes for major improvements. These creatures are fast, as you can see, have pinpoint smell once they know what they're looking for, they've a hunger for blood and they're much easier to control. Ideal weapons. It took a while to get them to this point, but it's all about learning, don't you agree?"

Violet's heart pounded as she tossed and wriggled, trying to break free.

"Best stop that now, dear. He's as strong as ten men and you, pet, are nothing but a miserable child! Take her inside!" Powick ordered. "Bring her to my surgery. No, hold on, I'll need to free up a bed first. Bring her to my room – at least she can't cause trouble up there! Imagine the look on everyone's faces when their miniature hero parades into Town, a freshly made zombie, determined to destroy them!"

Violet squealed, struggling to free herself as her captor turned and marched straight across the grass, passing beneath the gigantic stone arch into the castle courtyard.

She was being held securely, like a squirming baby, in the thing's crusty arms. This close she could see the small gaping wounds that dotted the creature's purplish face and the thread-thin petals of its eye-plant eyes moving like creepy lids when it blinked. Was Powick going to do this to her – turn her into one of her monsters?

She closed her eyes and tried to shake off the image, only opening them again as the temperature changed.

They were inside. The monster carried her through a large entrance hall and stomped up ornate wooden stairs that swept round onto a wide flagstone landing. The long corridor in front of them, lit solely by candlelight, was dotted with dark wooden furniture – the table legs sprouting roaring lions' heads or monkeys' feet. The walls were decorated with what looked like dirty hanging carpets. Small holes were worn through the images of war, where woven red-coated men rode white horses into battle.

She thought of Boy. If he'd gotten away, maybe he could get help, before...before...

The monster stopped outside a low door, crouched and shouldered it open. It grunted, then released Violet onto the cold stone floor. She landed painfully on her shoulder. The creature kicked her out of the way before locking her in the room.

CHAPTER 14

DR A. ARCHER

The room was pitch black.

Violet lay listening to her racing heartbeat while the zombie's heavy footsteps disappeared down the hallway. Silence engulfed the space. She eased up to sitting as pain seared across her back where she'd hit the floor.

All sorts of terrible thoughts skulked round her imagination.

What if Powick really did turn her into a zombie and make her attack Town? What if Boy had been captured too and the nurse was operating on him somewhere right now? What if she never saw her parents again?

The what-ifs tumbled round her mind as Violet crouched in a cold corner, trying to cocoon herself against anything that might be hiding in the darkness.

But she couldn't give in to fear, she told herself, as her body began to shiver. If she had learned anything from her encounters with the Archer brothers, it was that fear controlled people and made them do stupid things. She had to take back control, she had to think straight and get out of here.

Her racing pulse slowed. Her eyes adjusted to the dark and, aided by a trickle of light from under the door, she was just able to make out her surroundings.

Clambering up from the floor, she felt her way across Nurse Powick's room to the door. She slid her fingers along the wood until they caught on a thick iron ring – the doorknob. She twisted it, the rust scaling off in her hands. Nothing budged.

She looked round for anything that might aid her escape.

The place was cavernous and grey. There was a thin slit window in the thick stone wall and freezing air spilled into the space, making it cold and miserable.

A steel-framed single bed rested by the far wall underneath the window. Next to it was an old wooden desk and chair surrounded by a pile of cardboard boxes.

Lying across the top of the desk was a worn leather-work belt, similar to something Mr Hatchet, the butcher, often wore strapped round his expansive waist. Hanging from it were sharp, stainless-steel implements.

Violet grabbed a long thin tool resembling a giant knitting needle from the belt and walked back to the door. She was sure she'd seen Boy and Jack pick locks enough times to be able to do it herself. She twiddled the needle in the lock while pulling at the handle. Nothing happened.

After a while, she flung the needle with a clatter on the floor. She was locked in. Unless help came, there was no way out.

Her chest tightened and she strained to breathe. She needed hope. The boxes! Maybe there was something in them that might help her.

Quickly she kneeled by the pile of battered cardboard and opened the nearest box. Soft fur greeted her fingers and she pulled out a purple teddy bear bandaged round the head. Violet hadn't had a soft toy in years – she was too old, she insisted. Now she hugged it close, glad of the company as she continued to rifle through the rest of the contents.

Next she found books – some on sewing and knitting, others on surgery, and lots of stuff on faerie tales, myths and legends. Tucked under the books was a small brown box engraved with a heart. Violet opened it. Folded neatly inside was a pile of letters tied together by brown string.

She cuddled the purple bear as she pulled out an envelope. It was yellowed and worn, as though many years old, and was addressed in finely swirled letters to *Nurse Powick, Dr Spinners' Office, Hegel University*.

She gasped. Hegel University, where the missing scientists all worked. Had Powick been there too? Did she have something to do with their disappearance?

Violet nervously unfolded the page inside, watching under the door for any sign of an approaching shadow.

Dear Priscilla, she read.

I am flattered that you admire my work greatly. It is becoming ever more difficult to get a hearing amongst my colleagues. I think the field of life sciences scares them all, and none more so than your boss, my once esteemed friend, Dr Spinners.

I thank you greatly for your interest in helping me further my career. I assure you, the work you are doing for me is greatly appreciated and I promise Spinners will not hear anything about it. It's our secret.

I wanted to thank you for your recent inclusion of papers on the Divided Soul in regards to my son William. You are quite right, my luck has been out since that infant was born. I don't often delve into the realms of myth and legend but I am open to all kinds of thinking and some of your research does show merit.

I look forward to our debates and your kind ear. I am

becoming increasingly frustrated at the way my work is now received, even amongst my own family, but your letters give me some solace.

Yours gratefully,

Dr A. Archer

She shivered. The writer mentioned his son William – could that be William Archer, Boy's dad? Did this mean the letter was from Boy's grandfather to Nurse Powick? And they mentioned the Divided Soul. She'd heard about that before.

Violet pulled out another letter. Again, it was addressed to Nurse Powick.

Dear Priscilla,

They are trying to take my licence. They say my work is that of a madman! My friends and colleagues have all turned against me. Thank you for your latest kind words – they are all that keeps me sane. As you say, the GREATEST MINDS are ridiculed the most and someday they will recognize my greatness. However, in the midst of this onslaught it is hard to step out of the fog.

Dr Spinners is making life very difficult for me now. Again, your warnings and your work are of the upmost importance to me and are forever our secret.

William is causing more trouble at home. There is something off with that child. You might be right about him, my dear friend.
    Arnold

Her hand shook. The writing was the same on both letters, one signed Dr A. Archer, the other Arnold.

Arnold Archer. She had heard that name!

Edward had talked about Arnold from the steps of the Town Hall only a few months ago. He'd said Arnold Archer was his father and he accused William of killing Arnold with a shoelace when he was just a child. She knew she'd heard about the Divided Soul before too! Edward had mentioned it in the same speech – he'd said William's different-coloured eyes were an indicator that he was a Divided Soul and that meant he was cursed and evil. Violet didn't believe Edward's story then. Iris said it wasn't true either, and the old woman never said anything more about it.

But now there were letters from Arnold to Powick, letters that said there was something wrong with William, letters that talked about the Divided Soul. Violet had been looking for a reason for all of this, a reason why Powick was planning whatever she was planning. Maybe somehow this was it? But how did it all fit together?

Violet's head went into overdrive as she tried to make

connections between what she knew about the Archer family's history and what was being said in the letters.

Suddenly something knocked against the door. Quickly she stuffed the letters in her pocket and threw everything else back into the box, then stood up and hurried to the corner just as the door clicked open. There was no one there. She inched across the room and gingerly looked outside.

"Quick, come on!" someone said.

The person stood silhouetted a little down the hall, his back to her.

"Boy!" she gasped, trembling with relief. "How did you find me?"

"This way! Now!" he whispered, ignoring her question as he darted forward.

Violet sprinted after him down the stone corridor. Boy seemed very familiar with the place as he ducked behind a carpet-like wall hanging and down a concealed set of spiral stone steps to a corridor on the ground floor. Violet spotted the army of motionless zombies in the courtyard outside as she shot past a window.

Suddenly a door banged nearby. She jumped.

"What's all that racket about?" a deep voice boomed.

She hadn't time to think as Boy raced back and, without a word, shoved Violet roughly into a dark room. Her nose tickled with dust and she stifled a sneeze.

Her friend remained in the hallway. What was he doing? She opened the door slightly and peered out.

"Have I not warned you about running inside before?" a man shouted.

A small squat figure moved down the corridor towards her friend, a large candle in his grasp. Violet felt sick. Edward Archer? But how could that be? How had he gotten out of his cell in the Town Hall?

As the man moved closer, she noticed his face was heavily lined and strands of neatly combed white hair were pulled across his balding head, as though trying to hide his bare scalp. It wasn't Edward but someone who looked just like him, only years older.

"I'm sorry, sir," her friend mumbled, his hands shaking. "I was in haste to check on the troops. They are almost fully charged. I didn't intend to disturb you!"

"But you did disturb me, boy! Intention or not!"

"I know, sir. I'm sorry, sir. It won't happen again."

Violet squinted out at the person who'd helped her, his shoulders slumped and head bowed. She couldn't see his eyes but she knew his stance. She suddenly understood – this boy wasn't her friend, this boy was Tom!

"You're right, it won't! Now come with me, I need a dummy for the DeathDefier. I've been tweaking it all night. Purrs like a kitten!"

"But I…" Tom shuffled awkwardly.

"You dare to answer back, boy? Follow me!" the man ordered, storming towards him.

Boy's twin cowered, just like a dog Violet had seen once who'd been badly treated.

The stranger thundered past.

"Go home – it's straight back through the maze to the Outskirts. Evacuate Town tonight! It's all happening in two days," Tom whispered quickly to the air, before following after him.

She waited, breathless and stunned. Who was that man? What was the DeathDefier and why was Tom trying to help her again? She knew for sure now, he had to be the one who'd left the note.

But what was happening in two days? Violet needed to get out of the castle, find Boy and get home! Whatever it was, Town and everyone there was in danger!

CHAPTER 15

ARNOLD

As Violet waited to ensure the coast was clear, a green light flashed in the room behind her, catching her attention. She turned around and gasped.

The walls of the space were covered in small TV screens, just like the ones in Powick's stables in the Outskirts, only way more of them. Each of the monitors had a number stuck to the top left-hand corner. Most of them were blank but about five – the ones marked with tiny green lights – played grainy black-and-white video.

This had to be the control room where Powick could see everything her zombies did.

Violet looked at the nearest screen to her. It was strange to think she was seeing what one of those creatures was seeing. This zombie appeared to be in the maze, moving quickly through the pathway lined with tall trees. She searched every live screen for signs of Boy and was relieved when she didn't see any. Maybe he'd gotten away?

She snuck from the room and crept along the hall until she found a door to the courtyard and eased it open to peer outside.

The air buzzed with a sound like a thousand bees as the zombies charged in their stations. No other soul seemed to stalk the night.

Silently, she stepped outside. It was cold and clouds of condensation followed every breath. The hum of the batteries seeped through her skin and grated on her mind as she skirted round the edges of the dead, heading towards the main castle gate.

Suddenly a hand grabbed her shoulder and drew her into the shadows of the wall.

"It's only me!" Boy whispered urgently as she grappled for breath. "Don't scream!"

She whipped round and glared straight at her friend. His eyes were jet black. It was him.

"How did you get away from Powick?" he asked. "The second zombie chased me. It was fast, much faster than Hugo. It was hard to shake him and when I did, I couldn't find you."

"Tom… Tom saved me," she panted, still breathless.

"Tom? Are you sure?"

"Yes." She nodded. "A zombie locked me in Powick's room – she said she was going to turn me into one of her monsters! Tom let me out… Well, I thought it was you, but then this man came and shouted at him and…"

"Slow down, Violet. Tell me exactly what happened."

Violet filled her friend in – she told him about Powick's room, Tom's rescue, the control centre and the strange man in the hallway.

"Who was he?" Boy asked.

"I don't know. He looked just like Edward. I even thought it was him for a second, until he got closer. But he was old, like Iris-old! Tom was afraid of him. He left to help the man with something called the DeathDefier?"

Boy shook his head. "But why would Tom save you? I don't understand!"

"Because he's good, Boy! He doesn't want to hurt anyone, not really. I'm sure Powick is making him do it, just like your mam thought! He left that note on my bike, I know he did, and he warned me again just now. He said we have to get out of Town tonight, whatever is going on is happening in two days' time!" Violet insisted. "And I found these…"

She pulled the letters from her pocket and handed

them over to Boy to read, looking around nervously as her friend skimmed the pages.

"Arnold Archer?" he looked up, confused.

"Your granddad!" Violet whispered.

"But I've never heard of him before," Boy replied. "I think somebody would have told me about my own granddad!"

"Well, I only know his name because Edward said something about Arnold at the Town Hall last year, when Tom was pretending to be you. Remember, when he had you locked in the caravan in the Outskirts…"

"Of course I remember, Violet! Why do you keep reminding me of that?" Boy said impatiently.

"Don't you see though," she continued enthusiastically, "I couldn't figure out why Powick was involved, but then I found those letters. Arnold Archer has to have something to do with all of this!"

"Do you think the man in the hallway was him?" Boy's question was blunt.

"Oh…yes, maybe, it could be. I mean he did look just like Edward but…ahem…" Violet blushed, hesitating. "Edward said he…um… Well, it doesn't matter, Boy, we need to get out of here before someone spots us!"

"Edward said what?" Boy pressed.

"Look, Iris said Edward made it all up and that it wasn't true. I didn't believe him, Boy, nobody really did, honestly," Violet mumbled. She could feel the red rising on her cheeks. "He was just trying to convince everyone in Town that he was nice and that things were better when Town was Perfect. He wanted everyone to turn against William so that he and George could take back Town, that's all, Boy. Nobody listened to his story, not really..."

"Violet! What did Edward say? Just tell me!"

"Ahem...he said...he said that William killed Arnold when he was a boy," she blurted.

"What! He said that Dad killed his own father?" Boy was furious. "Why didn't you tell me this before?"

"Because it didn't seem important then, it was all lies, Boy! Iris said so. Edward was just trying to turn Town against William! Saying all that crazy stuff about the Divided Soul!"

"Tom talked about that too when he kidnapped me," Boy said, thinking out loud. He paused for a moment then continued, "If Iris said Edward's story wasn't true, then did she say where Arnold is now?"

"I-I don't think so," Violet stammered.

Boy was about to reply when a zombie jolted beside them. The pair jumped. The battery by its foot read ninety per cent.

"We need to go. We have to get help!" Violet stated. "The zombies are almost charged. Whatever Powick is planning, it's only two days away, Boy, on your birthday! We've hardly any time left."

Another zombie jerked beside them, its arm hitting Violet. All around them the creatures stirred, jarring and jolting as though their reflexes were sparking up. Deep, almost painful moans and long drawn-out groans filled the air as the mass of gruesome creatures slowly moved their heads, as if waking from a deep sleep. A monster turned and looked straight at them. One of its cheeks was rotten through and Violet could see its back teeth grind together as it growled.

"They're awake!" she whispered, petrified. "We need to go right now. The main door!"

Violet's whole body trembled as they snuck along in the shadow of the wall. In the middle of the cobbled courtyard hundreds of zombies stomped their feet and clawed at the air, straining against the cuffs and chains that kept them tethered to the ground.

"You won't get out that way unless you have a key!" someone hissed as they passed by an iron-barred window.

"Did you say something?" Violet whispered, looking round at Boy.

A bony arm poked out from between the black bars and a long, thin finger pointed to a door behind them.

"That's the nurse's workroom. The keys must be hanging up in there somewhere, they have to be! They're a large set on a ring – you can't miss them," the voice croaked. "If you do find them, old chaps, would you mind terribly letting us out before you leave?"

"Who are you?" Violet asked curiously.

The ghostly face of an old man appeared at the bars, his sunken eyes and hollow cheeks made worse by the shadows of the torchlight on the wall beside his cell.

"Dr Joseph Bohr…" he replied.

"You're one of the missing scientists?" she gasped, "Your walking stick. I found it in the house. I knew there was a link. I knew you had to be with Tom!"

She glanced at Boy.

"Oh my cane, I wondered where that had gone. I must have lost it as those brutes dragged me here, those…"

"We haven't time." Boy pulled Violet away towards the room the old man had indicated. "We'll come back for you, I promise," he hissed.

The nurse's workroom was unlocked. Boy turned the iron handle and peered inside.

"I'll keep watch at the door while you search for the key," Violet said urgently.

The space was dark and freezing cold. The light from the courtyard reached inside and Violet could make out four wheeled steel tables in the middle of the room. One of the tables was empty but laid out on the other three were decomposing figures just like the courtyard zombies.

The steel frames had not been attached to these bodies yet and somehow this made them more human. She retched.

"Have you found the keys, Boy?" she whispered, itching to leave.

"Not yet, it's hard to see properly," he said from somewhere in the darkness.

Suddenly a shrill cry cut across the night. Violet jumped and peered out round the door frame. Powick was across the courtyard in her white apron and was heading their way. Violet quickly shut the door.

"She's coming here, I think!"

"Hide!" Boy panicked.

He stumbled in the darkness towards the back of the room, knocking against tables. Violet followed his sound, stopping by a rickety free-standing cupboard.

"In here," he stuttered, yanking open one of the long double doors.

Quickly she shuffled after him and the pair squashed together in the cramped space, pulling the door shut just as the nurse pounded into the room.

"Tom, Tom!" Priscilla Powick screamed.

Long fluorescent lights flickered, blinked and burst to life, illuminating the chilling space. It must have been the only place in the castle that had electricity, or at least the only one Violet had seen – everywhere else seemed to be lit by candle or torchlight. She peered through a tiny gap in the cupboard doors, afraid to make a sound.

"Tom, come here now!" the woman hollered angrily.

A solid square figure darkened the doorway.

"Oh, Arnold..." Powick's voice changed. Now she was almost whimpering.

Violet's heart thumped wildly. It was the man she'd seen earlier.

"Stop screeching, woman! I can hardly concentrate with all that racket. Between you and those creatures waking up outside, this place is a madhouse! Can't you calm them down!?"

"Oh I'm sorry, I didn't realize you were up, Arnie," Powick said, softly wheedling. "Your genius needs rest."

Violet had never seen the nurse this way. The hard lines that usually edged her eyes and divided her forehead had all but vanished, along with her scowl.

"Rest? Rest! How could I rest now, when I'm on the cusp of greatness!"

"But everything is ready, Arnold, there's no need to fret. The army is almost primed, prepared to march. We'll take Town tomorrow and set up the scene for your heroic entrance on Monday morning, when you'll become living history!"

Violet grabbed Boy's arm, squeezing tight as the words sank in. Tomorrow? They were planning on attacking

Town tomorrow? But why had Tom said it was happening in two days?

"Don't rush me, Priscilla. You're always pushing."

"But...you know time is precious, Arnold." Powick's softness was now tinged with urgency. "This moment won't come again. It has to be now, when Tom passes from a boy to a man. The world needs to witness your genius!"

"And the world will, Prissy, but I won't be rushed. Right now, the DeathDefier still needs a little tweaking. When all of this comes together, the science must be undeniable. The world will scrutinize my machine! I won't be left red-faced, not again!"

"But the twins' birthday..." Powick insisted. "The Elixir of Life can only be made then. There's no other way, otherwise the curse... This is our divine destiny! It's what we've been working towards, sacrificing our lives for all these years. Don't you want to claim what's rightfully yours, Arnold?"

"What's the elix thing?" Violet whispered.

Boy shook his head angrily, silencing her.

Arnold Archer clenched his fists in tight angry balls. Powick moved closer and softened her voice even more. She was taller than him and stooped a little, as if conscious of their height difference.

"It's just nerves. Those on the verge of greatness always falter before the last hurdle. There has never been a greater mind than yours, Arnie. Forces outside of this world have conspired to give you this moment. A perfect storm. The curse, coupled with your DeathDefier, will enable you to bring Spinners and then the army back to true life, to claim your place in history and be the first scientist to conquer death. Those non-believers, those mockers, they will watch and weep and then they will cower before us and beg for mercy when they see the strength of what we've created. That's why I've dedicated my life and my work to you! I am your devout disciple."

"You're right of course, Prissy," he muttered. "Everything's coming together nicely. I'm just on edge. We've gone over the plan, I know. You'll let out those idiot sons of mine, George and Edward, then secure Town with the Watchers tomorrow and begin setting the stage for the big day. Which is when I'll march in with our glorious army and give everyone a show they'll never forget! Using your elixir, I will raise Dr Spinners from the dead – the idiot who mocked me most, brought back to life by his 'lunatic' friend! And it will all be broadcast far and wide so that the world will be my witness! I can picture the faces of my naysayers now. They thought it couldn't be done, jeered me from the hallowed halls of Hegel as I revealed my invention. Well, I'll show those spineless excuses for scientists! They'll rue the day they ever ridiculed me. And remember, Priscilla, you must ensure you're not seen – people aren't ready to embrace what they don't understand. It must look like my science alone has conquered death!"

"And the army, then you'll bring them back to life…" Powick encouraged gently.

Arnold walked over to one of the creatures laid out on the steel table. He lifted up its arm and let it fall back down; it banged stiffly off the cold metal. Then he grabbed its head and turned it roughly left and right.

"You haven't fitted this thing with its transmitter and control chip yet?"

"No, it's a fresh one," Powick answered, nodding to the bars on the floor, "but it won't take long. I'm ready to attach the frame and chip, patch it up a bit, charge it and then it'll join the others. But imagine, Arnold, when these creatures can think for themselves, when they won't need their frames or a chip, when they're truly alive. They will be indebted to us, their re-creators – and with this army behind us, we can achieve anything together."

Arnold lifted up the body's arm again and wriggled it around in the air, making mock scary-zombie sounds. "Nobody will laugh at me then."

"Of course they won't, Arnold. I saw your genius from the start. When others fell away, even Iris, I was there. The universe has seen it too, otherwise you would never have been granted this rarest of opportunities.

Together we'll see this through. Real greatness rises from our most difficult challenges. What was once your weakness will become your strength!"

"You're right, Priscilla...of course. I am great!" Arnold smiled.

Powick sighed as though relieved. "So your machine will be ready? We must get it into position for your grand entrance, Arnold."

"Yes, as planned, just before sunrise." He nodded. "Have you arranged everything your end? Will the Watchers know how to control those creatures when we march in? I don't want any zombies going rogue on us! Are my sons briefed? There won't be any problems with that boy, will there? He's proving a little difficult lately. I have my doubts..."

"Doubts?" Powick swallowed.

"That you took the right twin... He doesn't appear to have the desired demeanour. At times I think he's weak."

The nurse looked away, pausing before she answered.

"Everything's prepared," she stated. "Trust me. Tom will do what he's destined to – he'll do what he's told. The Watchers are primed too." She pulled a small black box from her pocket and waved it around. "They each have one of these already – that was sorted weeks ago, the same time Tom briefed your sons on our final plans. The zombies will listen to them now."

Boy shifted uneasily.

"Good." Arnold nodded before marching to the door. He stopped suddenly, looking back round. "Oh, and Priscilla…"

"Yes," she said, her smile full of expectation.

"Your stitching is growing sloppy!" He nodded to one of the laid-out bodies. "That one could do with more work."

The nurse's face fell. And without another word, Arnold Archer left the room.

Powick stomped over to the zombie indicated, picking up a small pink teddy that rested on the table beside the monster.

"Arnold loves me, I know he does! We're always hardest on those we love most," she snivelled, pulling at one of the bear's arms. "I know it's painful, you poor thing, but I just need a small patch of your fur. Imagine all the help you're giving Mammy right now."

The nurse yanked the arm from the teddy. Setting down the dismembered limb, she grabbed a bandage. Then, with great care, she wound the white material round and round the bear until the newly opened hole in its shoulder was fully covered. Next she took a small brown bottle from a metal shelf beside her and syringed liquid from it onto the bear's stitched snout.

"You called for me?" Tom poked his head in the door, breaking her concentration.

Powick looked up and snarled. "Yes, I cleared a table for that girl Violet and when I went to get her from my room she was gone. You'd better find that excuse for a human child before she causes any more trouble. And do not tell Arnold! Take some of the zombies and scour the place. I want her disposed of once and for all!"

Tom nodded and disappeared as Powick picked up a long sharp needle and began to thread it.

"Would you lot ever shut up!" she roared at the zombies clanking their chains in the courtyard.

Slamming the needle onto a steel-topped counter, Nurse Powick stormed out of the door.

CHAPTER 16

CHANGE OF PLAN

"We have to get out of here now, before Powick comes back. We need to tell everyone in Town. They're going to release the Archers and the Watchers – and that whole zombie army!" Boy said jumping, from the cupboard and racing to the door.

Violet was behind him when he peered out onto the courtyard.

"But the keys, the scientists…" Violet grabbed his elbow as he was about to move.

"There's no time, we have to go before she comes back. We'll figure another way out!"

The pair slipped from the room, keeping to the edge of the courtyard while the zombies still twitched and strained against their straps. Ducking low, they snuck in behind an old stone drinking trough.

Nurse Powick, in her brown-stained white apron, stood at the top of the courtyard just in front of the main entrance. She clapped her hands twice and all the zombies turned immediately to look at her.

"Shut up," the tall woman barked, "I am trying to work!"

A sudden silence fell on the courtyard. Each zombie dropped its head and stared at the ground. Violet shivered as Powick marched back through her frozen army; the only sound the nurse's feet clobbering the cobblestones.

Violet and Boy crouched down as the woman passed their hiding place and headed back into her room. The door slammed, echoing round the walls.

"Did you find the keys?" someone hissed.

Violet jumped.

She turned to see the same thin, wrinkled arm waving through the iron-barred window behind them.

"No," she whispered, sneaking over, "but we're going to get help...somehow!"

"Please don't leave us here," a woman cried. "Arnold Archer is a madman! Who knows what he'll make us do!"

"He doesn't want us to do anything, Teresa, I've told you that already!" someone else grunted from inside the same cell. "He just wants to show us he was right all along!"

144

"There's more of you?" Violet whispered, grabbing the bars and pulling herself up onto her tippy toes to squint into the darkness.

Joseph Bohr, looking a lot older than his picture in the *Tribune*, stepped aside to reveal four shadowed figures behind him.

"Yes, there's five of us," Dr Bohr replied.

Boy yanked her sleeve.

"We have to go now, Violet!" he insisted.

She shook him off. "Are you all the missing scientists?" Violet questioned. "I knew you were involved somehow!"

"We're not involved!" Bohr darted forward so she could see his kind brown eyes. "Not even slightly involved in this fiasco."

"But why are you here?"

Joseph shook his head. "Some of us believe Archer wants to prove a point. He always said he would. I used to get threatening letters from him, we all did. They stopped when he disappeared, after Iris and the family left him. I presumed he'd given up on his obsessions with raising the dead, decided to go quietly into the night with whatever dignity remained. I never expected after all this time he'd follow through. Stubborn old mule!"

"Do you mean Iris Archer?" Violet asked.

"Yes, Iris had the misfortune of marrying young Arnold. Although none of us would have expected things to turn out quite as they did. He went mad, you see, and tried to attack their youngest son. He seemed convinced that the family was cursed because of that boy's birth. It was tragic really and of course Iris had to get away…"

"Nurse Powick mentioned a curse too. Is it about the Divided Soul?" Boy stopped trying to force Violet away and hauled himself up to join the conversation.

Bohr gasped and stepped back.

"You're the boy who took me, the one who's helping them!"

"No, that's Boy's twin, Tom, he has blue eyes. Boy's are nearly black," Violet corrected.

"The curse…" Boy said urgently, prompting the man to continue.

Bohr eyed Boy suspiciously before speaking again. "Yes, the Divided Soul, that's what he called it. Arnold said his son had brought bad luck on his research, something to do with his different-coloured eyes. He blamed him for the scientific community turning their back on his latest work. Of course, it wasn't his son's fault at all. He was just a toddler. Arnold had invented a machine to bring back the dead – that was the reason he fell from grace. The Death something, I think he called it…"

"The DeathDefier?" Violet prompted.

"Precisely! Yes, the DeathDefier! I remember Arnold had a dog called Arnold – he'd named it after himself,

146

that's the type of man he is. Anyway, the poor thing died. And shortly after, Arnold called us all into Hegel's main lecture theatre to reveal his latest work. We had no idea what was going on until we saw the body of Arnold the dog strapped up to this monstrous machine called the DeathDefier. Arnold, the man of course, told us he was about to raise his beloved pet from the dead. Well, you can only imagine our reactions. Iris was there too and she turned a ghastly shade of green, as did many of us. Anyway, he pressed the button, the machine shook and nothing happened. I think the poor dog may have belched once which was rather impressive, though it was probably just trapped wind."

"So what happened to Arnold?" Boy asked, now fully engrossed.

"We buried him!"

"The man?" Violet gasped, all sorts of ideas running through her head.

"Heavens no! The chocolate retriever! Arnold, the man, was disgraced. His downfall had been coming. He'd been dabbling with death for a while, and it wasn't winning him any friends. His research papers were being rejected and he was losing funding fast. He had really started to descend into madness. He began to blame William for everything. He even approached me one day with a book of faerie tales and showed me some pages on the Divided Soul. He asked my opinion on the facts behind the folklore. I was horrified when I read that the only way to break the curse was to kill the bearer, meaning his son William…"

Violet looked at Boy.

"Of course I told him then it was all madness," the doctor continued, "but I never actually thought he believed any of it. I mocked him, trying to make light of it – all in good jest, you see – but it appears he was a little more obsessed with such things than I realized. After his DeathDefier failed, he tried to attack William. I felt utter guilt. I mean, I knew what the article said, but I never believed Arnold could do such a thing. Then poor Iris disappeared with her young family – she had no other choice. She was never heard from again. A terrible tragedy really but…"

The man stopped suddenly, his face changed. "Your twin, that other boy, he's coming! Quickly. Hide!"

Violet and Boy ducked down and sprinted back behind the trough. The pair stayed completely still as Tom passed by. He stopped outside Powick's workshop door and knocked. Violet watched as he shuffled his feet nervously.

"Come in," the woman called.

Tom pushed open the door and disappeared inside. After a few moments, there was a loud shriek and Powick stormed out into the yard.

"I'm surrounded by fools," she cried, flinging her apron onto the ground in a fury.

The zombies didn't flinch.

Tom stepped out gingerly into the yard, his head bowed. Powick grabbed his chin and yanked it upwards so she was glaring down into his pale face.

Violet quivered; she could feel tears welling behind her eyes. She wanted to reach out and grab Boy's brother. Who was there to help Tom when he needed it?

"I told you to find her and you couldn't even do that! Now we'll have to improvise. After all this planning, you let a stupid thing like this happen! Were you born useless? I'll have to explain this to Arnold!"

She paused for a minute, breathing deeply, as though steadying her thoughts.

"Take a small party now, twenty of my creatures. Go fast. Hopefully the maze will have slowed that girl down and you'll beat her to Town before she has time to warn anyone. Free George and Edward tonight – it's earlier than planned but now we have no choice – then release the Watchers. Tell them what's happened! I want everyone in Town pulled from their beds and moved into No-Man's-Land so they can't create any trouble, then the walls must be guarded so no one can escape and raise the alarm."

"What about the machine and the—"

"No questions, Tom! I'll come later and we can get things ready for the big day! I should have you..." The woman raised her fist as if to smack him.

Tom cowered. Powick laughed then turned and charged to the top of the castle courtyard, facing her zombies.

"Ready yourselves, my creatures!" she roared.

The zombies snapped to attention, staring at Powick. Violet shivered.

Powick glared at Boy's brother. "Release the first twenty!"

Violet gripped Boy's arm as Tom raced along the first two lines of bodies. He unplugged their metal spines from their batteries and pressed a small black button on their ankle cuffs to open them.

"Creatures, grab your torches at the gate and light them as you leave. I want the Townsfolk petrified when they see you! Put fear into everyone you meet, just like we practised. Show me, darlings!" Powick roared.

The zombies snarled and stamped their feet, clawing the air. Those still chained strained forwards, the veins on their heads and necks popping out like purple rivers.

"My dwellers of the night," Powick boomed, her voice now echoing around them, "your time has come. Help us achieve our greatness and I will give you a town to call home!"

"Not our Town?" Violet trembled, squeezing Boy's arm even harder.

"Make them weep when they see you! Show your fury, show your rage!"

The monsters roared and the sound crashed off the walls and windows, rocking the castle. Violet cupped her ears and tears raced down her cheeks as Powick drove her army into a frenzy.

On her orders, Hugo heaved open the large door of the castle and stepped aside.

"I am your mother," Powick cried, "now make me proud!"

The dead army threw back their heads and screeched into the night. Their wild eyes popped in twisted faces and saliva flew from their snarling and blackened lips. The ground vibrated as hundreds of bare, maggot-ridden feet stomped the cobblestones.

The first two lines moved swiftly into formation, collecting their carved wooden torches from a pile at the gate. Setting them aflame as they passed outside, they followed Tom Archer on their journey towards Town.

The creatures that remained behind struggled against their restraints, eager to join in. Powick cried out for silence and clapped her hands. Every head dropped and once more the courtyard fell into a sudden and eerie quiet.

CHAPTER 17

WARNING TOWN

Violet felt sick, as the world began to spin.

"You okay?" Boy asked, shaking her shoulders. "You've gone white!"

She nodded, grabbing the trough to steady herself.

Powick was inspecting the pile of torches at the top of the courtyard. The remaining zombies were quiet, staring blankly at the ground. The castle gate was open.

"We have to go, Boy! We might still be able to get home before them!" Violet panted, pointing at the arch. "We could distract Powick and sneak…"

Suddenly a loud bang echoed off the walls. Violet jumped, her nerves still rattled.

"Would anyone mind telling me what is going on?" a voice boomed.

Violet and Boy peered round the edge of the trough.

Arnold Archer stood facing Powick and the entrance gate, his back to the courtyard. The nurse, who moments before had been terrifying, now cowered a little in his presence.

"I can explain, Arnold…" she said, walking up to the man.

"Some of the zombies are gone. You've split the army, Priscilla. Explain that." He sounded furious.

"It's Violet Brown." The nurse stuttered now. "I-I didn't want to alarm you, but she's been sneaking about the place. I had captured her but somehow she got away. I was afraid she'd gone back to warn everyone. Tom is leading a small crew in tonight. They'll release the Watchers and secure Town just a little earlier than planned. We won't be far behind, we just need to pack your machine and bring the scientists."

"But I wanted to lead the whole army in myself. I wanted to see her face when…"

"Whose face…? Iris? I knew it!" Powick sounded prickly.

"What do you mean, you knew it? Yes, of course I want Iris to see me lead the army in." Arnold was flustered. "You know what she did to me, Priscilla, how she destroyed my career by insisting on protecting that son of hers. If she'd just allowed me to kill William, I would never have fallen from grace – and then, to add insult to injury, she tried to murder me! Why wouldn't I want to watch Iris suffer as I take her perfect life and home away, just like she did so callously to me…"

"But…but you said you'd chosen this town as my gift after all of this was over, and that it had nothing to do with Iris. I created this army for us, Arnold, so we could secure the perfect place to live out our days together, basking in your glory after we'd proven your genius, after you'd gotten redemption. A place where we could build on everything we've created so far. With our army, Arnold, we could be so very powerful – imagine all the things we could do…"

"Why are you always so needy? It *IS* for us, Priscilla! You're acting just like her now, thinking of yourself instead of me! I know all of that – but first, what about my revenge, my triumph? You're taking my moment away and turning it into yours." Arnold was angry. "Sometimes I wonder if I'm an idiot in all of this, putting my trust in someone who's just a nurse. In fact you're really just… just a simple seamstress!"

Violet could see that his words bit deep. Powick's face fell. She looked down for a moment, then composed herself before looking back up.

"I'm sorry, Arnold. I didn't mean to take anything away from you. I was trying to save our plans. You *will* march the army in. Most of my creatures are still here, look around you! I'm sure Violet Brown won't have enough time to warn anyone either. Things are still going as planned. No one can stop us now."

"We'd better get moving then!" Arnold barked. "Before a child and a band of brainless dead creatures ruin everything!"

"Are you coming now? The plan was that you'd make your entrance on Monday morning when everything was set up."

"Well, plans clearly change, Priscilla! I'm coming to oversee the operation before it's destroyed altogether. I'll return for the army once I'm happy and then march back in glorious triumph!"

"Yes, of course." Powick looked flustered. "Hugo, bring the scientists now!"

"And my machine," Arnold ordered.

The nurse pointed at three other zombies, the ones Tom had followed to the forest earlier. "Get the DeathDefier."

"And be careful with it!" Arnold snapped as he paced behind the zombies into a room at the far side of the castle.

"We need to go," Boy whispered as Powick and Hugo strode dangerously close by, unlocked the scientists' cell and stormed inside.

"What will they do to them?" Violet quivered as someone screamed.

"We can't worry about that. The gate is still open," Boy said, his face pale. "We need to get home. Come on, we won't be spotted now!"

He crept out from behind the trough, Violet just behind.

Everyone was preoccupied so nobody spotted the pair as they sprinted across the cobbles and out under the stone arch. They were neck and neck as they raced down the path to the door in the strange invisible fence and climbed through into the circular field beyond.

Violet shook her head as she turned back towards the castle. The whole building had vanished as if all the horrors she'd just witnessed were only a dream.

"The maze." Boy pointed to the treeline ahead. "If we're quick we might catch up to the zombies and be able to sneak past them."

He ran into the forest and burst through the middle of the first line of trees. Violet followed, her face nicked by branches.

"Aren't we staying on the path?" she asked, uncertain.

"It's quicker if we go this way!" Boy insisted. "If we keep straight we should come out the other side, maybe even ahead of the zombies!"

He continued forward, ducking and diving under

branches or around thick trunks, all the time keeping them on course. Violet followed, her face and hands scraped raw as she beat her way through the foliage.

They broke out of the maze onto the path just by the pile-up of tree trunks. The frayed net still hung open above them. Violet could just see the zombies in the distance as they moved towards Powick's old cottage in the Outskirts.

The pair sprinted on, finally stopping a little way back from Tom and the group of zombies. Breathless, they dropped to their stomachs and edged forward in the grass, watching the scene.

Tom stood beside the well that would take them down into the tunnel to the graveyard, directing zombies onto the platform. The creatures were calm and quiet, a contrast to their earlier display at the castle. Each held a lit torch in its right hand, the flames warming the night sky above them as they waited their turn.

"We'll never get ahead of them to warn everyone now," Boy sighed.

Violet's mind raced for solutions.

"Remember in the stables when you were able to order Hugo around because he thought you were Tom?" she said, suddenly excited. "Maybe that'd work here too. I could distract Tom and get him away from the well for a second. Then you could jump up on the platform and go into the tunnel with some of the zombies. I bet the zombies will just think you're him and they'll obey you. Then you could run ahead and warn everyone in Town…"

"That might just work," Boy replied. "These zombies don't seem any more intelligent than Hugo. I'll hide behind the tree until you distract Tom. Then I'll go for it!"

"Okay." Violet nodded, suddenly nervous.

Without another word, Boy slipped away. She watched him as he kept low, creeping through the grass and hiding behind the large twisted tree beside the well.

Tom was busy ordering more zombies onto the platform as Violet inched forward on her elbows. She tried to concentrate, though her body was shaking. She was tired, cold and scared.

She kept an eye on Tom until she couldn't go any closer or he'd surely notice her. Powick's cottage was on her left. She rolled under the nurse's yellow fence and snuck round so she was looking at the twin's back, ducking down by the wild rose bushes.

Violet could see Boy poking his head out from behind the tree on the other side of the track.

How would she distract Tom? She searched the ground for a stone or something to throw, but couldn't find anything. Then she noticed a green gardening glove resting in the grass little way away. She scrambled across the lawn, grabbed it and crawled back to her cover.

The material was flimsy and she wasn't sure it would fly any distance so she pulled up clumps of grass and stuffed the glove until it bulged.

Tom was going to be suspicious – a grass-filled glove can't just fall from the sky – but she had no other ideas. Part of her also trusted what Macula had said – Tom was good, Violet felt it in her gut. He'd saved her again in the castle. That was three times and counting.

She got into position, steadied her arm just as more zombies were climbing on board the platform, took aim and fired.

CHAPTER 18

THE AMBUSH

The flying gardening glove caught Tom smack on the shoulder. Violet wasn't normally a good throw but under pressure it seemed she was much better!

Tom turned and she ducked down behind the thorny rose bush. Holding her breath, she gripped the grass as footsteps headed towards her and stopped a little way away.

She could just see the bottom of his legs through the bush. Tom looked around, then, after what felt like an age, he turned and walked back to his position by the well. Violet released a long slow breath.

"Next," Tom shouted at the remaining zombies, who were standing obediently in line.

There were no signs amongst Powick's creatures that anything had disturbed them and Violet wondered if Boy had followed through with their plan.

She watched through the gap in the thorny bush as two creatures stepped forward and climbed onto the platform, followed by two more. Then Tom ordered one of the zombies to tap out the letters D, O, W, N, with its bare foot and they zipped into the tunnel.

She couldn't see Boy behind the tree. She checked up and down the overgrown lane, but there was no sign of him there either. The plan must have worked – he had to have gotten onto the platform and into the tunnel.

Relieved but still uneasy, she slipped to relative safety around the side of the cottage and waited by the whitewashed wall for Tom and the last of the zombies to disappear into the ground.

Though she tried to stop it, her mind wandered to Boy and Town and what was happening right now. She laid her back against the wall and gazed skywards to steady her racing thoughts. One of her dad's favourite things to do was spot stars. It was a crisp, clear night and as she looked to the heavens, the Plough gave her comfort. She hoped he was looking at it too and that somehow her dad and mam would be okay. That somehow Boy would get word to Town and they could escape before anything really bad happened.

Eventually, Tom saw the last of the zombies onto the platform and climbed up after them, before disappearing down the well.

She waited impatiently for a while before pulling herself off the ground. Tom and those creatures had to be out of the tunnel by now. She ran to the well and looked into a pitch-black void. The platform remained below in the darkness with nobody to send it back up. She hadn't thought about that.

How was she going to get home? She tried not to panic. There had to be a way to call the floor up. She remembered the first time she'd discovered this passage with Jack – how they'd had to figure out puzzles to get to the Outskirts. Maybe this was a puzzle too? She traced her fingers over protruding stones in the well wall but none of them budged; she searched the grass at its base for anything unusual but found nothing; she even hung over the side of the wall into the pitch-black shaft, looking for clues, but all to no avail.

She investigated the tree nearby for any strange knots or branches, then inspected the road sign that marked the Outskirts in strong black iron letters. There was a slight gap between the words OUT and SKIRTS. Curious, Violet pushed on the first three letters. They shifted easily across, closing the gap with a click. She heard a slight rumble and her heart skipped as she rushed back to see the floor of the well moving upwards.

Quickly she climbed on board and pressed the floor tiles. The platform zipped back down, the circle of night sky shrinking above her. Once in the tunnel, Violet ran for the graveyard, her footsteps echoing around the small space. She reached the steps, opened the tomb and sprinted outside, back into the clear night, and cut quickly through the headstones to the turnstile.

As she pushed out the gate, dots of light caught her eye on the horizon. The graveyard was on a hill and she could see right across the river into Town. A small group of flaming torches moved, like fireflies, up Wickham Terrace. It had to be Tom and the zombies headed for the Town Hall, where they would release George and Edward Archer and their Watchers.

She shuddered as she watched the group pass into the Market Yard and distant crashes and screams carried on the wind to whip round the graveyard.

Her legs were on fire as she cut across the grass and down the hill through the Ghost Estate, hoping against hope that Boy had managed to get word out.

"You're too late!" someone shouted as she turned onto the road through the eye-plant field.

Violet stopped suddenly; the voice familiar. Slowly she turned round. A boy stepped out of the shadows near the estate pillars, a black raven on his shoulder.

Tom's cold blue eyes were stark in the darkness. A large disfigured zombie hung back behind him and snarled like a threatening dog.

"But… Town, the zom—"

"Town is in trouble, just as I warned you! I expect the Watchers have been released already, and my uncles too. I'll join them directly, but first I have to deal with you. You didn't think I'd believe that glove simply fell from the skies, did you, Violet?" Tom sighed.

He looked so much like Boy. She struggled for something to say but the words wouldn't come.

"I warned you to make haste, to flee while you could, but you didn't take me seriously, did you?" Tom's voice was measured and slow. He used words Violet had only ever heard fall from the lips of very posh adults.

"But I…" Her throat was desert dry.

Another huge crash and some screams shattered the night and she looked round towards Town.

"Why didn't you pay heed to the note? The instructions were simple!" Tom seemed confused.

"I didn't know if it was real!" she pleaded, desperate now to get to her family. "Boy said it was probably just a trick. How could I know you were trying to help me?"

"I wasn't trying to help you!" he snapped, his face suddenly wild. "I was just…I was just…" Tom stumbled over his words, grasping for an explanation.

The zombie moved forward, hovering just behind the boy's left shoulder. Its eyes were trained on Violet as one side of its lips rose threateningly to reveal black toothless gums.

"What do you want, Tom?" she asked. "I know you're not like Powick or Arnold. I don't think you want to hurt anyone. You gave Boy back to Jack when Powick was trying to escape after...after she killed Macula. You must have gotten in deep trouble for that. And I know you visit your mam's grave. I've seen you there..."

Silence hung between them.

"I...I killed my mother," he stuttered suddenly, staring straight at her.

"No...no you didn't, Tom, Nurse Powick killed your mam. She pushed Macula. I was there, I saw it happen!" Violet stepped towards him, reaching out her hand.

"But I killed her too. I pretended to be Boy and helped Edward. If I hadn't, then she wouldn't have had to fight for Town. If it wasn't for me, none of this would have happened! I'm not good – I'm the evil twin, she told me so. You need to get away from me!"

"It's not your fault, Tom, you were just following orders, like now. Macula knew that. She died trying to get back her family. She died trying to save you. When she was in the Ghost Estate she wrote to you all the time – I saw the letters – and after she got out of there, she told me she searched for you constantly."

"That's a lie!" Tom shouted, suddenly shaking with rage.

She inched back, afraid. The zombie seemed to sense the change and moved forward again, locking eyes on Violet.

"Macula never searched for me! She said I wasn't good enough for her family. She didn't want me around. She picked Boy as her son!" Tom spat the words at her.

"Did Nurse Powick or Arnold tell you that? They're lying to you," Violet replied. "Whatever they're telling you is not true! They're crazy, Tom, don't listen to them. Please tell me what they're making you do. What is all of this about?"

"You'll see." Tom was calmer now, a slight smile played on the edges of his lips. "On our birthday, Boy will pay."

"What's happening on your birthday?" Violet quivered. "What is Arnold doing with his machine? Powick talked to him about a curse – what does it all mean? Is it the curse of the Divided Soul? Why are they taking over Town, what are they planning, Tom…? Please! You need to help us!"

Another loud bang rattled the night sky. Tom looked over her shoulder towards the sound.

"She says I'm special," he whispered now.

"Special how, Tom? Is it something to do with the DeathDefier, Arnold's machine?" Violet willed him to tell her.

He shook his head. "The machine doesn't work – not fully. She says I possess the real power. But I can only claim it on my thirteenth birthday, when I cross from being a boy to a man. It is my fate, thanks to the curse. I was born for this moment. We've been working towards it since…since memory serves me. It's my destiny to…"

He stopped suddenly, as if catching himself.

"What's your destiny, Tom? What are they making you do?"

"Why do you want to know?" he snapped, growing angry. "It's not as if you care! You wouldn't be my friend before, why should you pretend to be now?"

The zombie twisted its head at an impossible angle and its growl grew louder.

"Before?" Violet asked, confused. "Do you mean a few months ago?"

She'd had a feeling when things began to go wrong in Town the last time that someone had been following her. She noticed a black raven everywhere she went but at the time didn't know it was Tom's.

"Every time I saw your bird, were you there? If you wanted me to be your friend, Tom, why didn't you say? Why didn't you stop all of this?"

"I couldn't! I can't." His hands clenched in tight white fists.

"I care, Tom, I do. I know you're not bad!" Violet

pleaded urgently this time. "I...I promised Macula I would find you and bring you back to your family. I even wanted to do it as a birthday present for Boy before all of this happened. I believe in you, Tom, just like your mam did."

"Don't lie, that's a sin!" His cold blue eyes grew wilder. "Priscilla says it's impossible to care for someone like me. She said I've a black soul!"

"Don't listen to her, Tom!" Violet urged. "I've seen you with your bird. You don't have a black soul – someone like that would never care for an animal the way you do! Please, Tom, listen to me. Powick is the bad one."

"Don't say that! She's the only person who cared when Mam didn't want me." Tom's face hardened. The zombie crouched as though ready to pounce. "I've given you so many chances, Violet, but you just don't listen! I've had enough. Grab her!" he roared.

Violet turned on the spot but, tripping on the edge of a deep pothole, she stumbled forward. Her hands scraped along the gravel, breaking her fall. The zombie grabbed her. She screamed, wriggled and squealed as she was hoisted into the air.

"You should have listened!" Tom snarled.

Then he stepped round the monster and marched towards Town.

CHAPTER 19

THE DEATHDEFIER

The zombie flung Violet over its shoulder so her legs dangled down its back. She wriggled and twisted as they followed Tom through the eye-plant field, but she couldn't free herself – the creature's grip was too strong.

The sounds of chaos grew louder as they approached Town, mixed with the mechanical clicking of her captor's steel frame and the noise of the rushing river nearby.

Tom was already entering Wickham Terrace when the zombie mounted the footbridge, the boards creaking under every step. They were nearing the middle of the bridge when footsteps raced towards them from behind.

Someone flung themselves onto the zombie's metal spine. There was a loud pop, a sharp, short yelp and a clatter of metal. The zombie collapsed forward.

Violet screeched as she was dropped onto the footbridge, landing roughly on her shoulders. The monster buckled, pinning her to the boards. Boy gripped her wrist and pulled her out from under the heavy, motionless creature. Disorientated, she was scrambling up when the zombie grabbed her ankle. Boy kicked the creature's bony hand until it let go, then dragged Violet across to the riverbank.

The zombie didn't give in. Though she could now see that its metal spine was detached from the bottom of the creature's back, making its legs useless, the thing pushed up onto its arms and hauled itself across the bridge, growling as it slithered towards them.

"This way," Boy said, heading to the Ghost Estate.

Violet panted, trailing behind her friend, and almost tumbled again checking behind on the zombie's progress as it clawed after them.

The sky was streaked in the lighter blues of the coming morning as they passed through the pillars to the estate.

"Where are we going?" Violet asked, looking round again. "We need to go to Town. We have to help!"

"Yes, but we can't go that way. They've blocked off the Market Yard, we won't get in or out without being seen. We'll use the other tunnel, the one to Archer and Brown."

Violet could almost have forgotten that the tunnel existed if she hadn't seen Iris Archer use it the previous morning. It led back to her dad's workshop and up the spiral stairs to the optician's shop. It would bring them right to the heart of Town, where Edward Street met Splendid Road.

"Okay," she puffed as they powered up the hill past the lone lamp post, "but tell me what happened. Did you get a chance to warn anyone?"

"No, the zombies were too quick. Tom gave them their orders and they took off. I couldn't keep up and by the time I got there the place was blocked off, so I waited for you. That's when I saw Tom and the zombie and…"

"How did you knock the zombie over like that?" Violet interrupted, remembering how the monster had collapsed.

"I yanked out the wires at the base of its metal spine! I was trying to figure out how I'd rescue you and then I thought, well, the zombies aren't really living, it's just the metal frame that makes them move. They're more like robots than anything else. So I tried it – I pulled off the metal bar at the base of its back and it cut the power to its legs!" He grinned as they reached the turnstile to the graveyard.

"Violet!" Somebody called her name.

She looked around and saw Tom standing on the estate path, another zombie with him.

"Violet, I'll find you!" he cried again.

Boy quickly pushed open the creaking gate. The noise sounded sharp in the quiet of the graveyard. Tom looked up and spotted the pair at the top of the hill. He chased after them.

Violet panicked and hurried Boy through. As the pair darted by the broken headstones and crosses, Violet's head spun trying to remember exactly where the tunnel was hidden.

Tom was already at the turnstile when a loud boom shook the graveyard, rocking the ground beneath them. The pair were jolted forward by a powerful force, both landing face down on the grass. When Violet looked up, there was a huge plume of smoke rising into the sky from the other side of the cemetery.

Her ears were ringing. She struggled onto her knees and crawled to Boy, who was lying ashen-faced behind a nearby tomb. A trickle of blood ran from the corner of his bottom lip. His mouth moved but she couldn't hear what he was saying.

Suddenly shadow-like figures began to emerge through the clearing dust.

Nurse Powick was standing in the middle of the graveyard, the shoulders of her long navy cloak covered in a fine powder of debris. Her hands waved about as if she was directing an orchestra. She appeared to be shouting, but Violet couldn't hear a word through the throbbing in her head. Beside the woman, where the tomb that led to the Outskirts had stood only moments before, there was a huge cavity in the ground that Arnold now clambered out of.

"What are you doing here?" Powick ordered, spotting Tom just inside the gate. Violet's hearing had returned a little and she could just about make out the words.

"I...um...I came to check if you needed help," Tom stuttered.

"You're meant to be making sure things run smoothly at the Town Hall!" Powick barked, a slight note of panic in her tone. "Get back there at once!"

Violet held her breath, waiting for Tom to give them away. Red-faced, Boy's brother glanced around at the graves one more time.

"I said now, Tom!" Powick roared.

※　　※　　※

Violet breathed out in relief as the blue-eyed twin backed away, turned and disappeared down the hill without saying a word. He could have given them up but once again he hadn't. She looked at Boy. He didn't react.

Then another figure emerged from the dark hole. Hugo, the zombie, stomped through the smoke, dragging someone behind him.

Violet was sure it was Dr Joseph Bohr, the man she'd

spoken to through the iron bars of his cell. She could see him better now. He looked old, really old, his white hair thin on top and wispy round his ears. His brown eyes were large in his sunken face and his clothes hung loose over his shoulders and hips as though he were nothing but bone.

"Get your ghastly hands off me," the doctor said, pulling away from Hugo. "I can walk by myself, thank you very much!"

Four similarly aged men and women followed behind him, each escorted by their own zombie. They had to be the other scientists who had been kept in the cell with Joseph Bohr. One of the men whimpered and coughed as he stumbled through the smoke before falling forward onto the grass.

"Magnus, you were always a coward," Arnold laughed. "Imagine a nuclear physicist who couldn't harm a fly. I remember you were forever herding them out of the windows of Hegel instead of swatting the things. What a waste of a good mind!"

The old man looked up from the ground. "*I* wasted *my* mind?!" he snorted, incredulous. "Arnold, you lost your marbles long ago. Why don't you just do away with us now and save all of this commotion?"

"Do away with you? Why would I do something like that when the best is yet to come?" Arnold smiled.

"You lot threw me out on the rubbish heap long ago, you laughed at my discoveries and made nonsense of my science. Finally I will prove to you all what Arnold Archer is capable of. This time the world will watch. Nobody will be able to deny my genius!"

"Nobody cares about your genius any more, Arnold," Joseph Bohr rebuked. "This is stuff of the past. Move on, old boy. We're all a bit long in the tooth for these games!"

"Move on?" Arnold shouted, his face now fit to burst, like a shiny red cherry. "You might have moved on, Bohr, but I couldn't. You ridiculed me and you think I'd let you get away with that? I certainly didn't allow Spinners off the hook, so why should I allow you?"

"Dr Spinners?" a woman asked, stepping forward behind Joseph. She wore a long purple nightdress, pink slippers and still had curlers in her slightly orange hair. "What did you do to him? His accident was highly suspicious at the time. I wondered if you were involved… Oh, Arnold…please tell me you didn't… Not murder…?"

"Shall we just say Dr Spinners has served Arnold well these last few years, Teresa." Nurse Powick smiled widely.

"But he…he died," Magnus stuttered.

"Died?" Arnold smiled. "Yes, technically he did, but he won't be dead for much longer!"

"Stop this madness or—" Joseph Bohr stepped forward, but Arnold Archer pushed right past him and strode towards the large hole in the earth.

"Why do you think they blew out the entrance to the Outskirts?" Violet whispered, her words sounding swallowed.

"To fit that through, I'd say!" Her friend pointed.

"Mind my machine! Be careful, for God's sake!" Arnold instructed as four zombies, sharing the weight of what looked to be a large glass cylinder, stomped out of the enlarged tunnel.

Powick ordered the zombies to set the object down as Arnold walked around, inspecting it closely.

The machine looked like a huge test tube turned upside down so that its rounded end faced skywards. The glass sat on a round gold base that had what appeared to be a control panel screwed to its surface. Inside the tube was a large gold plate cut in the shape of a human body with leather cuffs at the hands and feet. Blue and red wires snaked through small pierced holes in the plate.

"What is it?" Violet whispered.

"It must be the DeathDefier," Boy replied.

"We've seen all this before, Arnold." Joseph Bohr was dismissive. "Your machine might look a little different now but I'm sure it still doesn't work. You're playing with the impossible. You're a fool, Archer!"

"Nonsense!" Arnold snapped. "I'll show you what's possible! Soon my machine will purr and our esteemed colleague, Dr Spinners, will live again – if only to eat his own words!"

"No, Arnold, you didn't...not Spinners, not my..." Teresa stuttered.

She broke down sobbing. Joseph Bohr comforted the orange-haired woman while she clung feebly to his arm.

"It's okay, Teresa!" the doctor soothed before changing his tone. "You don't scare me, old boy. You're still just a crank in a white coat!"

"A crank who happens to be in control of your life right now, Joseph. I'd be a little less frivolous with my words if I were in your position!" Arnold Archer turned back towards Powick. "My machine looks fine!"

"Okay, move out!" the nurse announced, signalling to the four zombies.

The creatures bent down and picked up the DeathDefier with ease, making it look feather-light as Powick and Arnold lead the group from the graveyard and down the hill towards Town.

CHAPTER 20

THE WATCHERS RETURN

"Who is Dr Spinners?" Violet whispered, pulling Powick's letters from her pocket and scanning through them for the name. "Look, Arnold wrote about him in his letter to Powick. He said he was Powick's boss and that he was giving him trouble. He must be dead, Boy. Maybe Arnold murdered him like that woman said!"

"I don't know, Violet," Boy replied quietly, "we can think about it all later. Right now we just need to get help."

Boy stood up and dusted off his clothes. "Let's go find Dad and the others and figure out a plan!"

He grabbed her hand, pulling her up, then they raced across the grass, sliding onto the ground by a hole just in front of the back wall. It was the entrance to the tunnel that wound back to Archer and Brown's. Boy slipped wordlessly into the darkness. Violet followed, dropping down beside him. Her feet stung as she hit the floor.

A chill wrapped her bones. This tunnel passed under the river and she'd forgotten how cold it could be. The pair ventured forward, the hollow sound of the wet walls dripping onto the stone haunting their journey.

"Powick told Tom nobody could ever care for him because he's got a black soul," Violet whispered into the dark after a few minutes. Her conversation with Boy's brother was still playing around her head and she felt she needed to tell Boy. "She told him that Macula chose you instead of Tom because he's bad. He said he's the real power, not Arnold's machine, and that Powick wants him to use that power on your birthday! It was weird and scary, Boy!"

Violet didn't mention what Tom had said about making Boy pay.

"What does that mean though, saying he's a black soul?" her friend questioned, his voice echoing round the small stone tunnel.

"I don't know, but it has to have something to do with what Powick said to Arnold in the castle about your birthday and the curse...but what curse? The only curse I've heard anyone talk about is that crazy one Edward mentioned and Arnold wrote about – the curse of the

Divided Soul – but I thought that had to do with William, not with Tom or you?"

As the words slipped out, a memory hit Violet – it was something to do with Macula but she couldn't quite put her finger on it.

"If Tom thinks he's the real power and not Arnold's machine, does that mean he believes he can raise the dead?" Boy sniggered, interrupting her thoughts.

Violet shrugged. "I tried to ask Tom what they were going to make him do but he didn't tell me. Whatever it is though, I don't think he wants to do it!"

"Not this about him being good again, Violet. He just got that zombie to capture you. Who knows what would have happened if I hadn't been there!"

"But Powick has told him he's bad ever since he was young… Imagine if someone was telling you that all the time, you'd believe them too. He just needs someone to tell him different, someone to tell him that he's good and that everything will be okay! He needs someone to love him, like a proper mam—"

Violet stopped suddenly. She hadn't meant to say it that way. Why didn't she think before she spoke, like her dad always told her to?

"Well, he should have thought of that before he killed mine!" Boy snapped, just as the pair broke out into Eugene Brown's laboratory at the end of the tunnel.

Violet kept quiet.

She squeezed past the metal tables crowded with miniature eye plants and walked to her father's desk. His handwriting swirled across the blackboard beside it. Where were her parents now? A lump rose in her throat as she thought about them. Maybe this was how Boy felt about Macula all the time, though probably much, much worse. She would get her parents back, but he'd never see his mam again.

She reached under the chunky wood desk. Stretching her fingers, she felt the large metal key hidden below the lip of the middle drawer and grabbed it, then headed for the spiral stone steps up to the shop.

Suddenly Boy pulled her back.

"What are you doing?" Violet shook her arm free.

"Listen." He pointed up the stairwell.

A door banged, followed by a dull thud of footsteps as people entered the room above. Crashes filtered down through the stone ceiling.

"Sounds like someone is searching the place," Violet whispered.

Another door slammed and four large shadows prowled down the spiral steps towards them.

"Hide!" Boy gasped.

Violet crawled under her father's desk as her friend dived for cover behind the large armchair, just as four men, dressed all in black, burst into the room.

"Well I never!" one of them roared, kicking over a coffee table by the large fireplace. "They've let this place go downhill, haven't they?"

"Remember when it was our spot?" another one said, shoving her father's papers to the floor and plonking down on the table, his legs dangling just millimetres from Violet. "Cheek of 'em, turnin' it into some kind of posh science lab!"

"I'll show 'em," another one laughed, hurling a metal table across the space.

Violet flinched as a loud crash ricocheted off the walls, rattling her eardrums once more. The room exploded in laughter, then another of the men began to draw all over the blackboard. They were acting just like some of the older boys in Violet's school did whenever they were trying to be cool.

"Did ya see Ed and George just now – think they're cock of the walk, tellin' us all about their da and how they'll be runnin' this place again. Bet they'll be quakin' in their boots when he turns up though. They'll be all 'Yes Da, no, Da, three bags full, Da'!" another snorted. "I didn't even know they had a father. Sounds like a right weirdo too, if ya ask me!"

"Well, Arnie's won me over already and I've never even met the man," another replied. "Them Townsfolk woulda never let us out! And there's rumours he'll pay a darn sight better than his tight-fisted sons!"

Violet felt sick as she pulled back further into the shadows of the desk. The Watchers were out!

❋   ❋   ❋

The Watchers, a gang of rough and burly men, had been George and Edward's guards when Town was called Perfect. They'd made sure the No-Man's-Landers stayed inside the walls of No-Man's-Land and used an invention called the Hollower to steal the imaginations of the Perfectionists through their glasses, keeping them under the brothers' control. Ever since Perfect fell they'd been locked in the basement of the Town Hall on the orders of the Committee.

Now, as Powick had planned, they'd been let out.

Violet quivered. How could the people of Town ever take on the zombie army and the Watchers together? Tom was right – maybe their only chance was to escape and lose their home for good.

The Watchers began to play games around the cellar space. They were knocking the steel tables off each other like bumper cars.

"Well I never would have called this place luxury when we was living here, boys, but it was a damn sight nicer than it is now!" one of them said, just before crashing his steel table into his friend's hip.

"Oi, what was that for?" the round-tummied man moaned as the culprit laughed.

One of the potted eye plants tumbled to the ground. The laughing Watcher stood on the plant's head. There was a loud piercing shriek and a mass of white and red gunk splattered across the stone floor.

"Oh yuck," he howled, lifting up his shoe to pull off the squashed and oozing eye plant before flinging it across the room.

"Serves ya right," the injured man sniggered.

"Come on, fellas, stop yer messin'. That Boy's not 'ere. We best get up to the street and report back!" the Watcher sitting on the table above Violet announced to the room.

"Don't be a stiff, Fists – give us a bit longer, we've only just got here! They said to search the place with a fine-tooth comb and that means 'well good'. They'll think we didn't do our job properly if we come out so soon and empty-handed! You know what George an' Edward's like!"

Fists? Violet flinched. He was a leader and one of the scariest Watchers. She remembered how his fiery red hair poked out from under his black knitted cap.

"We still have to go to Will Archer's place on Wickham Terrace to search there too, remember," he answered. "They're desperate for that Boy. Wonder what he's done now? Coulda wrung his neck meself in Perfect. Always climbing in over that wall like a dirty squirrel! We'll catch 'im this time! Feed 'im to them zombies, I reckon! Might catch that Will Archer too – could never stomach that fella neither, like father like son!"

"I don't like the look of them zombies though. One of the lads reckons a nurse made 'em, Powell or something – he said she sewed 'em together!" another Watcher said.

"I wouldn't exactly call 'em zombies, more like robots with flesh on and not a brain between them," Fists replied, holding up a black box like the one Powick had shown to Arnold earlier. "That's why the other young Archer, the twin with them weird blue eyes, snuck us these weeks ago! Said once you have one, you can control those creatures, you see! There's loads of 'em comin' in for a show later I'm told. Oh, I'll put on a show all right when I've a few of them zombies under my control – I'll have fun getting 'em to chase the No-Man's-Landers!"

"They're moving everyone to No-Man's-Land now, I heard. Even them annoying Perfectionists won't be wandering free this time. I always thought Ed and George should have locked 'em all up from the start. Makes stopping a rebellion much easier! Reckon that's where the twins got it wrong," the heavier Watcher stated.

"Come on," Fists said again. This time he jumped from the table and walked to the steps. "We've a job to do!

This place is clear, but we'll find Boy Archer before the day is out!"

"Killjoy!" one of the men huffed quietly as the four climbed back upstairs.

The landing door slammed and, before Violet had time to crawl out, Boy poked his head under the table. She jumped, hitting her head on the wood.

"Argh, don't do that!" she gasped.

"Sorry." Boy looked serious. "Did you hear what they said?"

"Yes." She nodded. "They're looking for you!"

"But why?" he asked, his face lined with worry.

"Well, at least we know they don't have William yet," she said quickly, grasping at a silver lining. "If we find him and the others, they'll know what to do. We have to get into No-Man's-Land – that's where they said they're putting everyone."

The pair raced up the steps, through the solid-stone door and into the long thin room beyond. This place had once been lined with metal shelving filled with jars of stolen imaginations. Violet remembered how they had glowed, lighting up the space.

The tinkle of a bell and a distant bang reached them.

"I think they're gone," Violet whispered.

They passed through the next room and waited, listening for signs of life on the shop floor before entering.

The door brushed over the thick red carpet.

Her parents and William hadn't changed anything about this space since they'd taken it over. They'd kept the dark mahogany shelving that traced the walls and the gleaming gold and sparkling glass cabinets that housed the glasses' frames for customers to browse.

Something crunched under Violet's foot as she stepped out. She looked down. The carpet was covered in shattered glass. The cabinets were smashed open and frames were strewn across the floor.

"They've wrecked the place," Boy said angrily.

Violet was just picking up a stray lens when a zombie prowled by outside. She ducked behind the reception desk and gestured to Boy to hide.

The zombie stopped and stared in the window, sniffing the air as if sensing something. Violet watched, petrified, as the creature marched backwards and forwards across the shopfront, clawing at the glass. Then a flaming torch passed by outside and the monster turned, racing after it.

Violet ran to the window. Two zombies stood sentry-still outside the butcher's across the road as some Watchers hustled inside.

A large balding man was dragged roughly from his home over the shop, while his wife and two children cried frantically behind him.

"That's Mr Hatchet and his family," Boy whispered, horrified.

"Look over there!" Violet pointed down Splendid Road.

Watchers were pulling pyjama-clad Townspeople from their houses all over the street. Some put up a fight but many were too terrified to do anything but scream.

CHAPTER 21

FAMILY TIES

"We have to help them!" Violet croaked.

"What can we do? Go out and take on all the Watchers and zombies by ourselves? That sounds like a great idea!" Boy replied sarcastically. "We should stick to the plan to find Dad and the others. They'll know what to do. They're probably working something out already!"

"Well then we have to hurry – we need to get to No-Man's-Land fast." She hesitated. "But it means going outside." Violet looked through the window. People were now being herded up the street like cattle. Some shouted at their captors while others cried and held tight to their families. She eyed a band of Townspeople, half dazed, passing by the shop.

She pointed them out to Boy. "If we leave now we can try to blend in with them."

Boy nodded and gently opened the front door. The terrified sounds from the street were suddenly amplified. The pair snuck out, keeping to the shadows of the shop, then skipped quickly down the steps and slipped unnoticed into the line of petrified people.

A woman in the middle of the group – Violet recognized her as a teacher in their school – held on to her young daughter's hand, trying desperately to calm her as she wailed.

"Shut up, you snivelling fool," a Watcher leading the group roared.

He pulled the small child away from her screaming mother and shoved her roughly ahead. Violet felt sick as they continued in tense silence, broken only by the girl's sobs. They passed the Town Hall and turned onto Archers' Avenue.

Boy grabbed Violet's hand as the group veered down Rag Lane and pulled her into the cover of the high wall that surrounded No-Man's-Land.

"What are you doing?" she whispered urgently. "I thought the plan was—"

"We're near Iris's," he interrupted. "Maybe she's still there? She'll know where Dad and the others are."

Quickly they snuck down the avenue, raced round the

side of Boy's grandmother's house and climbed into her garden. Boy poked his hand into the bright-yellow flowerpot that rested by her back door and pulled out a dirty key, then placed it in the lock.

"Iris?" he whispered as they tiptoed inside.

Nobody responded; the house was eerily quiet. They entered the kitchen, where the table was laid, a half-eaten plate of toast and a pot of tea on its surface. Violet felt the pot with her hand.

"It's warm," she said. "She mustn't have left that long ago."

Violet went into the hallway. Iris's long black coat was still on its hook and her flat leather shoes sat on the mat in their usual place. Though the old woman went barefoot inside, she'd normally put her shoes on if she was leaving the house. Maybe she was still here.

Violet was just rounding the first step to check upstairs when someone pounded on the door.

"Iris, I've come back to haunt you," a familiar voice called from the street outside. "Open up! This is not a dream, darling, though I'll bet you'll wish it were!"

The hair on the back of her neck stood up. Violet locked eyes with Boy in the hallway as the door rattled, shaking on its hinges.

"It's Arnold," she mouthed.

"Get that creature to break the door down, Father!"

another voice grunted.

"Edward!" Boy whispered, alarmed.

Violet nodded to the stairs. As quietly as possible, the pair snuck up the wooden stairs and along the landing to Iris's room, creeping inside as the banging continued below. Boy slid onto his knees and crawled under the double bed. Violet followed, the space just big enough for both of them.

There was a louder bang this time, followed by the splintering of wood and a huge crash as the front door burst open. Violet stiffened as what sounded like a small group of people pounded into the hallway below.

"Search the place," Edward Archer ordered.

A few minutes later, heavy footsteps plodded into Iris's room.

Violet held her breath and Boy squashed in closer as bruised bare feet walked round the edges of the bed. Most of the toenails on one foot were green and crusty, while on the other they were missing and a cracked bone protruded awkwardly from the creature's heel.

She tensed as the zombie stopped, groaned and then pounced onto the bed above them. The springs creaked. The pair flattened to the floor as the mattress sagged and the creature moved around on the bed. It sounded as though it was sniffing the air like a dog.

"Hey, you lazy lump, you sleepin' on the job or somethin'?" a voice boomed from the doorway.

The round bulbous tip of a Watcher's black boot stepped into the room.

"Get out here and check the rest of the house!"

The mattress sprang back as the zombie's bare feet planted on the floor. The creature groaned again and pounded back outside.

Violet released a long slow breath. They were just above the sitting room and she peered down through a small gap in the floorboards as Edward – the short, stout twin – stomped inside, stopping by the marble mantelpiece. Behind him was his brother George, who was tall and spindly and slightly crouched because of the low ceiling.

A third figure followed behind them. It was Arnold Archer. He made a beeline for Iris's wall of gold-framed family pictures above the fireplace.

"Oh the lies we tell ourselves!" He laughed as he pulled one of the images down and flung it across the room.

Violet flinched as the glass smashed.

"We'll thoroughly search the house, of course, but it would appear at first glance that Mother is gone." Edward coughed, clearing his throat.

"You'll have to track her down then, won't you, Ed!" Arnold snarled.

"She might be in No-Man's-Land already. I promise we've followed your instructions to a T, Father. We put the Watchers into action the minute we were set free. They've been moving people from their homes since the early hours…"

"Are you looking for a pat on the back?" Arnold snapped abruptly.

"No…ahem…I'm just—"

"I gave you numerous chances!" Arnold Archer raised his voice. "I rescued you when your plans fell apart in Perfect. What would have happened if I hadn't been watching and sent Tom to the graveyard that night to bring you to me? I let you in on my plans, even allowed you some of your own, which backfired yet again. Where would you be now had I not come to your rescue a second time when turning Town against your brother didn't work either? I'll tell you where, still locked in the Town Hall with George while that cursed brother William ran this place!"

"But, Father—"

"No buts, Edward. You swore you'd prove yourself to me last time and I foolishly believed you, but all you managed to do was release that brainless brother of yours before you both got caught again! I won't allow either of you to mess this up now. This is not a trial run! If you step a foot out of line I'll have no qualms about locking you in the Town Hall myself."

"Just let me expl—"

"No, Edward, not another sound!" Arnold moved menacingly close to his son.

The stout man flinched and George backed away towards the fireplace. The twins looked more like trembling children than the terrifying men Violet knew.

"You may think you're big shots around here – that was always your problem when you were children. Playing up to me, showing off your experiments, trying to impress me with juvenile science. You know, at your age I was heralded all over the world for my research into the workings of the mind. What have you two done? Controlled a few people in this measly little place. Grow up, Edward, and you too, George! You will not make a single decision around here. I am taking over Town. The timing is too important to me now. I didn't waste years of my life hiding in that dilapidated castle just for everything I'd planned to be ruined at the last moment because of childish mistakes! You will do as you're told and there will be no backchat. Understood?"

Silence filled the room.

"Understood?" Arnold roared.

"Understood," Edward and George whispered, bowing their heads.

"Good." The old man smiled. "Now find your mother and bring her to me! And Boy too, before tomorrow! Priscilla needs him if this is to work. I'll be in the Town Hall."

Arnold Archer stormed back out onto the street.

"*But, Father…*" George mocked after Arnold had been gone a few minutes.

"You didn't say a word, George, so don't laugh at me! Let's just find Iris – I bet she's in No-Man's-Land. That'll keep him happy!"

"Keep our father happy, Edward?" George scoffed sarcastically. "I heard that nurse raving to him earlier about how lovely this town is. She said it'd make a perfect home for them. I bet he plans on giving it to her and her zombies when he's through with his show. You said he'd promised to hand it to us if we helped him with this idiotic scheme. Perfect is all we've ever worked for. Perfect should be ours!"

"He'll come round, George," Edward replied. "You remember what he was like when we were younger, before he submitted research? He's just stressed. When this is all over, he'll change his mind. He's only stringing Priscilla Powick along to keep her onside. We're his family, we're his flesh and blood!"

"So is Boy." George tutted, shaking his head. "And I heard about their plans for him!"

CHAPTER 22

WHY BOY?

Boy shuffled out from under the bed as Edward, George and their crew left the house. Violet crawled out beside him and sat on the dark wood floor, suddenly feeling very tired as she tried to gather her thoughts.

"We have to get into No-Man's-Land." Boy ran to the window to peer outside. "He wants Iris and…"

"And you." Violet looked over at her friend. "You heard Arnold, he said Powick needs you for their plans to work! I know they want to raise the dead and prove to the world that Arnold's one of the greatest scientists to ever live, but the DeathDefier can do that… Why do they need you?"

"Maybe Iris will know – she was there when he did his

experiments years ago. And she must know how he thinks – she was married to him! If we can find her, Dad and the others, we can try to figure it out. They might know more than we do already! We have to go to No-Man's-Land."

"Okay, but before we go anywhere you need a disguise – you can't be caught, Boy!" She stood up and took one of Iris's black knitted shawls from the wardrobe, wrapping it round his head and shoulders.

"Now," Violet teased, "you look beautiful!"

"No way," her friend said, pulling it off him.

Violet yanked the shawl back on. "Do you want to be safe or sorry?" she tutted, repeating something her mother said whenever Violet refused to wear her cycling helmet.

"Fine," he huffed, "but you better not tell anyone about this!"

Violet tried not to laugh at Boy, who looked like an old woman as he sidled down the stairs in front of her. He disappeared into the kitchen as she climbed out over the destroyed front door into the street. A few seconds later Boy rejoined her.

"I was starving," he said, handing Violet a cold slice of toast.

Her tummy growled as she took a bite.

The pair snuck along Archers' Avenue until they reached Rag Lane. Violet slipped ahead of Boy to scout around the corner towards No-Man's-Land, before turning back almost instantly.

"We can't go that way," she gasped, beckoning Boy to follow her back to Archers' Avenue, where she ducked in behind an iron bench on the cobbled street for cover. "There's a line of zombies blocking off the entrance, and there's a Watcher there controlling them."

Another group of confused people were marched past their hiding place towards Rag Lane.

"Get a move on, you lazy swines!" a Watcher shouted as he shooed them by.

"But what are you going to do with us? What's going on? I demand an explanation!" a blonde-haired woman said bravely, stepping from the line to confront the Watcher.

"You're going back where youse belong. These streets are ours again!" The man laughed in her face.

"That's Madeleine Nunn," Violet said, "but Anna's not with her!"

Madeleine Nunn was Anna's mam and one of the Committee members. Violet's dad had told her once that Madeleine worked harder than anyone else and knew everything that happened in Town. Even lots of things she shouldn't know, Violet's mother often said.

"We could slip in behind that group?" Boy inched a little out of hiding.

"No." Violet shook her head. "They mustn't find you. Let's go over the wall!"

Boy had shown Violet his secret way in and out of No-Man's-Land when she'd first met him in the days of Perfect.

Her friend smiled, his eyes lighting up. "Okay!"

They raced down past Iris's house and stopped at the bend in the stone wall on their left. Violet gulped. She'd forgotten how high it actually was.

"I'll climb up and throw down the rope!" Boy said, already scaling the stones.

"But how do you know the rope's still there? That was ages ago!"

"Because I still go up there!" he replied.

"Oh." Violet was surprised – he'd never told her that before.

Using small crevices for foot- and finger-holds, Boy climbed the wall like a cat. Violet kept one eye on her friend and another on the street, hoping nobody would round the corner and spot them. She jigged nervously from foot to foot and pounced on the rope the minute it popped down beside her.

"My climbing skills are definitely rusty," she panted, finally heaving herself over the top of the wall.

She lay back against the stone, her muscles aching. The rooftops gave a perfect view of Town.

"I love it here." Boy half smiled. "This is where I come to talk to Mam."

"Oh." Violet was unsure what to say.

"People always do that."

"Do what?" she asked.

"Go quiet. Whenever I talk about Mam."

Violet thought for a moment. "Well it's hard to know what to say – you gave out to me last time I mentioned her," she replied honestly. "What if I upset you again or something? I thought you might not want to talk about her."

"But I do. Just 'cause she's gone, doesn't mean she was never here! Everyone's afraid to talk about the dead." His voice was strained. "Except for Arnold... What if..." Boy hesitated.

"What if what?" Violet encouraged.

"What if Arnold's not mad? What if he could beat death? Maybe he could bring Mam back!"

"But he can't, Boy," Violet whispered, tears welling in her eyes. "Nobody can."

The pair fell silent. The sound of the chaos below filtered over the rooftops; screams and cries cut the morning.

"Why does Powick need me?" Boy quietly asked as though the weight of the thought had only just hit him.

Violet shook her head.

"I don't know," she said softly.

"I'm…" Boy hesitated, looking away across the rooftops.

"What?" she encouraged gently.

"I'm scared." He blushed, not meeting her eyes.

"She can't hurt you, not if… That's it!" Violet sat forward. "What if you stayed here hidden until after your birthday? Then Arnold and Powick's plans surely wouldn't work. If we stayed up on the roof until then, they'd never find us and you'd be safe!"

A terrified cry cut through the streets. Violet shot up onto the wall, shivering as she watched a small band of people breaking onto Archers' Avenue and racing for Edward Street. Three zombies gave chase and pounced on them, easily knocking the escapees to the ground. Violet looked away as the terrified Townsfolk were dragged, screaming, back down Rag Lane.

"No." Boy shook his head, suddenly firm. The fear had left his voice. "Mam didn't hide, not when I needed her! We can't either, Violet, now our family and Town need us!"

Her friend stood up and, without another word, the pair picked their way across the slanted rooftops until they reached the old bathroom window that used to be part of their escape route during Perfect. Violet, less sure-footed than Boy, wobbled on the windowsill as she climbed awkwardly inside and tumbled forward onto the broken white floor tiles of the snot-green room.

"Shush." He darted a look back at her.

"Thanks for the sympathy!" she huffed, pushing herself off the floor.

They had just snuck out onto the orange-wallpapered landing when a noise startled them. Violet inched forward and leaned over the loose wood banisters. The stairwell was dark but she could just make out two shadowed figures climbing up the steps below.

CHAPTER 23

REVELATIONS

Violet started looking for a weapon, something to defend themselves with should they need it. When she glanced up, Boy was disappearing down the stairs. Unsure if he'd seen the shadows, she picked up the nearest thing – an old bottle top – and flung it after him as a warning. It just missed her friend's shoulder and rebounded off the banisters with a *ting*.

She flinched, afraid whoever was below had heard.

"Jack…?" Boy's voice drifted across the darkness.

There was a shuffle on the landing.

"Jack?" he hissed again.

"Boy…? Boy, is that you?" someone whispered nervously.

There was a flurry of movement on the second floor. Suddenly Anna Nunn's small, round face was illuminated in the darkness. She was staring up at them, holding a torch beneath her chin, which, from Violet's point of view, gave her enormous large black nostrils. Then she moved the torch and Jack lit up beside her.

"Anna, you scared me!" Violet gasped, almost toppling over the railing.

"Got ya!" The little girl laughed.

A giggle slipped from Violet's lips and suddenly all four friends were in convulsions.

"What...what are you doing here?" Boy managed to say a few minutes later.

"Sneaking out of No-Man's-Land," Anna replied, as though the answer were obvious.

"We were looking for Anna's mam. Madeleine isn't here yet and everyone's getting a little worried," Jack explained.

"We saw her," Violet said. "The Watchers are bringing her now! Any minute."

"Is she okay?" Anna asked, cupping her hands to her mouth.

"She's fine," Violet replied, trying to ease the little girl's worries.

"You said *everyone*?" Boy probed, looking straight at Jack.

"Yes." The older boy nodded. "Everyone is back in Merrill's old shop in No-Man's-Land. We were worried about you two as well. William's been asking around, but nobody had seen you at all. We thought maybe—"

"Is Iris there?" Violet interrupted.

Anna nodded.

"Let's go then," Boy instructed, descending the stairs ahead of the other three.

"No!" Jack grabbed his friend's sleeve before he had time to step outside. "The Watchers are looking for you. We think some of the old Perfectionists are helping them."

"What…? Why would anyone help the Watchers?" Violet asked, confused.

"It's Vincent Crooked and his friends." Anna looked straight at Boy. "Nobody else. Everyone said Mr Crooked's just annoyed about losing his place on the Committee after he tried to help Edward take over Town again. Violet's dad said Mr Crooked was lucky he wasn't locked in the Town Hall with the Archers last time and if we all get out of this situation he'll make sure he is this time! He was really angry, Violet, he even—"

"Do you know why they're looking for me?" Boy asked, cutting Anna off.

The little girl shook her head.

"No," Jack replied. "I overheard some Watchers talk

about an Arnold Archer on the way here, as though he had something to do with all this. Do you know who he is?"

"Sort of," Boy replied, heading for the door again, "but we think Iris knows more. We need to talk to her."

"No." Jack pulled him back. "I said they're looking for you. You need a disguise!"

"Well, it's lucky we have one." Violet smiled, grabbing the shawl roughly from Boy's grasp and wrapping it back over his head and shoulders.

Jack tried to muffle a laugh.

"You look just like your granny!" Anna smiled.

"Thanks." Boy fumed, red-faced, as the foursome snuck outside.

Forgotten Road in No-Man's-Land was quiet in the early morning light. Some people huddled, whispering, in groups by the walls, while others walked around confused, as though not knowing what to do with themselves. Watchers patrolled the cobblestones, picking random passers-by to intimidate. Violet watched as one of the hulking men grabbed a young boy by the collar of his shirt and reprimanded his parents for allowing him to play with his toy car in the street.

There were zombies too – a small number of them were stationed at all the main crossings. They stood straight and menacingly still, as if awaiting orders.

"They're scary," Anna whispered as they passed a creature with half an arm and no lower jaw. "I didn't know Hugo had any friends!"

"There are loads more where he came from," Boy replied quietly.

"Has anyone been told what's going on?" Violet interrupted, hoping that Anna hadn't heard Boy's response.

"As far as we can piece together, the zombies invaded during the night. They released the Archers and the Watchers and since then the whole of Town has been forced into No-Man's-Land. The people who already live here are offering to share their homes." Jack nodded at a group entering Lucy Lawn's house just ahead. "But it's getting really crowded. At the moment people who don't have a place are finding spots in the Market Yard. But we haven't a clue what the Archers are up to or why they are doing this."

"How long have you been here?" Boy asked.

"Not long," Jack replied. "The Watchers burst into my home a couple of hours ago. I thought I was dreaming when I saw them coming up our stairs. Mam screamed – there was a zombie there too and it was pretty disgusting to look at. I tried to calm everyone down but it was horrible. It's like Perfect all over again, except people can see the Watchers this time!"

"I saw them coming," Anna added. "I snuck out and was looking for you, Violet. I knew you'd gone to the Outskirts without me, even though you promised you wouldn't! I was hiding in the Market Yard behind the Rag Tree when the zombies marched in. They all had torches and their eyes were huge; some growled like dogs and they had all this spit coming from their mouths, and then one of them tried to bite me but I got away. It was pretty scary and I've seen scary films – this was worse. Tom was with them. He ordered some of them to stay in the yard and the others to get Edward and George, then he disappeared!"

"That's when he must have come back for me," Violet said as they walked quickly past a zombie that was standing at the top of the first laneway to the Market Yard.

The creature turned its head at an impossible angle to follow them, kind of like the owls they learned about in school that could twist their heads the whole way round. Violet shuddered as they passed.

The murmurs of a large crowd reached them. Violet stopped at the mouth of the lane to look out at the Market Yard. The place was packed. Angry people sat in groups all over the cobbled ground. Whispers and suspicious glances flew around the space as the Watchers patrolled.

Jack directed them forward. Everyone kept their heads down as they cut through the masses straight for

Merrill Marx's place in a lane tucked away at the far end of the Market Yard. Merrill, the Town toymaker and a Committee member, had kept the place as a storage room for his materials since moving back to his shop on Edward Street after Perfect fell.

As Jack turned the brass handle and pushed open the door, a small bell tinkled. There was a fluster of movement and Merrill looked a little flushed as he stepped out around his workbench.

"Boy, Violet, it's you!" he exclaimed, rushing forward. "Thank goodness."

The man was barefoot and wearing white-and-red striped pyjamas. Violet might have laughed had she not been so worried.

A noise stirred under the stairs, from the small cubby where they'd stored the imaginations during Perfect. Slowly the wood-panelled door opened. William Archer poked his head out gingerly before bursting into the room.

"Boy, where have you been? I looked for you everywhere! Oh, I'm so glad you're safe."

"Why are you hiding, Dad?" Boy asked.

Another head appeared from under the stairwell.

"The Watchers don't like congregations, Boy, especially not a Committee get-together." Eugene Brown winked. "They're a suspicious lot. Might think we're planning a rebellion!"

"Dad! I wasn't…I didn't…" Violet stuttered as she ran into his open arms.

"Violet Brown," her mother scolded, peering down from the top of Merrill's rickety staircase, "you have an awful habit of going missing! I promise I'll chain you to my wrist if you continue to insist on heading off on dangerous adventures!"

"We were just—"

"You were what?" William interrupted, also annoyed now that the relief of seeing them had passed.

"We were just looking for the scientists," Boy explained.

"What scientists?" William asked, clearly confused.

"Not the missing five?" Eugene butted in.

"Yes, Dad." Violet nodded, launching into an explanation. "You see, I saw Tom near Town – well, Anna saw him first – and then we found this walking stick!"

"I knew it." Anna stomped her foot angrily. "I knew you were on an adventure!"

"And then I got this," Violet rambled, ignoring Anna as she took the crumpled paper from her pocket and handed it over to her dad. "I persuaded Boy to come to the Outskirts with me. The note's from Tom. He's trying to help us, I think…"

"Slow down," William insisted, holding up his hand as Eugene examined the message in his grasp. "Tell us exactly what happened."

Violet launched into her story about how they'd gone to the Outskirts, making sure to explain that Boy hadn't wanted anything to do with it but that she'd convinced him. She talked about the empty cottage and the forest, then the trap in the trees and seeing the zombies. She explained about the maze, the eye-plant lookouts and finally the invisible castle and Nurse Powick.

"So that woman is behind all of this," William interrupted, shaking his head. "What does she want?"

"No, it's not just her, Dad," Boy replied. "It's a man named Arnold Archer. We think he's…he's…"

William's face turned sickly grey.

"He's your father, William." Iris Archer stepped onto the stairs from the landing above.

CHAPTER 24

IRIS'S SECRET

William sat down as his mother slowly descended the stairs. Iris looked weak and Rose Brown caught her elbow as she rounded the bottom step.

"I think there might be a need for some tea, Merrill." Iris nodded. "Arnold is not the nicest of subjects."

Merrill walked to a roughly made counter at the back of the shop and turned on the kettle.

"Tell me, did you meet Arnold?" Iris asked both Boy and Violet seriously.

"No." Her grandson shook his head. "But we heard him speaking to Nurse Powick. He's got some strange machine…the Death something."

"So he is alive. I knew it," Iris whispered, taking a

moment. "That machine is called the DeathDefier," she continued. "So that's what all this is about. His ego never could take a battering. He's got the memory of an elephant and a huge thirst for revenge, that man."

"He has the scientists too," Violet said quickly. "We met Joseph Bohr…"

"I suspected as much. Tell me, is Joe okay?"

"Yes. But he said to get help! Arnold and Nurse Powick marched the scientists here earlier, along with his machine. They must be being kept in Town somewhere."

"What does he want with them?" Eugene Brown asked, his face lined with worry. "They're great minds – they could cause huge devastation if made to work together for some awful means."

"No, no, no, Eugene." Iris smiled, shaking her head. "My ex-husband only believes in his own genius. I suspect he wants them as witnesses, to prove a point. They were all his peers at Hegel University, you see, when he fell from grace. They laughed at him and at his science. He vowed he would get revenge. I just didn't…"

"What's going on, Mam?" William asked, red-faced. "You told me… You told me that Arnold was dead… You told me you killed him!"

Everyone gasped.

"I knew this would come back to haunt me," Iris said, as she started to pace the floor. Violet had noticed before that pacing seemed to be the Archer family way of working things out.

"What's going on, Mam?" William repeated, standing up this time.

"Well how do I know, William?" Iris snapped, a little flustered. "I'm only hearing this for the first time too! I suspected he was alive when the scientists started disappearing but… Yes, I had thought I killed your father, but I see now I was wrong!"

"Killed him?" Boy asked, confused. "But you…you couldn't kill anyone!"

"It was an accident, Boy, but a lucky one for me," Iris replied. "You see, your grandfather Arnold was a great scientist. Once. He was heralded throughout the world. Fascinated by the brain and the mind, an area not many studied or knew much about really. He made all kinds of valuable discoveries, some still used today. His research led him down the road to mortality…"

"What's that?" Violet whispered, engrossed.

"It means death, Violet." Iris sat down heavily on a stool by Merrill's workbench. "For all his studies into the mind, I suspected Arnold was starting to lose his. He became fascinated by death and what it meant to be alive. He wanted to discover where the essence of life came from. He knew how the body worked, mechanically, but life – that spark some call the soul – eluded him. He never could figure it out. So he began to toy with death, a dangerous endeavour. He took dead animals and tried to revive their souls. This work got him the wrong kind of attention. He lost his friends, his scientific standing and his licence to practise."

"But that doesn't explain anything, Gran. Why did you kill him...or try to kill him?" Boy corrected himself, clearly still horrified.

"Please don't look at me like that." Iris shook her head. "The shame and guilt have followed me ever since but I tried to make peace with it. Arnold was a nasty man..."

The old woman seemed to play with her thoughts before continuing.

"Around the time Arnold's career began to show cracks, William was born. Arnold started reading all sorts of mystical books on the spirit and folklore tales. He brought them home from work. It confused me at first, as he'd never been interested in anything non-scientific before. He began to talk about something he'd read called 'the Divided Soul', which occurred in a person born with different coloured irises. This person, folklore said, brought a curse of bad luck on those around them."

"Edward talked about it from the Town Hall when he pretended to rescue Beatrice, Conor and me, remember?" Violet said enthusiastically.

Iris nodded and continued. "Our lives were falling

apart, we had no money or food because Arnold's work was dwindling, so I ignored his ramblings at first as I tried to keep everything together. Until he began to look at William differently and I realized: he was blaming our son for his downfall. Then one day, when William was just a small tot, Arnold attacked him."

The room was utterly silent, the stillness broken only by Merrill, who shifted awkwardly as he made tea.

"Fortunately I was able to stop him before William was hurt but I couldn't stay around. I fled. One night while Arnold slept, I packed up the three children and left. My family were originally from Adequate, as Town was called back then. I'd never been there but when I was growing up I'd heard stories of it being beautiful and secluded, just what we needed. We were always engrossed in Arnold's life and achievements so I was sure I had never mentioned Adequate to him. We had a new start. I had family money which I'd hidden from Arnold, so I bought the Emporium and set up an optician's – I had studied at Hegel myself, you see, and my original degree was ophthalmology.

"All was good…until Arnold tracked us down. He told me he was taking us home, that he'd break the curse and we could return to our old lives. The kids were older then and thankfully William was still at school. So, while Arnold waited for him to return home, I pretended all was normal and began to cook my husband dinner. In the midst of that I grabbed the frying pan and hit him smack across the head. I meant to just knock him out and run again, but he didn't make a sound and I was sure in my panic I'd killed him. So I lumped him in a barrow and wheeled him through the Emporium tunnel, which I'd discovered some years previously, to the graveyard above the Ghost Estate. I found an old tomb…the lid was broken and there was a space just big enough to drop his body inside.

"That was the last I heard of Arnold until, like Violet just said, Edward spoke about his father from the Town Hall steps and mentioned the Divided Soul. I wondered how he'd known about the curse, as I certainly never mentioned it to him. Then Macula told me of Powick's strange letter to her about Tom and the curse. She also told me about an unwanted visitor she'd had to her home after the twins were born. The man said he'd been watching her and he mentioned the curse too. It gave Macula such a fright that it made up her mind and she left the twins in the orphanage that night all those years ago. I thought it sounded like Arnold. I got nervous, but I couldn't believe he was back – it seemed impossible. Then the scientists, all our old friends from Hegel, started to go missing…"

Violet had forgotten Powick's letter to Macula after Perfect had fallen, the one she'd shown Jack, Anna and herself after they'd found the picture in the orphanage and asked her if Boy had a twin. Something about that letter niggled at the back of her mind.

"Why did the missing scientists make you think of Arnold?" Violet asked, trying to piece together the story. "Is that why you were in the graveyard yesterday morning?"

"You saw me?" Iris looked up.

Violet nodded.

"Well, yes. I thought if I could find the tomb I'd put him in, I'd locate his body and know that this was all just a coincidence – but I couldn't remember where it was. The place looked different and it was a long time ago…"

"But why did news of the missing scientists scare you?" Violet asked again.

"Because they were his peers. They were the ones who had laughed at him and the DeathDefier. He constantly spoke about how one day he'd prove to them that he could raise the dead with his machine and take back his place as one of the world's most renowned scientists."

"That's what he's trying to do now!" Violet said, her heart thumping. "We saw the DeathDefier."

"And Powick said something about him showing the whole world his invention," Boy added.

"How could he do that?" Rose asked. "We're only a small town!"

"The Brain." Eugene spoke quickly, his mind obviously on overdrive. "He could use that to broadcast to the world. Just train some of the eye plants on the event and…"

"Perhaps more than the world, he'll want me to see it. He thought I never believed in him." Iris sighed. "The funny thing is, I did – he was a great scientist, a genius really, before he went mad!"

"He's looking for you," Violet replied. "We were in your house when he broke in, and he told Edward and George to find you. Edward seemed afraid of him."

Iris sighed sadly. "Edward and George always feared and idolized their father in equal measure. They blamed me for leaving him and hated that I protected William so much. I never told them anything about what happened – I didn't want to turn them against their own father or to carry his legacy of madness, but perhaps that was a mistake. I fear it's the reason they are the way they are – I fear it's my fault. I've let my family down badly."

"No you haven't, Mam," William insisted, grabbing her hand.

"So your ex-husband wants to raise the dead, is that what all of this is about?" Rose asked, confused. "It sounds like madness to me!"

"It is madness." William was irate now. "Nobody can raise the dead. It's impossible! And he'll be a laughing stock once more if he tries to pass off those zombies as really living. They are simply robots. If you were to take their metal frames and batteries away, they are nothing but corpses. And what will he do then – what's his plan for us and for Town?"

"Powick thinks he's giving Town to her and all her zombie friends," Violet whispered, "but Edward thinks he'll give it back to him and George."

"Neither option sounds great to me," Merrill said, handing out mugs of tea.

"But why wait this long?" Eugene asked. "Has he been sitting in the Outskirts all this time, plotting revenge? If William is his problem and he really believes in the curse, why not just try to kill him again long ago?"

"Thanks, Eugene!" William huffed, half smiling.

"I don't think the curse has to do with William any more, Dad. For some reason he needs Boy and Tom, and on their birthday," Violet answered, "but we don't know why. Tom said Arnold's machine, the DeathDefier, doesn't work, that it's just for show…"

"You were talking to Tom?" William choked on his tea.

"Yes." She nodded. "He saved me from Powick. He told me he has the real power and we'd see it on his birthday. He said this has all been planned for years. It just doesn't make sense!"

"But his…their…birthday is tomorrow!" William gasped.

"That must be why the Watchers are looking urgently for Boy," Anna announced.

"I found some letters too," Violet said, not sure she should mention them in front of Iris. "They were from Arnold to Priscilla Powick. She had them kept safe in her room in the castle. I think they were written around the time when Arnold's job was starting to fall apart. I think she was telling him to blame William."

Iris flushed, looking a little surprised. "That might make sense. I thought someone was influencing him during that time. He would never have looked at folklore books had he not been encouraged. He was secretive too then – he didn't tell me much, but I did wonder… How did he know her back then? We had the same circles of friends, and I'm sure I never met her…" Iris fell quiet.

"So if I understand all this correctly, Arnold is going to try and raise the dead zombies tomorrow?" Eugene was flustered. "Using his machine?"

"He said something about bringing a Dr Spinners back to life first, Dad, then the zombies, I think!"

"Dr Spinners?" Iris startled. "When did he—"

"So Town will become a zombie town!" Anna gasped, interrupting the old woman.

CHAPTER 25

A TOWN UNITED

The bell above the door jingled and Violet turned around in time to see a frightened Madeleine Nunn enter the shop.

"I met Billy Bobbins in the Market Yard. He told me you were here!"

"Mam!" Anna raced to her mother's side, throwing her arms around her waist.

"Anna! I was so worried – you have to stop sneaking out of the house like that!" Madeleine scolded, then embraced her daughter tightly. After a few moments she looked up and addressed the room. "Can someone please tell me they know what's going on? I was pulled from my bed by zombies and the Watchers have been released from the Town Hall. Billy even reported seeing Edward and George as he was dragged through Town!"

"We're just trying to work that out ourselves, Madeleine," Eugene replied.

Anna launched into an explanation of everything she'd heard so far, Violet correcting whenever the little girl exaggerated, which tended to be a lot.

Madeleine sat down on an old toy box as her daughter stopped for a breath. "Well, that explains a few things," she sighed, shaking her head.

"What things?" William asked, stopping mid tea-sip.

"They were lifting in some sort of huge machine under the canopy of the Town Hall. The Watchers were fiddling with it, running masses of wires to the thing. It looks like a giant test tube, the same as some of the ones you use, Eugene." Madeleine nodded. "But person-sized and turned upside down. And there's a strange metal cut-out of a human shape inside the glass—"

"That's the DeathDefier," Boy interrupted. "We saw them bring it through the graveyard!"

"They're planting new eye plants too, all around the base of the Town Hall," Madeleine continued.

"It'd be simple enough to have the world see Arnold's experiment," William said worriedly. "The Brain is very powerful. If he can disconnect the eye-plant beds from around Town and tune the new ones he's planting into the

Brain, then they can code my machine to transmit what the plants are seeing to the world. Just a matter of simple tuning and frequencies really. Everyone would see whatever Arnold has planned. He'll be a laughing stock the world over!"

"And if he is a laughing stock again, William," Iris said seriously, "don't underestimate what your father will do to us and to the rest of Town. He's not one who deals well with failure."

"But we can stop him," Violet insisted, "and get our town back."

"Not while we're locked in No-Man's-Land." Jack shook his head.

"Are they going to keep us in here for ever?" Anna asked nervously. "Just like in Perfect?"

"Not if we can help it, Anna." Eugene stepped forward and picked up a piece of spare wood from Merrill's work table, brandishing it about. "Violet's right, we can stop him! We've stopped the Archers twice before, we can do it again…"

"But how?" Rose asked. "Arnold seems even more deranged than his sons – excuse my bluntness, Iris. And he has a whole army of zombies behind him. We'd never be able to tackle them and the Watchers together!"

"But what if we can stop the zombies?" Jack said, standing up. "For now at least they work on battery power. They're not alive! What if we could run down their power somehow? They wouldn't be able to move. We'd only have the Watchers to face then, and we beat them the last time when everyone worked together."

"Before they left the castle, Powick said the zombies were super-charged," Violet interrupted, "and shouldn't need charging for a long time... Boy did stop one of them at the footbridge though. He disconnected its metal spine from its legs. It kept moving, but it couldn't get very far on just its arms!"

"It took a lot of force, Violet, and the zombie didn't see me coming. I don't think we'd be able to do it for the whole army... But the frames are made of metal..." Boy was thinking quickly. "What if we could use some kind of magnet that their frames would get stuck to? Arnold is planning to raise Dr Spinners from the dead first and then the army. That means the zombies will all have to be together somewhere near the DeathDefier outside the Town Hall tomorrow."

"Hugo Spinners..." Iris whispered to herself, as if toying with a memory.

Violet was about to ask Iris to repeat herself when Anna laughed loudly. "How could we make a magnet that big? It'd need to be bigger than the moon to fit all of the zombies on it and the only magnets I know of are the ones on my fridge!"

"Hold on…" Eugene looked up as though pulling a thought from his head. "Boy could be on to something. I know I've read about it… There was an article recently about a magnetic force field… I know, it was in the *Tribune*! Written by Dr Joseph Bohr, one of the kidnapped scientists – his work is mainly on magnetism!"

Boy replied excitedly, "Then he could help us! We need to find him – he has to be in Town somewhere!"

"Well wouldn't that be wonderful," Iris laughed. "I bet Arnold didn't think about that when he kidnapped Dr Bohr. If Joe can figure out a way to stop those zombies, Arnold's own lust for revenge will be his downfall!"

"We'll have to start searching now – there's hardly any time. Nobody will notice us. We'll go in and out of No-Man's-Land over the wall, just like we did in Perfect." Boy spoke hurriedly as if piecing a plan together.

"Being an orphan had its advantages." Jack smiled, standing up. "I'll go with you!"

"Me too!" Violet and Anna chorused together.

"We can split up," Boy continued. "We'll cover Town better that way – the scientists could be kept anywhere."

"I'm not sure about all this – we're letting the kids do our dirty work again. It's too dangerous this time. Those zombies don't look friendly and we know from old what the Watchers are like." Rose stepped forward, shaking her head.

"We went up against the Watchers before, Mam, and the zombies aren't that clever. We'll be fine!" Violet replied.

"They'll be okay, Rose." Eugene grabbed her hand. "We'd never be able to sneak in and out of Town like they can. They've done this before and are far more capable than even we know."

Rose sighed, bending down to cup Violet's face. "Promise me you'll be careful, pet. You are so very brave, but please don't be foolish. Those zombies might not be clever, but that nurse surely is!"

Violet hugged her mother. "I promise, Mam," she said, and this time she didn't cross her fingers. "We'll find Joseph Bohr and see if he can help us. Then we'll come straight back!"

"I'll go home and see if I can rummage up some books on magnets – I know I have at least one somewhere." William walked to the door. "Hopefully between us all we'll have an answer, and soon."

"I'll go with you." Eugene followed his friend outside.

William, Eugene, Violet, Anna, Boy and Jack left Merrill's old toyshop as the sun was shining over Town. They kept their heads down and bid each other goodbye at the Rag Tree, the two adults heading for 135 Wickham Terrace.

"Right." Boy nodded at his friends. "We'll look

suspicious in a group. Let's split up and meet back on the rooftop beside the wall."

A woman who'd been sitting on the ground near them shuffled closer to their group. She was looking intently at Boy. He pulled the shawl further over his head as the foursome split up.

Violet was just passing into the first laneway when someone cried out behind her. She turned just in time to see the same woman pulling on Boy's jumper. The pair tussled in the middle of the yard, creating an unwanted fuss.

"Get off me!" Boy struggled to release her tight grip.

"The Watchers are looking for him! It's him!" the woman cried.

People began to move towards the activity. Violet raced back and grabbed Boy's arm, tearing him away. A zombie nearby started to groan and look around uneasily, as if waiting instruction. From the corner of her eye, Violet noticed two Watchers moving towards the commotion.

"What's going on here?" one of them snarled, elbowing his way into the gathering crowd.

"Nothing," an old man said, stepping in front of the Watcher to block his path. "Just a silly fight."

"Let me be the judge of that," the Watcher snarled, shouldering his way past.

"He said it was nothing," another woman announced, pushing Boy behind her back to shield him.

Violet recognized this woman from the school gates. Her daughter was a few classes ahead of them.

"Go quickly. We heard there's planning going on in Merrill's. Whatever it is, young ones, we're behind ye!" the older man whispered to Violet and Boy, before stepping in shoulder to shoulder with the younger woman to confront the Watcher.

"It's Boy, it's him." The first woman pointed behind her, frantic now. "Vincent Crooked said the Archers have a reward out, says you're looking for him!"

The Watcher grimaced, clapping eyes on the pair, and grabbed for Violet. Boy yanked her away and they broke from the commotion towards the first laneway. The Watcher yelled out to the zombies to stop them as they sprinted past. The creatures sprang to life, snarling as they beat a path down the cobbled lane behind the children. Violet could smell their rancid bodies as she pushed frantically through a group of people approaching from the other direction.

Suddenly she heard the crowd in the Market Yard boo and jeer, then an unearthly, bloodthirsty roar cut the air. The hair pricked on the back of her neck as she exited onto Forgotten Road. She glanced back over her shoulder – the group in the laneway were being tossed like rag dolls against the stone walls as they tried to hold back the zombies.

Violet spotted Lucy Lawn's house just ahead of them on Forgotten Road and in a panic she jumped the small picket fence into the garden. Lucy's dad was great with his hands and loved to turn old things into new. Her mam said he could make a masterpiece from a rusty old bucket, and his garden was full of his elaborate creations. Violet ducked down behind a giant flower pot that was once an old water cylinder and watched Boy scramble under an upturned wheelbarrow, now a quirky garden bench.

Four zombies broke out onto the road, their nostrils flared and their eyes protruding as they stopped and sniffed the air. Two Watchers exited the lane behind them, red-faced and frazzled. They barked instructions as they bent over, gasping for breath. People hustled inside their homes or hid in doorways as the zombies began to slowly prowl the street.

CHAPTER 26

OLD FRIENDS

Boy looked over at Violet from his hiding place under the makeshift bench. With his back to the street, he couldn't see what was going on. She shook her head, signalling for him to stay put.

The Watchers split up – one went left towards the orphanage accompanied by two zombies, and the other went right towards Rag Lane, exactly in the direction Boy and Violet needed to go.

Suddenly one of the zombies stopped and sniffed the air, as if catching a whiff of something. Violet froze.

"Violet," a voice hissed quietly behind her.

She turned around, shaking nervously. Lucy Lawn was peeking out of her front door. The girl quickly beckoned to the pair to come inside.

Boy hesitated. Violet knew what he was thinking – he didn't trust Lucy.

Lucy Lawn had accused him of stealing her bike when things started to go missing in Town a few months before, just before Edward Archer had reappeared. Lucy had been wrong – it wasn't Boy who took her bike but his twin brother Tom.

Boy was very upset that so many people in Town would believe he could do the awful things his brother did in his name. Violet had tried to persuade him that it wasn't anyone's fault. She said that nobody knew he had a brother and so it was easy to be confused, especially since they were identical twins, but Boy was still finding it hard to accept. Violet's mam said it'd take him some time.

"Quick," Lucy whispered again, watching the street.

Violet took one last look at her friend, then back at the skulking zombie sniffing nearby – they had no choice. She slipped across the garden and in through Lucy's front door. Boy seemed to come to the same decision and pulled himself from under the barrow, sprinting in behind her.

Lucy closed the door gently then took a few deep breaths, her back to the solid carved wood.

"I saw them chase you!" she panted, as if she'd been running herself.

Violet imagined that Lucy had never been in trouble before or done anything even slightly dangerous – all of this must be new to her.

"What are they looking for?" she asked Violet.

"For Boy." Violet nodded at her friend.

"Oh," Lucy said, not looking at him. "Why though? What's going on in Town? Who let the Watchers out? There's zombies in the streets!" The girl's large brown eyes seemed double their usual size.

"It'll be fine," Violet soothed, feeling the need to say something comforting. "We'll all be fine."

Lucy looked at Boy for the first time.

"I'm sorry about...you know," she whispered. "I thought it was you who stole my bike. I didn't believe you, but you were telling the truth all along. I got you in trouble. I understand why you ignored me when I tried to apologize before at school. I don't blame you..."

Boy blushed and his face softened a little. He looked at Violet, then back at Lucy.

"It's okay...I suppose," he replied. "Simple mistake."

"Simple mistake! That's a change of heart," Violet snorted.

"Well, I suppose me and Tom do look alike." Boy smiled, his face even more flushed.

Lucy relaxed and smiled now too. "I guess that's the trouble with twins," she added softly.

All three suddenly burst into laughter, the danger outside making them nervously giddy.

"So do you need my help? It's the least I can do," Lucy asked, serious now.

"Well," Violet replied, "if you really want to…"

She filled Lucy in on their plans to escape No-Man's-Land and how they needed to reach the house at the bottom of Forgotten Road to get to the wall. When she'd finished explaining, Lucy nodded and opened her front door.

"Leave it with me," she whispered, disappearing outside.

Violet and Boy watched anxiously from a long slim window by the side of the door as Lucy marched out of her gate.

With a bravery Violet was sure even Lucy didn't know she possessed, she walked straight past the zombie sniffing around her front garden and up to one of the Watchers. She talked to him for a few minutes, her face animated, then pointed towards the orphanage. The large bulky man shouted orders and the whole group turned and headed up the street into the old stone building. Lucy followed behind them.

"Now," Boy said urgently.

Without another word, he opened the front door, jumped the garden fence and sprinted towards the other end of Forgotten Road, ducking into the derelict house that would lead them to the rooftops of Town. Violet darted in behind him and the pair bent over against the wall, catching their breath.

"Where have you been?" Anna squealed, rushing down the dark stairwell and flinging herself around Boy's waist.

Jack stood up on one of the steps above. "We've been a little worried." He nodded at Anna. "What happened?"

"Someone in the Market Yard alerted the Watchers to Boy." Violet gulped in air. "We had to hide for a while. Lucy saved us."

"Not Lucy Lawn?" Jack sounded surprised.

"Yeah." Boy nodded. "And some people in the market too. They stepped in when the Watchers saw me. Maybe people are sorry for what happened last time."

"Isn't that what I've been saying all along?" Violet huffed.

"Yeah, but why would I listen to you?" her friend mocked, leaping two steps at a time up the rickety staircase past Jack, heading for the slime-green bathroom above.

A short while later, they'd all climbed outside, reached the wall and descended the rope to the cobbled street below.

It had to be lunchtime, Violet thought, as her stomach growled and she ducked in through the broken door of Iris Archer's house.

"What are you doing?" Boy hesitated before following her inside.

"I need food and we need to think this out properly," she whispered, rummaging through the kitchen cupboards. "It's daytime! Someone will see us sneaking around the streets. We can't get caught, Boy!"

"Violet's right," Jack said quickly. "There's a zombie at the top of Rag Lane and there seems to be loads going on up on Edward Street. How are we going to slip through all that?"

"I know!" Anna said, racing out into the hallway and up the stairs.

Grabbing some bread, Violet, Boy and Jack followed her into Iris's bedroom. Now that she wasn't rushing to hide from a zombie, Violet had a chance to take in the whitewashed walls and dark timber flooring. The large wooden bed they'd hidden beneath sat in the middle of the space, beside a single locker and facing a wardrobe.

"Iris has these!" Anna exclaimed, stepping out of an attached bathroom.

She carried two pink-labelled cartons. The little girl shook one and released lots of white powder into the air like perfumed snow.

"It's talc powder – my mam has some too! Old people use it all the time. I smelled it on Iris, so I knew she had to have it! We can dress up as zombies, just like at

Halloween! The zombies won't notice and I'm sure the Watchers won't either – how are they supposed to know what every zombie looks like? I've seen some smaller ones around too so our size shouldn't matter. We just need to stay out of their way a little so they don't see we've no metal frames. The only people we really have to avoid then are the Archers and Powick, and that should be simple enough!"

"Genius." Violet sneezed as Anna began to smear white powder all over her face.

Then the little girl ran out of the room and back downstairs. Violet had never seen her move so fast – she clearly loved playing dress-up. Anna returned with a fistful of coal.

"We can use this to make ourselves look dead like the zombies and we can draw their stitching lines on too. We'll have to ruin our clothes though," she said, pulling scissors from her back pocket. "I found these in the bathroom too!"

Anna set to work ripping her clothes, then she grabbed a brush and frizzed her hair, covering it in talc too. Finally she pulled off one sock, rubbed more talc on her bare foot, looked up at the others and growled.

"Does it work?" She smiled – her teeth were also coated in coal.

"Brilliant!" Boy laughed. "You look like Hugo's child!"

The other three then hurried to get ready. Boy and Jack helped each other as Anna sat Violet on Iris's bed and got to work. The little girl was riffling through Iris's locker drawers for some hair clips when Violet spotted a leather-bound photo album in the bottom one and pulled it out.

There were lots of photos of the Archer boys when they were children, including one of William sitting picture-perfect by the base of a Christmas tree, a cheeky smile plastered across his young face. There was another, which appeared to be from the same day, of all three boys together, Edward and George both scowling. She flicked further on as Anna pulled wildly at her hair.

There were gaps in the album as though pictures had been taken out and Violet wondered if they were ones of Arnold. She turned another page and stopped at a photo of a large group of youngish people. They seemed to be in someone's yard, smoke from a barbecue evident in the background. Everyone had weird hairstyles, like something from an old film. The girls wore short skirts and the boys had tight trousers that flared out round the ankles.

Violet studied the faces, stopping at a small pretty woman who looked a little like William.

"Iris," she gasped, touching the image.

She was sure it was Boy's granny, just a lot younger,

crouched down at the front of the smiling group. Everyone was waving happily at the camera except for a single figure. A woman at the edge of the gathering stood straight and stern in a stiff white blouse buttoned to the neck. Beside her was a tall smiling man in tartan green trousers, his elbow resting on one of her square shoulders.

Violet shook her head.

"It can't be! That would mean they knew each other…"

"Who?" Anna peered round.

"Nurse Powick! She's in this photo with Iris."

CHAPTER 27

THE MAKEOVER

"Show me." Anna reached forward and grabbed the photo from Violet's hand. "Is that her, at the back?"

"I think so." Violet nodded.

"You're right, it definitely is her, but then why didn't Iris say anything?" Anna pushed her face closer to the picture. "I think I recognize that man too." She pointed to the one in the tartan green trousers. "I'm sure I've seen him before."

"I don't think I know him," Violet replied uncertainly.

"What's going on, aren't you two ready yet?" Boy's face was even paler now and shadowed in coal as he stepped out of Iris's bathroom.

Suddenly Jack burst from behind him, his arms outstretched. He stomped around the room, dragging a leg while groaning like a zombie.

"Stop it, Jack!" Anna squealed in delight, hiding behind Violet.

Jack grabbed her sides. "I'll tickle you to death," he grunted as she rolled around the bed, kicking and laughing.

"Shush," Boy snapped, looking out the window. "We don't want anyone to hear us!"

"Show them the photo," Anna panted as she sat back up. "Violet found it in Iris's drawer."

"You shouldn't be looking in there, Violet!" Boy scolded.

"I know, it's just…"

He walked over and took the photo from her hands. "Is that Iris?" he said as Jack peered over his shoulder.

Violet nodded. "And look who that is." She pointed to the woman at the back.

"It couldn't be…" Jack shook his head, sending talc flying through the room.

"Powick?" Boy replied, disbelieving.

"Yeah, I think so." Violet nodded. "But that means Iris knew her already."

"She would have told us though, wouldn't she?" Jack questioned.

"Maybe not. Macula said that Iris was a well of secrets!" Violet answered.

Boy took the photo and put it in his pocket.

"We can't worry about that now," he said, moving back

to the window. "We're losing time – we need to find the scientists to see if Dr Bohr can help us."

"Right." Jack turned around in a swirl of white dust. "Everyone ready and know what they're doing?"

"Yes." Violet coughed, choking on the talc. "I'm heading to Splendid Road. I'll check out Archer and Brown too. We were there earlier though and didn't see any sign of them, but just in case!"

"I'm going with Jack to George's Road and the tea factory," Anna added.

"And I'll search Edward Street," Boy said, stepping out of Iris's room. "I might be able to sneak into the Town Hall too!"

"Don't take risks, Boy," Violet warned. "Remember they're looking for you. Don't look at anyone and stay out of the way as much as possible!"

"Yes, miss!" her friend teased. "Meet you all back at the wall in an hour or so?"

"Let's meet here, in Iris's," Jack replied. "It might be safer than all of us standing on Archers' Avenue."

They all headed from the room down the stairs, Violet jumping as she caught their reflections in the mirror by the front door. At a quick glance, they were convincing zombies.

"Right." Boy stepped outside. "I'll go first. It'll be better if we leave separately!"

Butterflies spun round Violet's stomach as she watched him turn left towards Edward Street.

"Right, you're next." Jack nodded at her.

She took a deep breath and stepped out onto the avenue. The cold on her bare feet sent darts up her body – she'd forgotten she wasn't wearing any shoes.

"Remember to walk like a zombie!" Anna hissed from Iris's doorway as Violet took her first careful paces over the cobbles.

Violet leaned forward and tilted her head a little. She held one arm straight out in front, the other left stiff by her side. Then she lurched forward, dragging a leg. Getting even more into character, she groaned long and slow, just like she'd heard Powick's creatures do many times.

Passing a real zombie on the corner of Edward Street, she hobbled by, hoping it couldn't smell fear. The thing didn't flinch and she relaxed a little, more confident in her disguise now. Her progress was slow – it'd take for ever to get to Splendid Road.

Edward Street was a hive of activity, with Watchers patrolling up and down. Fists, the head man, shouted orders at zombies who were erecting seating opposite the Town Hall. It looked like a mini-version of the viewing stand Violet had seen at a concert once.

At the Town Hall Watchers were hanging long, red velvet curtains across the stone arches, converting the canopy of the old building into a theatre stage. In the middle of the flagstone floor stood the DeathDefier, a mass of electric cables running into its gold base.

The glass tube sparkled as two heavyset men rigorously cleaned its surface. She stepped closer, pretending to be polishing too. The inside frame wasn't gold as Violet had first thought but more copper in colour, and it gleamed.

As one of the Watchers looked up from his work, she grunted and trudged away. She had to concentrate – she was meant to be looking for the scientists.

Violet went through one of the yet un-curtained arches and down the steps, passing a huge, freshly made eye-plant bed.

As she shuffled by the Brain, she was sure she saw Edward Archer fiddling with the screens inside. Like William had said, they must be planning to transmit Arnold's show via it to the rest of the world.

Violet kept up her steady plod towards the other end of Edward Street, reaching Mr Hatchet's butcher's. The door was ajar. With a shiver, she remembered Mr Hatchet being dragged out earlier that morning.

She slipped inside and ducked down beneath the large display window that faced out onto the street. Hand-scrawled advertising for delicious sausages was written across the glass, making her mouth water.

She decided to survey Archer and Brown from here

for a minute, looking for any signs that the scientists might be held inside that building. She had just sat down on a brown sack Mr Hatchet used to decorate the shop floor when a familiar zombie snuck past outside.

Boy? He couldn't have searched the whole of Edward Street already, so what was he doing here this quickly?

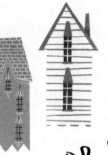

CHAPTER 28

DR JOSEPH BOHR

Violet crept back outside. There was no sign of Boy anywhere, though he'd only passed by moments before. She inched along the footpath and peered up Scholars' Road, catching sight of him climbing the hill towards her school.

She followed behind. The street was quiet but she kept up her limp in case anyone happened to spot her.

"Boy," she hissed. Her slow pace meant she couldn't catch up – her friend was moving quickly, seemingly having forgotten he was meant to be in character.

He kept going and ducked behind the school wall. His thick mop of talc-covered grey hair poked back up a few seconds later.

"Boy," she hissed again, a little louder this time.

"Violet?" he whispered, spotting her hobbling up the street.

She checked around. The place was deserted, so she broke from character too and raced behind the school wall to crouch beside him. Subconsciously she checked the colour of her friend's eyes.

"It's me!" he snorted, annoyed.

"Sorry," she replied, embarrassed, "I think it's a habit now!"

Ignoring her, Boy turned towards the school.

"I think the scientists are being held in there." He pointed. "I heard a Watcher talking about it."

"But why the school?"

"I didn't ask them, Violet!" he said – then darted across the yard to the large arched entrance.

She followed and stepped uneasily into the cream-painted hallway behind her friend. The place felt cold and empty. The huge space, usually filled with hundreds of voices, was eerily quiet. The silence scared her as they stole along the tiled floor, past the colourful collages and posters that decorated the walls.

"Check the classrooms," Boy whispered.

Violet stopped outside the first red-painted door and turned the knob, easing it open. Familiar rows of small desks and chairs were lined up facing the blackboard, which had the remnants of homework still visible in the partially rubbed-out chalk. She stepped back out. Boy shrugged, closing his door on the opposite side of the corridor.

They moved on separately, covering the rest of the ground floor. There were no signs of the missing scientists.

"Upstairs," she whispered, pointing above.

The pair snuck up the tiled steps and stopped at the top. In front of them, across the landing, was a cloakroom of coloured metal railings, normally filled with coats. To their left was a blue door into the girls' toilets and on the right a corridor that led to the science labs.

Violet stepped onto the landing, then ducked straight back into the stairwell.

"The science labs," she gasped. "There's a Watcher and two zombies guarding them."

She peered out and glanced towards the labs.

The Watcher had his feet on a chair and was reading a children's book that he must have taken from one of the classrooms, while the zombies stood on guard either side of the door. She relayed the information back to Boy.

"It has to be where the scientists are," he said. "We have to get in there, but how do we get past the guards?"

"If we can distract the Watcher," Violet whispered, an idea forming, "then we should be able to get past the zombies. They're programmed to listen to Tom – Powick said so. And remember Hugo believed you were Tom the last time and so did the zombies in the tunnel earlier? So it might work again – they might just let us past."

"The alarm!" Boy said excitedly. "If we can set it off, then the Watcher will have to leave to go figure out what's happening!"

"But how do we do that?" Violet asked.

"Easy." Boy smiled. "I did it once with Jack when I wanted to get out of a test!"

"Boy!" Violet was shocked. "That was you…?"

"Oh stop acting like such a Perfectionist! Remember you were almost a No-Man's-Lander too!" he mocked, slipping back down the stairs.

She followed, unsure where they were headed until they stopped outside the principal's office.

Violet shivered – she'd never been there before. Boy turned the handle and walked in, and she crept in behind. The room was nothing like she'd imagined it would be. It didn't have rules written up all over the place, or a dartboard with pictures of the school's most troublesome pupils, or confiscated items laid out across the shelves like trophies. The place was normal, boringly normal.

A large desk and chair sat at one side of the small space. A worn green carpet covered the floor and a picture of the principal's family and some sort of certificates hung on the cream-painted back wall. Boy walked behind the desk and opened the top drawer.

"What are you doing?" she hissed.

He pulled out a lighter and shook it.

"It's where the teachers keep things they take from pupils. I saw Mrs Moody take this from Conor Crooked last week! If we hold the flame under the alarm it should go off!"

"We might need a bit more fire than that," Violet said, looking around for some paper.

"See, now you sound like an orphan of No-Man's-Land!"

The pair crept back upstairs to the bathroom just off the landing near the science labs. The room was long and thin, lined on one side with cubicles and on the other with a row of white ceramic sinks. In the middle of the ceiling was a small round fire alarm.

Boy climbed onto the top of the front wall of the cubicles and shimmied along until he was near the alarm. Violet passed him up the paper. He set it alight, then reached across, waving the flames underneath the small sensor.

Violet waited nervously by the door, peeking out at the labs, until suddenly a loud sharp beeping pierced the air. She covered her ears. The Watcher dropped his book and looked up. Then he shot to his feet and marched down the hallway to the stairs, peering over. He barked something at the zombies before disappearing down the steps.

Boy was racing out the door when Violet grabbed him.

"Clean your face," she shouted above the noise, "you look like a zombie!"

He washed off the talc and coal and then slipped out onto the landing. Remembering her limp, Violet followed behind her friend towards the science lab, her heart pounding as they approached the two zombie guards.

One of the creatures was tall, its thin, brittle skin barely covering long, bony limbs. Its face was pockmarked and its head hung a little to one side, revealing a missing ear. It snarled at the air and shook its head, as if trying to rid itself of the sharp alarm sound. The other was just a little smaller and gaunt; its cheeks were hollow and dark purple circles enlarged its protruding eyes.

Boy stopped confidently in front of them.

"I've been ordered to speak to the prisoners," he said loudly.

The taller creature bent forward as if inspecting him, still throwing its head around like it was trying to swat a fly.

"I need to see the prisoners!" Boy shouted this time.

Violet winced and tried to cover her reaction with a grunt. She stared straight at the classroom door, willing it to open. Boy shifted uneasily.

"Now!" he boomed, then he reached forward and put his hand boldly on the door handle, turning it.

Violet's heart pounded almost louder than the alarm in her ears. The zombies looked at them as Boy stepped in, but made no move to stop them. Violet, breathless now, marched in behind him, closing the door with a bang.

The alarm was a little more muffled inside the classroom. Across the space, huddled in the far corner, were three men and two women. They brandished upturned stools, Bunsen burners and spatulas like weapons. Each of them wore a strange, pointed, paper cone hat with a D printed right in the middle.

"Isn't she the girl from the castle earlier?" the man Violet recognized as Joseph Bohr said, lowering his lab stool. "And you're the twin with black eyes, I remember!"

"Don't tell me that nurse got her too!" The orange-haired woman called Teresa sounded horrified as she pointed at Violet.

Violet blushed – she'd almost forgotten how she must look.

"Oh no, it's just a disguise," she said, pulling up her sleeves to reveal her healthy pink flesh. "I'm pretending to be a zombie!"

"Good show!" Dr Bohr smiled, banging down the stool. "Did you set off the alarm too? Clever, clever children!"

The beeping sound still rang on the air and Violet found she had to strain a little to hear.

"We need your help," Boy said urgently.

"Our help?" the man who Arnold Archer had referred to as Magnus asked, pulling off his white cap.

"What are they?" Violet nodded at the hat.

"Oh, something Arnold's been making us wear since we got here. He thinks it's funny," he spat. "The D is for 'dunce', you see. The last time I didn't have mine on, one of those monsters hung Teresa out the window. He's even stuck us in a children's science lab to drill home his point, while he plastered all of his so-called genius across these walls..."

For the first time Violet properly took in the details of her surroundings. While the brown-topped tables and steel-legged chairs of the science labs were familiar, the school science posters and children's experiments that normally adorned the room were covered over with large-scale drawings of what looked to be Arnold Archer's DeathDefier.

Pages and pages of writing and sketches hung from every corner of the space, displaying his research and outlining exactly how his machine worked. A banner on one side of the room above the posters read, "The Thesis of a True Genius" in large black letters.

Joseph Bohr held up his hand. "Not now, Magnus,

let's not get distracted – the children said they need our help…"

"Yes, Dr Bohr." Boy nodded. "We haven't much time. The Watcher at the door has gone to check on the alarm, but he might figure out it was a trick soon!"

"Arnold has taken over our town, Dr Bohr, and locked everyone away in a part of it called No-Man's-Land," Violet interrupted quickly. "He's released the Watchers, who are his sons' army, but we think he is also going to march all of his zombies in too. The people of Town need to fight back, but we can't take on the Watchers *and* the zombies – we'd never win. So Boy thought maybe we could create some sort of magnet that the zombies' steel frames could stick to, and then we would only have the Watchers to fight. We've taken them on before and won – we could win our Town back again. We need to do it before—" Violet stopped herself, unsure whether she believed what she was about to say.

"Before what?" Teresa encouraged.

"Before… Well, just in case he really can raise the dead, we need to do it before the zombies become real and can walk around without their frames or batteries."

"Ha," Magnus laughed, sitting down on one of the high lab chairs. "Don't tell me the people of this town believe that Arnold can do what he says. Arnold's a madman…"

"A madman who has you locked up, Magnus." Teresa tutted, silencing the scientist.

"Ah, I see, so you've read about my research." Dr Bohr stood up and pulled off his dunce's cap. "Yes, magnetic fields are my thing and you are on to something with this, but I'm afraid time is not on our side. Arnold is planning his show tomorrow, is he not?"

Boy nodded.

"I'd need more thinking time than this and these surroundings are not conducive to good work. Besides, that man you called the Watcher will be back soon and you two need to go…"

"What if we got you out? What if you came with us to No-Man's-Land?" Boy blurted.

Violet raised her eyebrows, unsure how Dr Bohr could pass unnoticed through Town.

"Go with them, Joseph," Teresa urged, stepping forward, "and take this."

The orange-haired scientist ripped one of the posters from the wall. On it was a layout of Arnold's machine with arrows explaining the working parts. Inside the glass tube was a zombie strapped to the large metal human-shaped plate.

"But what if they notice I'm gone?" the man stuttered, looking around at his colleagues.

"We'll cover for you." Magnus nodded, standing up.

"Teresa's right, just go. Arnold needs to be brought down, and you can help."

"But they might hurt some of you to find out where I am. Can't we all go?"

"It'd be too risky," Boy said solemnly, "but once our plan's in place and the battle starts, we will save the rest of you. I promise."

"Just go, Joseph, we'll be fine. Do it for Spinners," Teresa replied, tears welling in her eyes.

Joseph Bohr turned to Violet and Boy. "Right. I'm coming!"

Violet gulped and glanced across at her friend.

"Okay." Boy nodded, looking much more confident than she felt.

He walked to the door and opened it, the alarm attacking their ears once more.

"I've been ordered to take this prisoner to Arnold," he shouted at Powick's creatures and passed through without another word.

Violet grabbed hold of Dr Bohr's arm and, putting on her best zombie act, pulled him roughly out into the corridor, before taking one last look at the other scientists inside. They stood together in a line, arm in arm. Teresa nodded and smiled gently as the door closed.

The alarm blocked out all other sound as the three made their way down the corridor. Violet expected to see the Watcher at every turn. They descended the stairs and carefully checked the hallway below before heading for the exit. They were just passing the art room when she had a brainwave.

"In here," Violet whispered, ducking back.

She raced around and grabbed as many bottles of paint and props as possible, then, taking inspiration from Anna, began changing Boy back into a zombie. Then she turned her attention to Dr Bohr. Violet worked the gory details into his face, arms and feet as her friend grabbed scissors and began ripping holes in the old man's clothes. The doctor sat amused, watching them.

"I already had one foot in the grave – does this now qualify as two?" Bohr joked, looking at himself in the mirror.

The alarm was still ringing as all three snuck outside, through the school gates and limped their way down to Edward Street. As they approached the Town Hall, Watchers were erecting loudspeakers on two of its tall stone columns. Violet had to nudge the doctor forward when he lost concentration staring at the DeathDefier and momentarily forgot he was a zombie. He snapped back into character and they reached Iris Archer's house without another hiccup.

"Where have you been?" Jack asked, standing up as they walked in. "We thought you were—"

He stopped, as he noticed the third figure. Anna grabbed Jack's leg in fright.

"Very sorry, I don't normally look like this." The man smiled. "I'm Dr Joseph Bohr, reporting for duty!"

CHAPTER 29

THE ULTIMATE REVENGE

Boy was just explaining everything that had happened when a sharp sound cut across him. A voice ricocheted around the streets, clearly being broadcast through a loudspeaker. It was Edward.

"Boy Archer, come forward and give yourself up, unless you want your friends and family to suffer for you." His gruff tone hung cold in the afternoon air. "We are sending in the Watchers and they will search No-Man's-Land with a fine-tooth comb. Anyone found harbouring Boy will be punished."

The loudspeaker crackled, hissed, then cut out.

Violet shivered and grabbed her friend's arm. Boy didn't look at her as they heard a band of Watchers pounding the cobbles close by on Archers' Avenue.

"We can't go back," she whispered. "I mean, you definitely can't anyway, Boy!"

"I have to," he insisted.

"Powick and Arnold must be desperate now." She spoke quietly. "They need you by your birthday, by tomorrow."

"Well, I'll just have to stay out of their way." Boy stuck his head back through the broken doorframe to check the street.

"What do they need him for?" Anna asked.

"We still don't know." Boy sounded frustrated.

"Powick said something at the castle about an elix… something of life. Remember, Boy?"

"Elixir of Life." Boy nodded.

"What's that?" Anna asked.

"It's a formula for immortality," Joseph Bohr explained. "It's been sought through the ages by alchemists. It's a legend, of course, but even still, many have died trying to find it!"

"What's an alchemist?" Violet asked.

"Alchemy is an ancient practice shrouded in mystery," Joseph Bohr continued. "The alchemists' quest was to find the Elixir of Life, a substance that could raise the dead or grant eternal life to the living."

"Powick said she needed it to be Tom's birthday to

261

make this elixir thing. And Tom said that he was the powerful one, not Arnold's machine. Do you think they believe Tom can raise the dead? But then why do they need Boy?" Violet was still confused.

"It's all nonsense, Violet. The Elixir of Life is just a fantasy, the stuff of folklore," Joseph Bohr declared. "Mark my words, Arnold Archer is and always will be a madman. He was obsessed by this years ago and he's at it again, but no one can raise the dead and, in my opinion, the dead should be left well enough alone!"

"But does it really matter if they can or can't?" Violet insisted. "If Powick and Arnold believe they can, and they think they need Boy to do it, then Boy's in danger. He can't go back to No-Man's-Land. He needs to leave Town, now! I have a terrible feeling about all this."

"Do you think I'd just abandon everyone, all my family and friends? No way, Violet." Boy was determined. "Right now we have to save Town and that means stopping Arnold and the others."

"We really need to get going." Jack interrupted the conversation, looking nervously up the street.

More Watchers pounded by outside, heading off down Rag Lane.

"We can talk about this later," Boy said, and he slipped back out of the house, heading for the bottom of Archers' Avenue.

The other four followed behind him towards the wall into No-Man's-Land.

"I've to climb that?" Joseph Bohr craned his neck to look up. "I know I have a youthful glow but do any of you realize what age I am?"

"I don't think you have a glow, I think you look really old, Mr Dr Bohr, but there's no other way," Anna said, pulling on his sleeve. "And my mam says age is only a number."

"A wise woman." Dr Bohr laughed, shaking his head as Boy climbed the wall and dropped the rope down.

All four clambered up. It took the doctor much longer than the others but he'd a smile as wide as the footbridge when he was helped over the top of the wall.

"Well, I haven't had this much fun since I was spinning electrons!" he beamed.

They crept across the rooftops and in the bathroom window, down the three floors to the ground and out onto Forgotten Road. They kept in zombie character as they crossed the Market Yard towards Merrill Marx's place.

Violet looked away as a Watcher bullied a man near the Rag Tree.

"Where is Boy?" he growled, a fistful of the man's collar in his grasp. "If some of youse don't give 'im up, you'll all get it!"

The man was tight-lipped. Violet winced as he was

shoved roughly against a wall and his attacker stormed away. Someone rushed to his side to help. If the Watchers kept this up, someone would surely give Boy away. People knew there were meetings at Merrill's.

The bell above the door *ting*ed as Violet entered. The place was empty, stools overturned as if it had been deserted quickly.

"No," Violet gasped, "they've taken everyone, the Watchers must have—"

"Violet?" Rose rushed out from the cubby under the stairs. "I'd know your voice anywhere. We thought you were a group of zombies, pet!"

Shocked and relieved, Violet looked at her friends and burst out laughing. She'd completely forgotten how they must appear.

Slowly the others emerged from their hiding places to welcome them back.

"They're really looking for Boy now. People know he's here! Maybe we should move?" Violet said as everyone settled down.

"It's okay," Merrill replied softly. "I've spoken to most of Town – we've friends watching the streets. I promise we'll be alerted if anyone tells the Watchers anything."

"What if Vincent Crooked finds out where he is? He'll definitely give us away."

"We'll cross that bridge if it comes to it, Violet,"

Eugene said, pulling his daughter close. "Now what happened with Bohr?"

"Stay back," Madeleine cried, late to the gathering, picking up a sweeping brush and wielding it about as the doctor stepped forward from the shadows. "Come here, children, get behind me. One of those creatures has snuck in with you!"

"No, Mam, no," Anna said, running to grab Joseph's hand, "he's the doctor man!"

"They've turned him into a zombie?" the woman gasped.

"Oh no, my dear lady – like the children, it's merely a costume!" Dr Bohr said, rubbing away some of his make-up.

"Joseph?" Iris stared straight at the scientist.

"Iris?" he replied. "I hadn't imagined…I didn't know… oh, how good it is to see you again!"

He dropped Anna's hand, walked across the shop floor and embraced his old friend. Violet looked at Boy, who was blushing just a little.

"Ahem…" William cleared his throat. "Mam, would you like to…"

"Oh," Iris said, pushing back from Bohr's shoulder, "I must introduce you, Joe. This is my son, William…"

"The troublemaker." Joseph smiled, taking his hand. "I remember the last time I saw you, you were just a tot."

Iris introduced Dr Bohr to the crowd. Her dad turned into a stuttering mess and almost curtsied when it was his turn.

"I love your work, sir...Mr...Dr Bohr. It's just... It's just an honour, a complete and total honour to meet you, sir, doctor."

"Excuse my husband," Rose gushed, stepping forward to take the man's hand, "he's got quite a thing for celebrity scientists!"

"Rose!" Eugene huffed, embarrassed, as his wife stepped away.

"We need your help, Dr Bohr," William said, gesturing to a pile of books on the table in front of him.

"Ah, yes." Joseph picked up one of the titles. "Magnetism. Boy filled me in on what you would like to do, but how do we do it is the question..."

Violet watched as Iris slipped quietly away from the crowd. She seemed to be caught in her own thoughts and took up a spot on a small crate in the corner of the room as loud discussions began behind her. She was playing with one of Merrill's new toy experiments, a wooden elephant's head, jerking the lever up and down to move its hollow trunk. She looked as though she were somewhere else.

"I'll give you a penny," Violet said, repeating something she'd often heard her father say when he was trying to make people feel better.

"It's a penny for your thoughts." Iris smiled gently.

"You don't have to tell me your thoughts." Violet sat on a carved wooden drum beside her.

"You're a good child. I'm just stuck in memories," Iris sighed, reaching out to squeeze her hand.

Violet fell quiet and watched the elephant's trunk move up and down.

"I think Merrill wants it to be able to squirt water." The old woman filled in the silence. "It'll be one of his bestsellers then, I imagine."

Violet smiled. She wanted to ask Iris questions but she didn't know where to start.

"I'll give you a penny for yours." The old woman's eyes were kind.

"My what?"

"Your thoughts, Violet. Is there something bothering you?"

"Yes." She nodded, looking over at Boy, who was busy listening to Dr Bohr. "I'm worried about Boy and what Nurse Powick wants with him."

"That woman is crazy." Iris shook her head.

"Did you know her before all this?" Violet asked.

"No," Iris replied, sounding a little uncertain, "I think the first I heard of her was the letter she sent Macula about Boy and Tom. I've never doubted my memory till now, but since you told me about the letters you found from that woman to Arnold, I've started to question whether I did meet her before. I mean, I thought I knew all of Arnold's friends back then. Maybe it's old age!"

Violet walked over to Boy and asked him for the photo they'd found in Iris's house. He pulled it from his pocket and handed it over.

Boy's grandmother smiled, as though lost in memories again, when Violet passed her the picture.

"Where did you find this? It's the old gang from Hegel. Joe is in here somewhere."

Violet hesitated for a moment. "I hope you don't mind, but we were in your room, dressing up as zombies and it was in an album in one of your drawers."

"It's okay. I've not much to hide. I haven't looked at that album in a long, long time."

Violet shifted forward and pointed to the square-shouldered lady at the back. "We think that's Powick."

"Is it?" Iris gasped, drawing the image closer. "The eyes aren't as good at my age." She studied the picture before pulling it away from her nose.

"You're right, pet, it is Powick." Her face paled. "How did I not piece that together? I don't recall her much from back then. I think I only met her once – that day, in fact. They called her Prissy or something. I think she was Hugo's assistant – that man beside her, the one leaning on her shoulder."

"Oh." Violet nodded, moving closer. "Anna thought he looked familiar too."

"I doubt that, Violet." Iris sighed. "He was Arnold's best friend – Dr Hugo Spinners, a young man with quite an amazing mind. When Arnold started to go off the rails, they fell out. Hugo tried to persuade him away from his death studies, but Arnold wouldn't listen – he believed Hugo was jealous. They became arch-enemies, each trying to prove the other wrong. It was very sad."

Dr Spinners, the name rang a bell. Powick had mentioned him in her letters to Arnold but Violet knew she'd heard it somewhere else too, she just couldn't quite put her finger on it.

"What happened to him?" Violet asked, her stomach in a knot.

"He died a few years after this photo was taken. It was very sudden, an accident. I'm not sure what happened, but I remember some talked about it being suspicious. Things were not good for me then. Arnold was at the height of his madness. It was shortly after Hugo died that he attacked William and I fled here with the boys."

Suddenly the conversation in the graveyard came back to her. An uneasy energy passed through her body.

"One of the scientists, a woman called Teresa, asked Arnold if he killed Dr Spinners…"

"Killed him...?" Iris's face turned a slight shade of green. "What did he say?"

"He said something about not letting the doctor get away with mocking him and that he would raise him from the dead first."

"Hugo, his best friend! Oh, Arnold! And after all this time...surely he hasn't... Oh no, not like our dog, he hasn't kept his bod—" Iris reached out her hand and leaned against Merrill's toy elephant as if for balance.

"Hugo! That's Dr Spinners' first name?" Violet interrupted. "Hugo the zombie! Do you think...? You don't think...?"

She remembered the nurse saying that Dr Spinners had been of great service to them. And Anna recognized Dr Spinners in the picture. Now that Violet looked at the photo, remembering the creature's gruesome features, it did seem possible.

"You don't think Dr Spinners is Hugo, the Child Snatcher?" Her stomach churned as the words slipped out. Iris gasped.

"Of course!" she whispered, locking eyes with Violet. "That would be just Arnold's style. After they fell out, Hugo became Arnold's biggest opponent. He tore apart his research into death. Of course he killed Spinners! And now he plans to bring him back to life, to prove his point using the corpse of his biggest opponent. The ultimate revenge. Oh, Arnold, your madness knows no boundaries!"

Violet felt physically sick at the thought. If Arnold could kill his best friend and turn him into a zombie, what did he and Powick have planned for Boy? The others were still busy with Dr Bohr, trying to figure out a way to stop the zombies; nobody seemed that worried about Boy or the threat of his birthday. But she couldn't shake a feeling that something really bad was about to happen to him.

Iris was stuck in her thoughts, shaking her head as she muttered to herself, still in shock about Hugo.

"Powick wants Boy for some reason," Violet pressed the old woman, her tone urgent. "She said something about an Elixir of Life – have you heard of it? Did Arnold ever mention anything like that when he was working on his machine?"

Iris stayed silent for a while as though racking her brains.

"No, Violet. I can't say I ever heard him mention an elixir. In his maddest moments he would rant about William, the Divided Soul and the curse he brought on our family. But I don't recall anything else."

"Did he have notes or books about the curse that you might have kept, or anything that could help?"

Iris shook her head. "What is it, pet?"

"I'm just afraid they're planning something awful for Boy! The letter you talked about before – the one Powick sent to Macula after Perfect fell, telling her that she'd taken Tom – do you remember anything else it said?"

"No." Iris shook her head. "But I do remember Macula thought that Powick wanted to turn her against Boy. It was part of Edward's plan to divide Town and win back Perfect."

Violet nodded. She knew all that, but the letter said something else too. Something she wished she could remember.

"We'll watch Boy," Iris reassured her. "As long as he stays in our sights he'll be fine. You're a good friend, Violet. The best anyone could ask for. I won't let Arnold or that woman hurt my grandson. I promise you that. And once we've stopped them, they'll never hurt anyone again." She grabbed Violet's hand, squeezing it tight. "Boy will be okay."

Violet wanted to believe Iris but she couldn't. Something was playing heavily on her mind – she just wished she could pin it down. She was standing up to join the planning discussion, when she noticed a large black bird perched on the windowsill outside.

She walked to the window just as the bird launched itself up into the air. Violet opened the door and peered outside, up towards the Market Yard.

"Tom," she whispered. "Tom, are you here?"

The place seemed quiet, quieter than it had been when she'd arrived. A chill danced down her spine. She closed the shop door and walked back to the others.

CHAPTER 30

THE SELFLESS SCIENTIST

Dr Joseph Bohr was busy drawing something on a large flat piece of wood. They seemed to have run out of paper, Violet noticed as she walked through the scrunched-up balls of it on the floor. Jack was by Bohr's side as the doctor explained something about magnetism to him, while pointing to sections of his diagram.

William and Eugene were both arguing over a theory while Boy and Anna scrutinized Arnold's drawing of the DeathDefier that they'd taken from the science lab in school. Iris joined the children, peering over their shoulders.

"That's new," she said aloud. "Arnold appears to be using a lot more power this time round. I wonder where he'll get all of it?"

"He is, isn't he!" Dr Bohr smiled, looking over at her. "That much electricity could jolt a rock back to life!"

"Electricity…" Jack said, looking up the doctor. "What about electromagnetism? Didn't you say something about passing electricity through a metal to make a magnet?"

"Jack, my boy, you're a genius!" Joseph Bohr laughed, slapping him so hard on the back he almost fell forward.

"We've been trying to overcomplicate it!" Jack grabbed the poster of the machine. "Arnold has already made us a magnet! See the human-shaped plate in the middle of the DeathDefier? It's copper, a metal. And according to these plans, it'll be pumped full of electricity when the machine powers up!"

"My boy, I may give you an apprenticeship when we save this little town! Copper is not just any metal either, it's an excellent conductor too! Why, we could have quite a powerful magnet on our hands. The glass will hold the magnetism in of course, but if we can break the glass then it'll be released and those zombies will be sucked onto that plate faster than matter down a black hole."

Violet cringed as her dad laughed loudly at Dr Bohr's science joke.

"But Violet said there are loads of zombies," Anna interrupted. "They won't all fit on that piece of metal!"

"Well spotted, Anna," Dr Bohr continued, "but magnets have a kind of contagious quality, if you will.

275

The zombies themselves, or their frames should I say, will also become magnets. So some will stick to the machine, then their frames will become magnetized – others will stick to them until we've layers of zombies all sticking to each other!"

"I imagine we'd have to break the glass when the power is on in Arnold's machine?" William asked.

"Precisely, William, but that's a minor detail, of course. Something we'll get to in the fullness of time!"

"Not so minor." Rose was shaking her head. "Details are important. I'm a numbers person and I imagine even if we do manage to break the glass, we'd need to have quite a large number of people on the street at that precise moment ready to take advantage of the Archers' weak position and fight the Watchers. If we lose the element of surprise, the electricity could be cut to the machine and the zombies released, am I right?"

"Why yes, you are." Dr Bohr nodded as Eugene smiled proudly at his wife.

"But we're all stuck in No-Man's-Land," Madeleine said, catching up with the conversation.

"We can break out like before, Mam, and hide somewhere until it's time," Anna said enthusiastically.

"We'd need quite a large number of people – the whole Town, in fact, just like when we fought for Perfect – if we want to successfully take on the Watchers," Iris interrupted. "How can we hide that many people in plain sight?"

"They're building a stand…" Jack offered. "Maybe we could hide under it?"

"It's not large enough," Boy said. "I think they'd spot us anyway!"

"The castle?" Violet said suddenly, glad to be distracted from her worries about her friend.

"What do you mean? We can't go back to the castle, Violet," Boy said dismissively.

Everyone continued to argue about the best way to mount their attack.

"You're not listening!" Violet said, so loud this time all other voices came to a halt. "The castle, Boy! Remember, it was invisible. We couldn't see it, even though it was right in the middle of an open field! Right in front of our eyes."

"What?" Eugene furrowed his brow. "I remember you said something about this, but it didn't register with me, pet. You're saying it was completely invisible?"

"Oh yes, why didn't I think of that!" Joseph Bohr butted in. "Arnold developed it years ago before he went mad – it's a metamaterial, won numerous awards! He boasted to us one day when he visited our cell, explaining how he created a large metal wall around the whole castle and covered the outside of it in his material, making everything disappear. He was insufferable the way he bleated on about it, but I must give the man some credit, his product is ingenious!"

Iris cleared her throat, her face suddenly stern. "Arnold claimed he invented that fabric, Joe, and I was silly and naïve enough to let him! But that piece of science was all mine! I needed to keep my mind ticking over after I had a family and gave up my research, so I developed this material at home for fun. I used to trick the kids with it. Don't you remember, William? My disappearing hand! I had forgotten all about that until now."

"Oh yes…" Her son smiled as if being brought back to a moment.

"You three thought it was magic!" She laughed. "Oh I loved to watch your faces. Your old mother is no fool! I developed a silk that can bend light around itself. I used split-ring resonators. The spacing between them was less than the wavelength of light and I was eventually able to manipulate both the magnetic and electric fields of light. It meant that you couldn't see anything the silk encased but you could see everything in front and behind it. I have to say, I was pretty pleased with myself."

"Iris, that is impressive!" Joseph Bohr announced. "If only I'd known back then. The cheek of Arnold!"

"He saw it and, without telling me, submitted my research for peer review under his own name. It was picked up straight away and Arnold was lauded. I was annoyed, of course, but also in love with him, and he argued that what was mine was his and vice versa. I told myself not to be silly or have an ego and that whatever benefit came from it would also benefit the family, so I stayed quiet. Wasn't I a fool back then?"

Joseph wrapped an arm over her shoulder. "If only all scientists were as selfless, Iris," he soothed.

"Can you make more, Mam?" William asked.

"I can do better than that. If memory serves me right, I think I may have a few sheets of it in the attic at home. I took everything I had with me and even used it when I was escaping from Arnold. It can be hard to find though – but nothing a little searching can't sort, I imagine."

"I can go get them," Boy said quickly. "Granny will never be able to get over the roof."

"Excuse me!" Iris raised her bushy eyebrows. "I'm not past my sell-by date yet!"

"If I can do it, young man, so can your grandmother. In fact, I'll go with you, Iris!" Joseph Bohr butted in. "I thoroughly enjoyed my climb this morning. We'll take this young man too." He clapped Jack's back. "He can show us the route in case our memories fail us!"

"Okay then." William nodded. "This plan just might work. If we break into smaller groups, each could hide inside a moveable hoarding covered in one of the silks, a bit like the castle. Would you have enough material, Mam?"

"I might have, William. I think I made quite a lot of it for Arnold as journals were requesting samples to inspect to prove it actually worked."

"Brilliant!" Her son smiled. "So the groups will sneak into Town undetected tomorrow, wait for Arnold to fire up the DeathDefier, break the glass, let the magnetism do its work and attack!"

"We'll rescue our Town back from those lunatics!" Madeleine said, hugging her daughter close.

"Who's going to break the glass, William?" Rose asked cautiously.

"I know a few people that are good with slingshots." Boy smiled. "I'll round them up!"

"No," Iris said. "You're to stay here out of the way. Powick needs you for tomorrow, but she will not have you. Not as long as I live!"

Boy went quiet. Violet could see he was mad.

"I can get the sling-shooters if you tell me who they are. It's nearly your birthday," she tried to joke, "you can put your feet up!"

"Perfect." William nodded. "Myself and Eugene will spread the word about what's happening. Get people ready for a battle."

"I'll go too," Rose said. "You'll need a bit of charm to

convince some Townsfolk and I'm not sure either of you possess enough of that!"

"You might be right." William smiled, a little red-faced. "Boy, tell Violet who's good with the slingshot and she'll come with us and round them up."

Violet nodded, feeling just a little awkward as her friend remained quiet.

"I imagine we'll need about ten people with good aim. The glass on the machine, as per the drawing, isn't that thick, but they'll still need to be firing heavyish stones at it. Tell them to get a few practices in! Madeleine, Anna and Merrill, stay here and make about ten boards, big enough to shield a decent amount of people behind!" William continued his instructions.

"Right." Merrill nodded, looking around the shop. "I'm sure we'll be able to cobble enough bits of wood together!"

"Oh I love hammering stuff!" Anna said excitedly. "Mam never lets me do it at home!"

"It's just this once, pet," Madeleine warned. "It won't be a regular thing!"

"Perfect." William looked around. "Is that it? Does everyone know what they're doing?"

"I'm not doing anything," Boy sulked.

"It's safest this way – we don't know what Powick and Arnold have planned. You can help Merrill make the boards." William tried to sound enthusiastic. Then he addressed the room again: "Right, let's go then. We'll meet back here at midnight. That should give us enough time to finalize everything before tomorrow!"

CHAPTER 31

DESPERATE FOR BOY

Reluctantly, Boy filled Violet in on a group of orphans he knew who were great with slingshots. He barely looked at her as they spoke and she felt guilty about leaving him behind.

"It's for the best, Boy," she whispered, unsure what else to say.

"I'm not afraid of Powick or Arnold. I was an orphan, Violet, I never had anyone minding me and we beat the Watchers then and last time we beat Edward and Powick. I don't need anyone to protect me! I'm fine on my own!" He looked over his shoulder, checking no one was watching him.

"But this time is different, Boy. Arnold is crazy – he

killed his own best friend, and Powick has made a zombie army. Tom is even afraid of them, I know he is—"

"I'm not Tom!" Boy snapped.

"Please, just don't do anything stupid. Stay here and by tomorrow night it'll all be over!"

Her friend turned away and began picking up loose bits of wood to pass to Merrill and the others for their hoarding. Violet tried to get his attention again but he ignored her. She left the shop under a huge weight of guilt.

Night had settled in and the Market Yard had quietened when Violet stepped outside. Most people were asleep, huddled in small groups, some covered in blankets, whilst others walked laps of the area, trying to keep warm. There weren't many Watchers around and the same handful of zombies stood sentry, guarding the laneways.

Violet's earlier unease returned. Something felt off.

Lucy Lawn and her family were handing out hot drinks and bread to those awake. Her dad, Larry, had an outdoor clay cooker hidden round the back of their home and he'd been firing it up and feeding whoever was hungry.

Violet spotted William and her mam and dad stopping to speak to people before passing on slowly. They were being discreet as they shuffled from group to group – if the Watchers caught wind of a plan, everyone would be in trouble.

A bunch of kids sat huddled by the base of the Rag Tree – she recognized some as ex-orphans. Lowering her head, she walked towards them.

"Has anyone seen Billy Bobbins?" she asked. Before she left the shop Boy had told her that Billy had been the best in the orphanage with a slingshot and would be able to round up the other sharpshooters.

"I think he was over there with his family." One of the boys pointed.

She was just walking away when a commotion broke out by the bottom of the first lane up to Forgotten Road. Somebody was pointing out her dad to one of the Watchers.

"And there's Archer!" the same person shouted, pointing across the yard at William.

It was Vincent Crooked.

Her dad and William started to run just as someone screamed. Violet turned to see Madeleine and Merrill being dragged into the middle of the square, two Watchers holding them tightly.

People panicked, scattering back against the walls as William and Eugene were surrounded by a group of Watchers who had suddenly appeared from one of the laneways.

Violet spied a narrow track between two homes on the square and raced for it. The space was just wide enough to touch the stone walls either side with her fingers. Crammed with odds and ends, bins and a broken washing machine, Violet squeezed into hiding. From her position she could just see into the Market Yard.

It looked like the whole army of Watchers now trailed like ants out of the laneways encircling the yard. Some of them herded the terrified Townsfolk into the middle of the square, while others began to bang down doors and invade the homes of No-Man's-Land.

Clinging onto each other, people watched in a petrified silence as their houses were ransacked and William, Eugene, Merrill and Madeleine were manhandled over to the Rag Tree.

Then Edward and George Archer strode out from the first lane, through the crowd, stopping right beside Violet's dad.

George ordered Vincent Crooked to round up the rest of Town's Committee members and the smartly dressed, greasy-haired man walked through the crowd, smiling as he pointed them out one by one. The Watchers dragged each person over to the Rag Tree, shoving them roughly beside the others. Some, still holding onto distraught family members, had to be forced apart.

"I've just about had enough of you lot!" Edward announced.

An anxious murmur passed through the crowd.

"You had it easy under our rule," he snarled. "Most of you lived *perfectly* and those in No-Man's-Land, well at least we kept you alive. But things are about to change. Tomorrow brings a new dawn, one where I cannot promise your safety, unless I'm shown some loyalty! Bet you regret fighting against us now!"

"Yes, loyalty," George growled, echoing his brother as he prowled through the crowd.

"I need you to give me Boy Archer!" Edward roared, his face red to bursting.

Violet gulped. The Watchers had found Merrill and Madeleine, so they had to have been in the shop. But where was Boy? Had he gotten away somehow?

"You give him over to us and—"

"You'll let us go, I suppose!" someone bravely sneered.

Violet couldn't see where the voice came from.

"No, I won't let you go, but I'll let you live!" Edward spat. "I will make sure my father shows you mercy. You won't become fodder for his army or, worse still, be turned into one of his creatures. You've met them – we have just a small selection of his beasts helping us out at the moment!"

The stout man walked back and forth in front of the crowd. "And, Boy – yes I'm talking to you directly now – all those you care about are coming with me. If you don't show yourself before your birthday tomorrow, I promise that each of them will be turned into a member of Arnold's army. You've seen Priscilla's sewing skills! But if you do show, I will let them live too – so don't miss the party!"

Another cry rang through the market and Violet's mam was forced out of the crowd.

"This one's not on the Committee but she's as good as," Vincent sneered, dragging her over to the others.

Violet tensed. She wanted to scream and charge; her anger boiled. She scanned the area again, desperately trying to see Boy. If he was watching this, she was sure he'd give himself up. But that was exactly what Edward wanted.

"I need an audience for tomorrow's special event, so I'm taking your Committee," the short man continued. "See how this little town functions without its leaders! Now if you'll excuse us, we've work to do!"

"No, Mam!" someone shrieked.

A small child raced from the crowd and grabbed hold of one of the Committee members. A Watcher forced him back roughly, knocking the little boy to the ground.

The kid was screaming as Edward Archer clapped his hands. "Ah the sound of little children's tears never fails to make me smile! Now everyone move out. We've a briefing for tomorrow's activities up at the Town Hall. Our zombies will keep an eye on you lot until my Watchers get back. A warning though, put a foot out of line and I promise they'll eat you!"

Then, together with his brother, Edward marched out of the Market Yard, followed by the Watchers and their newly acquired prisoners.

Violet leaned back against the washing machine, breathless. What were they going to do now? All their plans... Everyone was gone. And Boy... A lump rose in her throat. No matter what Edward said, he wasn't a man of his word. Town would suffer whether they handed Boy over or not, but she was afraid others wouldn't see it like that.

"They've taken Mam!" a voice trembled, as a small shadow moved towards her from the yard.

"Anna!" Violet exclaimed, leaping up. "How did you get away?"

"I was upstairs looking for bits of wood when the Watchers came. I hid. They dragged Mam outside. I'm scared. I should have done something."

"There was nothing you could do, Anna. It'll be fine. We'll figure it out. What about Boy, where's he?"

"I don't know," she sobbed. "He wasn't there when I came down – the shop was empty. I was looking for my sister when I saw you in here. I thought maybe Boy was with you! They're all gone, Violet. Everyone. What if he hurts them? What about our plans? You said Arnold had a huge army – what if he marches them all in tomorrow and there's nothing we can do? What if he turns us all into zombies?"

Violet wrapped the little girl in her arms and led her back out into the market. "We'll save them, Anna," she soothed, unsure if she believed her own words. "Somehow we'll save them!"

A huge group of people were congregated round the Rag Tree. They were angry. The pair stepped closer to listen.

"We will not give him up! Wherever he is," a voice roared.

Violet could just see the scruff of brown hair above the gathered heads. Someone was standing on a chair addressing the crowd. Holding on to Anna's hand, she pushed forward through the sea of bodies.

"William and Boy Archer gave me back my family," a short-haired, pixie-faced girl said.

It was Pippa Moody, her teacher's daughter. "They gave us all back our freedom, both Perfectionists and No-Man's-Landers, so that no divisions existed any more. I won't sacrifice them now!" she hollered.

"Me neither," somebody else cried, stepping forward from those gathered. It was Billy Bobbins Senior, one of the first to get back his imagination after the Archer brothers' reign.

"Nor me," said Lucy, Billy's sister. She'd helped persuade the No-Man's-Landers to fight back during the battle of Perfect.

"I won't stand for anyone going against William or

his son. We will defend him just as he has defended us!" announced Larry Lawn, coming out of the crowd. He was joined by the rest of the Lawn family.

"I'll butcher any zombie that tries to harm a hair on their heads," announced Mr Hatchet.

"So will I!" said a smaller high-pitched voice.

Violet almost choked as Beatrice Prim came forward. Soon it seemed like everyone was on their side. Vincent Crooked tried to snake away at the back of the group, but he was surrounded by angry Townsfolk. Before he could do anything, he'd been bundled over to a nearby home and locked in to stop him making any more accusations.

Violet took Anna's hand and squeezed. She looked at the crowd with a deep sense of pride. Someone grabbed her shoulder.

She whisked around.

"Boy! You're okay," she gasped, hugging him.

Violet was sure there were tears in his eyes as Anna threw herself around his waist.

"So what are we going to do?" Pippa Moody announced.

"Um…" Violet cleared her throat and stepped forward, her two friends on either side. "We could do with some help!"

Suddenly a huge whirring sound filled the air. The light around them flickered, then blinked, and the yard was plunged into total darkness.

CHAPTER 32

SECRET MEETINGS

"What's happened, what's going on?" Anna asked, grabbing Violet's arm.

"The electricity," Boy gasped, looking around. "Iris said Arnold would need a lot of power for his machine this time. I bet he's taken it from Town's supply!"

"Everyone stay calm," Pippa Moody cried.

Violet could barely see her as she held her hands up, trying to quell the terrified crowd. People began to quieten but still shifted uneasily as they looked around the Market Yard. Anna squealed when a zombie lurched past in the darkness. Boy darted off and grabbed Pippa's arm, whispering something in her ear before returning to Violet's side.

"I've told Pippa to get word out that there'll be a meeting at the orphanage in about twenty minutes. People are to come in ones and twos so as not to be obvious. We can't talk here – the Watchers will be back soon!" he said.

"Oh, I've a key." Anna said excitedly, pulling one from her pocket.

"I knew you would." Boy winked.

The three passed word of the meeting around those gathered, then snuck through the darkness up the laneway to the orphanage. Anna reached on her tippy toes, opened the lock and they snuck inside, leaving the double doors slightly ajar.

They tried the light switch but nothing happened.

"I know where there's candles and matches," Boy whispered, crossing the large cold hallway.

Violet and Anna followed him to a cubbyhole tucked in under the ornate wooden staircase, the one he'd hidden in when Tom had pretended to be him. Boy opened the door and crawled inside, emerging a few moments later with a small tin box.

The threesome waited in the dark, sitting down underneath the wall of photographs that William had installed when the orphanage became a museum. The pictures were a visual history of all the things that had happened in their little town since the days of Perfect and served as a reminder to all, William said, never to repeat the same mistakes again.

As the minutes ticked by, people began to arrive, gathering in the cavernous main entrance hall. Anxious whispers rang round the space.

Then Boy lit the candles and Violet passed them out. The soft light warmed the cold and the uneasy voices started to settle.

"Violet, Boy, Anna," Pippa Moody panted as she found them, having been one of the last to get there, "how can we help?"

Boy pushed Violet forward. She shot him a look but he was nervous, paler and quieter than normal. He was never good at public speaking, even in class.

Violet took in the sea of shadowed faces. Sweat prickled her brow. She blushed and racked her brain for something to say. She was never good at public speaking either but that didn't seem to matter to her friend.

Something tickled her fingers – Anna had taken her hand and Violet's nerves suddenly eased.

"We have a plan," she announced. "Well, we had a plan, but now everyone is gone and it's falling apart, so we need help. Lots of help!"

"We can do that!" Pippa Moody said to a swell of agreement.

Violet cleared her throat and started at the beginning.

She told everyone about Arnold Archer and his history. Then she spoke about Nurse Powick and the zombies, the DeathDefier and their plans to raise the dead and take over Town. The only thing she didn't mention was the Elixir of Life, because she still didn't know where that fitted in yet.

The crowd sounded worried as the story unfolded and Violet had to wait for the mumbles to die down before continuing.

"You mean to say there's a whole army of those creatures…those zombies?" somebody cried.

Violet nodded.

"How many?"

"Ahem…" She wasn't sure what she should tell them. An image of the rows and rows of the creatures filling the castle courtyard flashed through her mind. "Lots," she replied.

"But then we're doomed. We've taken on the Watchers before, but those creatures are strong and fast, I'm not sure we—"

"But we can beat them!" Anna stomped her foot on the tiled floor, determined. "We have a plan, just listen to Violet, please!"

The crowd went silent and Violet squeezed the little girl's hand once more. Then she outlined their plan. She spoke about Arnold's machine, and how they could turn it into a magnet if they had people to break the glass once the power was on.

"I thought Billy Bobbins could get some sling-shooters together," Boy added after she'd finished.

"I'd love to," a small figure announced from the back of the group. "How many do you need?"

"At least ten, with really good aim," Boy confirmed.

"Sorted!" Billy smiled, waving his candle excitedly.

Violet was about to explain Iris's invention, the silk that would shield them from sight, when suddenly she looked around the hall.

"What is it?" Boy whispered.

"Iris," she hissed. "They're not back. What if they've been caught like the others? Then we've no chance of finding her silk or hiding everyone on Edward Street."

"Oh, don't skip over our part," a voice giggled from somewhere nearby. "We're waiting here patiently!"

Violet jumped, looking around to see who had spoken.

Suddenly a picture flew off the wall behind her, smashing onto the floor – it was a framed photo of Edward and George. The crowd looked terrified. Violet, Boy, Anna and Pippa backed away, pulling each other close.

Then laughter echoed round the hallway and Iris, Joseph and Jack appeared from thin air.

The crowd erupted in gentle applause, their fear turning to relief. The three newcomers smiled widely, and grabbed each other's hands to take a mock bow.

"We've loads of the stuff!" Iris said. "More than I remember!"

Violet explained to everyone about the silk and how it would work.

"Then, once all the zombies are stuck to the magnet, we take on the Watchers straight away, using the element of surprise!" Violet said, wrapping up. "We need to be ready to fight. Just like in Perfect!"

"Ready and waiting, pet!" Mr Hatchet, the butcher, cried.

The crowd cheered quietly again and silent high fives passed round the space.

"Right," Violet said, "we'll meet back here at sunrise. That should give everyone enough time to get ready. Then we can go over any final plans!"

The meeting finished, the groups were divided up and the hall was abuzz with whispers. Slowly people began to leave in ones and twos so as not to raise suspicion. They headed to separate houses to prepare for the coming day.

CHAPTER 33

TOM'S DESTINY

Back at Merrill's, they worked by candlelight, each taking it in turns to sleep. Violet and Boy, fresh from a short rest, were stapling Iris's material to numerous boards.

Violet noticed her friend looked lost and distant. She had an inkling what was wrong and broached the subject.

"Where were you earlier?" she asked, trying to make her question sound innocent.

"Earlier when?" he replied.

"When Merrill and Madeleine were taken."

"I was hiding."

"Did you hear what Edward said in the Market? About hurting the people you care about if you don't show yourself? You know we won't let that happen, don't you?"

He didn't reply.

"You're not planning anything stupid, are you, Boy?" she continued.

The question had been niggling her for a while.

"I can't let everyone suffer for me, Violet. I have to give myself up!" He stopped working and looked her straight in the eyes. "I'll help out until we're ready, then I have to go. I heard what Edward said."

"And you think that'll help us? Giving yourself up for what?" She was angry now.

He didn't answer or look at her.

Her anger rose and she snapped. "Edward is a liar, Boy! It doesn't matter if you give yourself up or not, he's still going to keep everyone captive here. Arnold will hand this place to Powick and her zombies no matter what you do! Don't be so stupid. Giving yourself up won't help anyone! If I thought it would, I'd be the first to shove you into his arms. He's taken my parents too, remember!"

Boy still didn't look at her, but his pale cheeks blotched a little. She tried to bring it up again but he continued his work in an awkward silence.

A little later, Larry Lawn arrived, laden down with bread and soup for everyone. The sound of slurping spread through the room as people filled their empty stomachs. Violet's worries faded a little, wafting away with the smell of freshly baked bread. She was just tearing a chunk off in her teeth when a loud screech cut through the night outside, so shrill it pierced the windows. Anna, who was standing nearest the door, opened it, allowing cold air to infiltrate the room.

"Happy birthday, Boy Archer!" Powick sang. Her coarse voice bounced off the stone walls as the microphone shrieked uncomfortably.

Violet looked at the clock – it was well past midnight. Boy's birthday!

"You still haven't shown up for your party, dearest, and to be frank that's tested my patience. So here is some encouragement."

The microphone screeched again and suddenly William's voice filtered through the night sky.

"Don't listen to her, Boy!" he shouted before a loud and painful cry rattled the airwaves. "I'm… I'm…" There was a thud, another painful groan and the broadcast stopped dead.

"Dad!" Boy cried, standing up and knocking his soup to the floor. His face was pale and his eyes hollow as his hands shivered.

Iris rushed to her grandson's side and grabbed him.

"He'll be fine, Boy, your father's made of strong stuff," she soothed, though tears watered her cheeks. "Don't allow that woman to rattle you. We just need to concentrate on what we're doing here."

Boy shook his head. "I can't let this happen. I can't, not after Mam, I can't lose Dad too!"

"And William can't lose you either, Boy!" Violet insisted, standing up now too.

"But she's hurting him. What use is any of this without him, Violet?" he asked, struggling against Iris. "I was an orphan, I never knew what it was like to have a family. I thought I was fine on my own. But then I found them, and then I lost my mam and I wished I'd never found them at all...! I know how awful it feels and I can't do it again. I can't lose Dad too. Please just let me go!"

"Please don't, Boy!" Violet was crying now too. "We don't know what Powick has planned for you. Just wait this out – once we've beaten her and Arnold they can't hurt you or anyone any more!"

"And while I stay here she hurts Dad and everyone else – maybe even your parents, Violet – just to get to me. Can't you see? The only way I can stop her is to go to her!"

Violet strode away. She couldn't argue with him any more. She needed to be strong and to figure out what the nurse wanted with her friend. If she could solve that, she might be able to help him.

Iris and the others eventually persuaded Boy to sit and after a while a strange calm seemed to settle over him. Violet ventured back.

"Maybe I can sneak into Town early and find out what Powick's doing? She doesn't need me so—"

"I don't want to talk about it! I just want our plans to start," he interrupted, his knees bouncing rapidly up and down, unnerving her.

"They will. Everyone is almost ready – we're leaving soon," she soothed. "Arnold and Powick and your uncles will be stopped… It's only a few more hours!"

Boy nodded, not meeting her eyes.

❋   ❋   ❋

It was still dark but birdsong had started to seep in the window, a sign that morning was approaching. Small groups had been arriving all night to grab their invisible hoardings. They were to practise moving with them in various homes around No-Man's-Land, making sure they stayed invisible before coming together.

When it was almost time for the final run-through in the orphanage, Violet made her way there across the quiet Market Yard. Boy had wanted to go too and promised he'd remain behind at the orphanage until the battle was won. He'd insisted they go to the orphanage separately so as not to raise suspicion but she had secretly asked others to watch him, worried he'd break his promise and try to sneak away.

She was just passing the Rag Tree when something

rattled the branches. She turned around, a little on edge.

A large black raven was perched on a branch nearby. Its coal-coloured eyes bored into hers.

She looked around for Tom but couldn't see him.

The bird moved its wings as she stepped closer. Something was rolled up and attached to its leg. She reached out. The raven flapped excitedly and Violet was sure it was going to fly away. Her throat tightened and every muscle tensed.

Then the raven bounced from the branch onto her extended arm. She tried to relax but her heart pounded. Slowly she moved her free hand for the note attached to the bird's smooth black leg. Its dark claws tightened, clamping her arm. She flinched and the creature opened its wings again and launched itself into the sky.

Panicked, Violet grabbed for the rolled paper but only managed to loosen it. She watched the raven swoop across the cobbles into the first laneway, the paper hanging precariously from its ankle. She raced after it to the narrow passage.

Someone was running up towards Forgotten Road away from her.

"Hello?" she called.

The steps stopped and the person turned around, silhouetted against the morning sky at the top of the lane. It was a boy, a bird perched on one of his slight shoulders.

"Tom," she whispered.

"Why hasn't he come yet?" Tom quivered. "Does he want Da— William to die too, just like Macula? I told you to go. I warned you to get them out of here and now look what's happening!"

"What is it, Tom? What's happening? Please, I can help you."

"There isn't time now, it's too late. She needs me. If only you'd listened then none of this would be underway. I wouldn't have to…" Boy's brother sounded scared.

"You wouldn't have to what?" Violet urged.

"To fulfil my destiny!" he barked, anger ripping through his voice. "Tell him to come. NOW! To give himself up. She's informed Arnold that she already has Boy – he's on his way with the army. She's desperate now! I know what she's like – she will harm our father and then yours, Violet! This is all your fault!"

Her heart stopped. Tom turned and raced away down Forgotten Road. She chased after him, her feet pounding the cobbles. His raven launched into the morning sky as they rounded onto Rag Lane and Violet watched the piece of paper fall from its leg and drift slowly to the ground.

CHAPTER 34

THE DIVIDED SOUL

Violet put her foot out to stop the note from flying away on the breeze. Then she picked up what looked like a page ripped from an old book. The paper was thin, yellowed round the edges and the type was really small.

What appeared to be the title of the book was printed in capital letters at the top right-hand corner of the page: *Eye Confess – Windows to the Soul.*

About halfway down she came across a section marked heavily in pen. Lines and squiggles highlighted paragraphs and tiny handwritten notes were scrawled in the margins of the page. Violet bent forward, squinting at the text in the half dark.

Her heart skipped as her eyes fell on the words "Divided Soul". It was written in a paragraph entitled

"Disorders of the Mind", which was underlined.

Divided Souls, it explained, were born with different-coloured eyes. They were extremely creative, with great minds, and could tend towards insanity. The piece went on to name successful people all through the ages who were Divided Souls.

She turned the page over. The back was also heavily marked, so much so it was hard to read the printed text. Her eyes scanned the title sentence. "The Curse of the Divided Soul."

Her hands shook, rattling the paper, as she read.

The Curse of the Divided Soul is written about in the folklore of many world cultures. The birth of such a weary soul is a bad omen; for the Divided Soul brings destruction to everyone it meets. To break the curse and rescue a family from its horrors, a Divided Soul was often given up as a sacrifice to the gods.

It is written that many divided persons succumb to insanity as they walk equally in the lands of light and dark, their souls torn between good and evil.

Many texts speak of two methods in which the curse can be broken. The first of note: the death of the Divided Soul, as mentioned above, lifts the curse from all who have been touched by it. The second: on the occasion a Divided Soul has twin offspring, their soul is split evenly between each infant. It is said that one child shall have the potential to master death and evil while the other can master life and good. The parent is left whole, their soul renewed, and regains their sanity.

Violet gasped. That's what she had been trying to remember. Powick talked about the Divided Soul in the letter she'd written to Macula after Perfect had fallen, telling her she'd taken Tom. The nurse said something about the curse being halved when William had twins and that it meant one boy was evil and the other good. Powick said in the letter that Boy was the evil twin. Macula believed that the nurse was just trying to turn her and everyone else against her son as part of Edward's plans to take back Town.

Tom told Violet that Powick said he had a black soul, which must mean she thought he was the twin who had the potential to master death. That's what he meant when he said he had the real power and not Arnold's machine.

But if the nurse believed all of this was true then why did she need Boy?

Violet read on.

The Rule of Worldly Balance

The Rule of Worldly Balance states that, if they so wish, only one twin can claim their gift, on the occasion of their thirteenth birthday when they pass from childhood into adulthood. But in order to claim this gift, one twin must kill the other. The blood of the deceased is then used to create an elixir. The blood of the twin whose soul is dark shall create the Prophesy of Death, while the blood of the twin whose soul is light shall create the Elixir of Life.

The Elixir of Life! That's what Powick had been talking about with Arnold, what Joseph Bohr said people had been for ever searching for – he said it was a potion to raise the dead!

Violet's head was spinning as everything fell into place. Nurse Powick wanted Tom to kill Boy! She was going to use her friend's blood to create a potion that'd raise the dead, and it could only happen today, on his thirteenth birthday. That's why Arnold had waited this long; that's why Powick was so desperate to find Boy. Like Tom said, they'd been planning it for years.

It was all crazy folklore, like everyone said, but if Powick and Arnold believed it, then Boy was in huge trouble. She needed to find him before the nurse did.

Violet shoved the paper in her pocket and was just racing up the laneway towards the orphanage when the loudspeaker crackled.

"Here's a little tune to welcome the birth of a glorious day, a day that will go down in history, a day when life will be put back into old friendships..." Priscilla Powick droned across the airways.

Suddenly music filled the skies over Town.

It sounded like one of Violet's mam's favourite songs, the one that crackled whenever she played it, by someone called Vera who sang about meeting again. Rose told Violet it was a song from the olden days. The soft tones and gentle music jarred eerily with the awfulness of the situation.

Violet bounded in through the double doors of the old building, where everyone had stopped what they were doing to listen.

"Right, we need to keep practising our positions," Iris Archer ordered, breaking the stillness. "Ignore distractions. Slingshots to the front, everyone else pack tightly in behind. We need to move out soon and be ready and waiting on Edward Street!"

Violet watched from the top of the hallway as small groups of Townspeople squashed in behind their hoardings and disappeared before her eyes. A tingle raced through her body as the song continued to play on repeat outside.

The paper itched in her pocket. Where was Boy? She raced around, asking if anyone had seen him, but nobody had.

Jack and some others, who'd been lookouts on the rooftops, ran into the orphanage.

"They're moving the Committee and scientists into the stands," Jack panted. "Edward and George are there too but I haven't seen Arnold or Powick yet! We need to go now!"

Suddenly everything started to happen. Violet was pushed into place in the front row behind the second hoarding; the first group contained the sharpshooters. Somebody in her pack started to hiss, "*One, two, one, two,*" and they moved like a centipede out through the double doors and down Forgotten Road. Violet's head was frazzled as she looked behind her for Boy. But she couldn't spot him anywhere and nearly tripped over herself trying. She had to concentrate or she'd ruin the plan for everyone.

Their first obstacle was the group of Watchers stationed on Rag Lane. Everyone stopped and allowed Mr Hatchet and a small bunch of other Townsfolk to sneak up and take the guards by surprise. They tied and gagged the men, then as swiftly as possible locked them inside a home on Forgotten Road.

The coast was clear as they left No-Man's-Land.

The groups stopped at the corner of Archers' Avenue and took great care working their way onto Edward Street. The slow, serene music still wafted eerily through the air. Violet shivered. The crowd shifted uneasily behind her.

Watchers lined the edges of the Town Hall, the arches of which were concealed by drawn red-velvet curtains. Over the canopy, hanging from the roof was a huge sign which read *Arnold Archer's Greatest Show on Earth: The DeathDefier*. It was rimmed in white bulbs, their halo glow in the early morning the only electric light on the streets.

Violet's heartbeat hammered in her ears as her group stopped just short of the tea shop. She glanced out past the hoarding that concealed them. The small stand was half full now. The scientists sat in the front row. George and a group of Watchers seemed anxious and were questioning them with what looked to be bully tactics – it seemed as though they had only recently discovered one of the five was missing.

"I do hope they don't rough them up too much," Joseph Bohr whispered to Iris, both just across from Violet in the front row.

Iris grabbed the old man's hand, squeezing his frail fingers.

Behind the scientists were Town's Committee. Violet

scanned the faces and spotted her parents. Her mum held firm to Violet's dad's elbow. William wasn't there.

The atmosphere was fuelled, like a kettle about to boil. A lump rose in her throat. How long was it since she'd last seen Boy?

She reached into her pocket for the page on Divided Souls but when she pulled it out a small folded piece of notepaper came too. Curious, she unfolded it.

The paper was worn and dirty crease marks stained the once white page. Tears welled at the edges of her eyes as she read the note. She remembered how Boy had carried it the first time she'd met him, how it was his prized possession. How he thought it had come from his mam though he was never really sure, until the day he met Macula.

So you will never be invisible, it read in his mother's neat handwriting.

She felt sick. Boy would never give this note away for no reason. What had he done?

CHAPTER 35

POWICK'S POISON

"Have you seen Boy?" she whispered, turning around towards Jack.

"No, not for a while," he replied earnestly. "Is everything okay?"

"I found this in my pocket." She passed the note across. "I think he must have left it there for me. He's gone to rescue William, I know he has, and…" She hesitated.

"And what?"

"And Tom's going to kill him. He has to do it today, on their birthday – it's part of Powick's plan!" Violet's voice trembled as the words spun out of her mouth.

She reached into her other pocket and handed over the page describing the Divided Soul. Jack scanned it, then turned over the paper and read the back before looking up.

"But this is madness, Violet, it's crazy!"

"Yes, but that doesn't matter! Powick believes it and so does Tom. It's all she's ever told him. It's why she took him from the orphanage. It all makes a weird kind of sense now, Jack. She thinks Tom is the twin who can raise the dead and make Arnold great again. But if it's to look like Arnold's machine actually worked, then Tom needs to kill Boy before Hugo steps out of the DeathDefier so he can be given some of that Elixir—"

A thought hit her.

"My parents, the Committee..." She looked over at the stand. "They might know where William's been taken."

"But they're surrounded by Watchers, Violet..."

"Not completely," she said, checking the street.

Without another word, Violet slipped from behind the hoarding and ran for cover under the stand. The structure was held together with lots of metal bars which were easy to scale if she didn't look down. Then she clambered over the top to the empty back row of seating, ducking just as one of the Watchers glanced up towards her.

Slowly she snaked her way down until she was just behind her parents.

"Mam, Dad," she hissed, "don't turn around."

"Violet!" her mother squealed before Eugene pinched her arm.

Her mother twitched then sat stiff and motionless as she forced herself not to glance over her shoulder.

"Violet, you're okay!" her dad whispered, relieved, staring straight ahead.

"Do you know where they took William? Boy is missing and I need to find him. I think he's gone to save William, but if Powick catches him she's going to kill him, Dad!"

"What...?" Rose gasped, almost swivelling round before Eugene stopped her.

"They took him to the Town Hall, Violet. I think I heard them mention the dungeons." Her father spoke quickly.

"Thanks, Dad." She paused, ready to slip away before she could be spotted. "We're fighting back, the plan's still in place!"

"Be careful, pet..." Rose quivered as Violet disappeared up the steps.

She was just climbing out over the back seats when the music changed to a drum roll. The sound beat through the air, mimicking Violet's racing heart.

Turning quickly, she caught sight of George Archer ducking inside the Brain. All the eye plants then stood to order and looked towards the front of the stage, where Edward Archer pranced out from behind one of the red-velvet curtains.

"Welcome one and welcome all to the 'Greatest Show on Earth'!" he announced.

Suddenly the stand began to vibrate. Everyone was panicking as they held on to each other. Violet gripped a seat as the vibrations grew deeper and the structure started to rattle. One of the Committee members jumped up screaming then stumbled backwards, pointing down Edward Street to where an orange glow filled the horizon.

The vibrations deepened even further. The curtains in the Town Hall shook like waves and the stand was now rocking from side to side.

Violet squinted; the glow grew brighter until she could just make out masses of flaming torches at the bottom of the road. They seemed to be streaming out from Archer and Brown and advancing towards them.

An otherworldly roar cut the morning sky.

Edward Archer danced around the stage, growing more excited as his audience became frantic.

Violet retched, petrified, as the creatures slowly came into focus.

Hundreds of Powick's zombies pounded the cobblestones towards them. Some tossed their heads from side to side, biting on the air; others dragged and lunged forward, clawing at the sky. Their eyes locked on the audience in the stands as they marched closer.

Becoming more frenzied, they drooled and snarled, snapping like rabid dogs looking at their dinner.

Suddenly they stopped and the sea of undead creatures parted.

A small, stout figure moved up through the path created; an animal on a leash limped at his side while a large zombie loomed behind him.

Silence engulfed Edward Street. Violet was shaking.

Arnold Archer stopped at the front of his army, just short of the Brain. Standing at one side of him was what must once have been a large chocolate brown Labrador dog and behind them was Hugo, the Child Snatcher. The animal was missing half its tail and two of its legs were eaten down to the bone. Its coat was caked in dirt, drool dripped from its gaping mouth and a steel frame, just like the ones on Powick's zombies, traced its stitched-together body.

"That's Arnold, his family dog! The one he used when he first revealed his machine all those years ago in Hegel! This man is crazy!" Magnus, one of the scientists, gasped as he gripped his colleague beside him.

"You've heard of the living dead, now watch the dead live!" Arnold Archer roared as he threw his arms into the air and the zombies stomped into line, closing the gap behind him. Then the creatures thrust back their heads and screeched into the skies. The sound cut through

Violet as she shut her eyes and prayed that none of this was happening.

They'd never beat them, not an army this size, she thought, doubting their plan. Her head spun in desperation. She needed to concentrate – if she couldn't save Town, at least she could save Boy. They could all escape and find somewhere else to call home.

"You've met my army, now meet my machine," Arnold announced. "This is a new dawn, where man no longer fears death. With my science, we will rule it!"

On cue, the red velvet curtains zipped back, revealing the DeathDefier in the middle of the Town Hall stage. Arnold strode confidently up the steps, his dead dog by his side, then turned to the zombies.

"Dr Hugo Spinners, come forward."

The Child Snatcher stomped heavily up to Arnold.

"Hugo!" Teresa, the orange-haired scientist, screamed from the stands, distraught, as her colleagues held her back.

Violet couldn't look away as Arnold beckoned his son Edward forward and a pale-faced Watcher handed them both white coats, just like the ones her dad wore in his lab. Then Edward wheeled a large stainless-steel table out from inside the Town Hall over to Hugo.

The zombie stood still as Arnold turned to address his audience once more.

"The creatures before you are dead. They can only

move using my metal walking frame and the power of battery. They have no consciousness and cannot think for themselves outside of their programming." Arnold pointed to a small black box at the back of Hugo's head. "Let me demonstrate."

He ordered the Child Snatcher to lie on the steel table and, together with Edward, began to remove his metalwork. Each time a chunk came away, Arnold held up the freed limb and let it fall back down, limp. It sent a chill through Violet. Hugo now appeared more human, more dead.

Her stomach queasy, she turned away.

Time was running short. She looked across the stage. From this angle it seemed as if the door into the Town Hall was open. A bunch of Watchers stood nearby, engrossed in Arnold's gruesome scene. She crept over the back of the stand, shaking with nerves as she descended to the ground. She checked round and just saw Iris quickly poke her head out, checking the street, before disappearing again behind her invisible hoarding.

Violet waited until all eyes were on Arnold as, together with Edward, he lifted the limp and lifeless Hugo inside the glass tube of his machine and began to strap him to the human-shaped copper plate using thick leather belts.

Taking her chance, she snuck through the groups of

hidden Townspeople, up the steps, passed behind the gang of mesmerized Watchers and in the unlocked door of the Town Hall, closing it gently behind her. The place was quiet except for the mumbles that floated through from outside.

A strange hum found her ears; low at first, it grew louder. Someone was chanting. The sound was rhythmic, the pitch rising and falling at regular intervals.

A door was hidden under the stairs – it led down to the ancient dungeons beneath the Town Hall where her dad said William had been taken. She'd never been down there before but it was where the Watchers were held after they'd been captured.

The door was black and metal with a small peephole hatch. Violet slid it open and the sound intensified. It was coming from the dungeons.

She pushed down on the cold handle – there was a small click and she held her breath, hoping the iron wouldn't squeak as she eased it open. A flaming torch mounted on the wall lit the darkness, casting shadows across the narrow spiral staircase before her.

She took a deep breath to steady her nerves, then put her hand against the right-hand wall and snuck down the steps.

The chanting stopped on a high-pitched finale as she reached the flagstone floor.

She was in a narrow passageway with a low vaulted ceiling. Her right shoulder almost touched the stone wall, which bore more flaming torches, while on her left was a row of iron-barred cells.

A strange purple light glowed in the half dark ahead. Violet inched forward.

Nurse Powick stood, arms wide, in the middle of a cell. Her head was cast back and the bottom of her cloak brushed the stone floor. She was standing in a ring of heaped white dust like table salt, whispering continuously. Outside this salt circle was a bigger ring of lit purple candles.

Tom stood behind her in the centre of his own smaller white circle. His hands were out and he was looking at the ceiling too, revealing his Adam's apple.

Strapped to the bars of the cell, his back to Violet, was Boy. Gagged, her friend groaned and mumbled as he struggled against his ropes.

Anger swelled inside her as she pulled back into hiding.

Suddenly the nurse stopped chanting and glared straight at Boy.

"I've called for help." Powick sounded different, lighter than normal. "The powers that govern this world and the next are swelling around us! Can't you feel them?" Her eyes were large and wild.

She bent down and lifted a purple velvet bag from the

floor. It was tied at the top with gold rope and from inside it her thick fingers took a tiny copper jug that looked to be decorated in delicate filigree.

"Tom!" the woman announced.

Boy's twin opened his eyes and looked forward. Violet disappeared further into the shadows – when suddenly something touched her ankle.

She startled, almost giving herself away. Fingers reached out from the bottom of the cell beside her. She squinted inside. William was lying on the ground, his hands strapped above his head, tied to the iron bars near her feet.

Violet glanced over at Powick. She was handing the ornate jug to Tom, both chanting something under their breaths. The sound made her shiver as she stepped across the path and into William's open cell. The ropes that clasped his wrists were tight, his skin red and raw from trying to force against them. Her fingers strained at the knots as she heard Powick hiss, "Once you've extinguished your brother, you'll steal his blood and the Elixir of Life will be ours. We'll master death, Tom! This is what we've been building to – this gift is your birthright! Your grandfather will be so proud!"

Violet worked frantically, tearing at William's ties.

She peered over as the nurse took a small brown medicine bottle from her pocket.

"The venom of a black widow – what a pretty way to die." The woman beamed.

She handed the small brown bottle to Tom as Boy fought against his restraints. Violet tried not to panic, pulling at William's ropes until the knots finally gave way.

Boy's dad climbed up from the ground, looking determined.

"Can you feel the energy, Tom? All combining for this very moment!" Powick was ecstatic.

Violet and William crept from the cell, hiding in the shadows as the nurse stepped out of her circle, ripping the tape from Boy's mouth.

"Don't do this, Tom!" his brother gasped.

"Shut up!" Powick snarled, slapping Boy's face.

He struggled, rattling the iron bars. Tom hesitated.

"Now!" the woman roared. "Arnold is waiting. There's no time to waste!"

"You said… You said that she abandoned me…just me…" Tom stuttered, his ice-blue eyes wide.

"What are you talking about? We haven't time for this now!" Powick cried as she wrestled Boy's mouth open.

"You said that she chose to rear him and not me, but Boy was in the orphanage too. I remember him, we both were… Mam gave both of us up!"

"There's no time for this!" the woman spat, her face flaming. "Pour the poison down his throat and claim what's yours, your gift! Your grandfather's waiting!" She grabbed Tom's arm and yanked him forward, forcing his hand towards Boy.

Still in the shadows, William whispered to Violet to untie Boy from outside once he'd distracted the nurse. Then he tiptoed forward.

"You're right, Tom, son," William announced, bursting into the cell. "Your mam gave both of you up because she loved you. She did it to save you, to protect you from my brothers." His voice shook and tears rimmed his eyes, but he was confident and strong – a different person to the dishevelled man Violet had first met on Wickham Terrace in the days of Perfect.

"What…how…?" Powick stuttered before quickly grabbing Tom's shoulder. "Concentrate!" she hissed.

Tom hesitated again, the bottle held millimetres from Boy's parted lips.

Violet started working desperately at her friend's bonds while they were all distracted by William.

"Don't listen to him," Powick snarled. "William comes here now just to save the twin he really loves, the one he actually calls his son. He's spinning lies. Myself and Arnold – we are your family. I'm the only mother you've ever known. Don't you want to please me? To please your grandfather? Don't let him steal this from us now. Claim your gift, Tom!"

Violet's fingers released the final knot holding Boy's arms and her friend ducked down away from his brother just as William lurched across the space, knocking Powick aside. The older man wrestled the nurse to the floor while Violet undid Boy's ankles and raced into the cell. She dragged her dazed friend upright as William hurriedly tied Powick to the iron railings. Tom stood motionless in the mayhem, the nurse's poison still in his grasp.

"Come with us," William pleaded to his silent son.

Tom backed away, locking eyes with his father. He seemed scared and uncertain.

"You're my son!" Powick screamed as she struggled against her restraints. "Free me, this is our moment. It has to be now, Tom, now!"

"William, we have to leave, the others need us!" Violet shouted, helping Boy out into the narrow passageway.

William grabbed Tom by the arm and forced him out.

"Tom, son! Don't leave me here!" The nurse's screams echoed as Violet reached the top of the spiralling dungeon steps, the other three in her wake.

CHAPTER 36

THE SACRIFICE

The foursome broke out onto the stage of the Town Hall as the DeathDefier rattled and shook in front of them. Inside the glass tube, Dr Hugo Spinners was strapped to the copper plate, his body dancing to the uneven beat of the machine. His eye-plant eyes were closed as blue darts of electricity zapped around inside the glass. The hair on Violet's arms rose in the electrified air.

The crowd in the stands watched, mouths open as if catching flies, while the Watchers inched closer to the machine, trying to get a better glimpse of the strange happenings.

"What is going on?" Arnold Archer demanded, spotting William, Violet, Boy and Tom onstage.

Tom stumbled backwards as if afraid of his grandfather.

"Where is she, where's Priscilla?" the old man roared. "That Boy, he shouldn't be here! What's going on, Tom? Where is my elixir!?"

Violet looked to her left where she knew the Townsfolk to be. She just caught sight of Jack's head floating in mid-air, the rest of him concealed, like almost all of Town, behind Iris's invisible silk hoardings.

"Jack, what's happened to Billy's group? They need to fire now!" she thundered, pointing at Arnold's vibrating machine.

Violet spun around as Powick broke out of the Town Hall door behind them, screaming for someone to grab Boy.

Suddenly the first hoarding dropped, revealing Iris's group, ready for battle. They wielded their weapons and charged forward.

"Leave my grandsons alone!" the old woman cried, leading the advance.

Then all along Edward Street, ahead of schedule, the hoardings fell and the Townspeople charged at the Town Hall.

Quick to respond to the onslaught, the nurse raced to the edge of the stage and faced her zombie army.

"My creatures," she screamed, "we can still rescue this day. Attack!"

A loud and unnatural growl filled the street as the zombies stomped their feet, then the whole army crouched down like cats ready to pounce. Their eyes locked on the Townspeople, drool dripped from their quivering lips and they launched forward, their metal frames propelling them powerfully over the cobbles. The clash of flesh and weapons cracked across the early morning.

The shocked Watchers took a while to wake up to what was happening, and only moved hastily towards the battle when Arnold started to roar at them.

"Billy, now!" Violet yelled, as a zombie lurched hungrily for her.

She ducked aside and sprinted down the steps to where the small group of slingshot sharpshooters were frozen in panic in the middle of Edward Street.

"We can't...can't get a..." Billy stammered, stunned by the scene around him.

The Committee and scientists had rallied now – having broken free of the stands, they were also in the thick of the action. Madeleine Nunn battled a crazed creature just metres away. The zombie was gnawing for her neck as she tried to break free of its clawed grip.

Violet grabbed Billy's shoulders and shook him. "Forget everything else, Billy. You can do this! For Town, for your family – you don't want to be an orphan again, do you?" The words slipped out as the zombies and

Watchers overwhelmed the people around them.

Something in the boy's face changed. He turned to his small group of scared friends and pointed through the mayhem to the DeathDefier. The machine was still surging energy through Hugo, smoke fizzling from the Child Snatcher's skin, and a burning smell swept through the air.

"Take aim!" Billy Bobbins roared, his eyes now locked on the glass tube.

Each of the team pulled back their thick elastic bands, wrapped taut around Y-shaped pieces of wood. Small arms shivered under the strain as they secured large stones in the launch pockets.

"Fire!" Billy thundered.

A shower of heavy rocks whizzed through the air towards the glass cylinder. Some smacked off the shoulders and shins of those who battled, but most hit their target, cracking against the glass.

Nothing happened.

Powick's creatures still overpowered everyone around them. Arnold Archer stepped out from behind the DeathDefier and pointed to the small band of boys.

"Stop them, Prissy!" he roared. "They're trying to break my machine!"

Panicked, Violet raced forwards towards the machine, looking for anything that'd crack the glass.

"Take aim!" Billy shouted again, undeterred. "Fire!"

Another flurry of rocks zipped through the air – and this time they all smashed through their target.

"No!" Arnold bellowed as the tube exploded.

Shards of glass scattered through the sky. Violet ducked, shielding her head as tiny fragments skewered her skin.

A blast of air surged like a giant wave through the street, the power so strong it knocked everyone off their feet. A deep rumble and boom shook the skies and the buildings vibrated around them.

Violet tried to stand but was knocked roughly to the ground by a zombie soaring above her. The creature thrashed against the invisible force that sucked it onto the exposed metal plate of Arnold Archer's machine. Now the morning sky was black with Powick's army as they were pulled, like a swarm of stinky flies, towards the DeathDefier. Other things flew through the air too, bits of jewellery, bikes, tin cans and all sorts of metal were attaching to the pile-up. A huge creaking sound then filled the skies and Violet watched, terrified, as parts of the viewing stand began to break apart under the pull of the powerful magnet.

"It worked, it worked!" Billy and his boys celebrated, jumping round as the zombies piled up under the canopy of the Town Hall.

Though the battle had evened out, it wasn't over. The streets were still frenzied as Townsfolk fought fiercely against the Watchers.

Powick wrestled Boy to the ground a few metres away just outside the tea shop by the Town Hall. Iris, hit by a flying zombie, was sprawled out by the steps, unconscious beside them. Arnold Archer had Tom by the wrist and was dragging him over to his brother, the medicine bottle still in his grasp.

Violet struggled up onto her feet as she tried to race to help her friend. Her back seared in pain and she stumbled forward onto her knees.

Powick was now straddling Boy, her face crazed as she pinned him to the ground. He tried to struggle free, but the woman was too strong. She forced open his mouth as Arnold flung Tom onto his knees beside his twin, shoving the poison bottle towards Boy's parted lips.

"You will take your brother's life!" The old man shook with rage.

Tom struggled for a moment, then suddenly stopped and looked straight at his grandfather.

"Okay," he said calmly, pulling his arm away, "I'll do it! I want to claim my gift. I'll do what's right."

"I knew you'd see sense." Arnold smiled.

The old man relaxed his hold. Then Tom bent forward over his brother's face and whispered something into his ear, before opening the small brown medicine bottle.

"No," Violet screamed, crawling across the ground towards them.

"You're a good child," Powick eagerly encouraged him.

Tom looked at the nurse and Arnold, then turned, smiled sadly at Violet, threw his head back and drank the poison.

"No!" Violet and Powick cried in unison now.

Forgetting her pain, Violet forced her injured body across the cobbles and up onto Arnold Archer's back. Fury raged inside her as she pounded her fists wildly on the man.

"Get off me!" Arnold cried.

She held firm, like a rodeo rider, as he flung his weight around, trying to knock her off. Powick grabbed her ankles just as Violet noticed Iris Archer was back on her feet. The old woman threw herself at the nurse, knocking Powick aside.

"You won't touch any of my family again!" Iris roared, gripping a sturdy red plastic bar which appeared to have once been the arm of a seat from the now-mangled viewing stand.

Priscilla Powick was stumbling up from the ground when Boy's grandmother crashed the weapon down on the nurse's back, flattening her to the cold stone.

"And as for you!" Iris locked eyes with her ex-husband.

She lifted her makeshift baton again, nodding at Violet to untangle herself from the man. "What were you thinking, Arnold? Why didn't you just leave us alone? Let us live here in peace?"

Violet jumped off the man's back and stepped behind Iris. She looked around for Boy and Tom but couldn't see them anywhere.

"This is all your own making, Iris!" he growled. "You never believed in my greatness. A wife should support her husband, not work to destroy him!"

"Destroy you?" she spat, still holding the metal bar aloft. "You did that yourself! You tried to meddle with life and death. Some things are not yours to control, Arnold!"

"I am the greatest mind that ever lived, but you couldn't accept that, could you? Jealousy ate you up and then you bore me that child who ruined everything!"

"That child! William? He's your son, Arnold!"

"A cursed child. Oh you relished it while he tore down my career and our family's future."

"He was just an infant! You showed your madness to the world, you destroyed your own future, Arnold!"

"My madness? You tried to kill me, Iris, don't you remember?"

"Of course I do. It's a pity I didn't succeed."

"That tunnel you dropped me into was an opportunity

– it led me to the Outskirts. It seemed fitting. All the greatest of minds are outsiders! The world conspired to help me, even when you didn't. The world could see my greatness. Priscilla showed me that!"

"So you plotted out there for years with that woman?"

"Prissy believed in me, Iris, even when she worked for Spinners. She knew I was meant for great things. When I called on her again, she came running, just like any good woman should!"

"And you both plotted for this fiasco?"

"William, once my curse, became my blessing. I told you the world conspired to help me – the Divided Soul spawned twins. I couldn't believe my luck when I saw the babies."

"So it was you! You were the man who visited Macula the night she gave up the boys?"

"Oh, I spied on you all with interest as my sons created Perfect. I was curious about their plans for a while, until I saw her belly grow. She thought she was hiding it from the world, the foolish woman. When she bore twins… well, Iris, you wouldn't believe the celebrations Prissy and I had when I told her. The curse of the Divided Soul was split and what was my failing could become my fortune."

Violet remembered Macula telling her and Jack that story after they'd found the picture of Boy and Tom in the orphanage. So Macula's mysterious visitor had been Arnold after all. He'd been plotting this since before the twins were born.

"My machine, though I tried hard to perfect it, never fully worked – beating death eluded me – but this, this was my chance," Arnold continued. "Nobody had to know about the elixir, everyone would believe my DeathDefier worked and all of you who laughed at me would be sorry. Priscilla got a job in the orphanage and watched the twins. Tom displayed all the characteristics of the darker soul so she took him. We reared that boy to fulfil his destiny – on his thirteenth birthday he would kill his brother and claim his birthright, his gift, the Elixir of Life. It was going to revive my career, Iris, don't you see? I would be the greatest scientist that ever lived. I would defeat death!" he cried.

"Listen to yourself, Arnold. All of this madness, it exists only in your mind!"

"You're mocking me again, Iris. What have you done with yourself since you left me? You've turned stagnant. You've no ambition, you're no one! You're nothing!"

"I'm a mother, Arnold, and a grandmother and I am surrounded by love! You could have had that, you could have had it all."

"And live in a town called Adequate. What a perfect place for someone like you. Why try to be anything more,

Iris, when adequate is all you were ever born to be!"

"I'm happy with adequate. But this...this *sham* is your great moment, Arnold? How the world will laugh now!" She pointed to the eye plants, which were still broadcasting.

Arnold's fury burst like a blister. He stormed forward and wrenched the seat arm from Iris, overpowering her. The old man raised the weapon over his head and glared down at his ex-wife. Hatred washed through his face. Before she could think better of it, Violet jumped and grabbed onto the plastic, holding tight as she was lifted from the ground. Arnold swung viciously and slammed her small body against the tea-shop wall.

Violet groaned, her grip slipped and she fell to the ground.

Arnold snorted dismissively and turned back to Iris. "I finally get to see this out," he sneered. "If I can't master death, I can at least take your life!"

His face contorted and he swung savagely for his ex-wife.

Suddenly Arnold was hit from the side and tumbled backwards. The plastic baton flew from the old man's grasp, clattering to the ground by Violet's feet as William Archer wrestled his father to the floor, pinning down his wide frame.

"Hello, Dad!" he said as Arnold struggled against him.

Thinking quickly, Violet scrambled up, raced to the dungeons of the Town Hall and grabbed the ropes that had held previously held Boy, returning as fast as she could. She tied up Powick, who was still unconscious, as William bound his father's wrists and ankles. Iris hobbled across to them.

"I see you've met your son. He's all grown up now," she whispered, bending over Arnold. "Maybe you were right after all. It seems he was your curse!"

CHAPTER 37

BROTHERS

The battle was easing off. Edward and George had been captured and the Townsfolk, bruised and weary, were overpowering the Watchers. The immediate danger over, Violet looked around frantically for Boy and Tom, unwilling to think about what she'd witnessed earlier.

A pair of feet, cut short at the ankles, rested in the middle of Edward Street. Violet recognized the shoes. She raced over and reached blindly through the air until her hands fell on Iris's invisible silk.

She pulled back the cover.

Tom was lying in the road, his head on Boy's knees. His face was pale and gaunt. Boy looked up, cheeks and eyes red from his torrent of tears.

"I brought him here to get away from the fight. I thought I could save him, Violet... He's, he's..."

Violet looked down at Tom. His eyes were closed, rimmed with deep purple circles. His arms lay limp by his side.

"He drank it," Boy stuttered, the words stumbling out. "He swallowed Powick's poison. He...he saved me, Violet. He's gone. Just like Mam..."

The tears traced a path down his face as he looked up at his friend. He was willing her to say something, but Violet's mind was blank, her heart empty as she sank to her knees beside him.

"He told me he was going to take care of Mam and that I should stay here and take care of Dad. He said we'd see each other again. Then he drank the poison. I thought... I..."

Boy bowed his head; his shoulders shook as a wave of grief engulfed him.

"He saved me and all this time...all this time I thought he was... I remember him, Violet. I remember him now. It's just snippets, but I think I remember swapping beds and how, that night, when Powick came, I saw her take him, and I didn't go after her. I thought she'd come back, but she didn't, she...she took my brother. And now...and now he's gone."

Violet's tears spilled now too. She grabbed Boy's hand

and squeezed it tight. He was shaking, his face red with rage and sadness, as if he wanted to scream at the skies.

The battle was a distant hum. A shadow hovered over them. She looked up. Dad.

"What happened?" Eugene asked, urgency in his tone.

"Tom saved Boy," Violet mumbled, searching for words. "He saved him, Dad. He drank Powick's poison."

Everything went hazy then. Later, she remembered people standing around them, her dad lifting Tom's body from the cold stone. She remembered her mam as she pulled Boy close under her arm, one of Violet's favourite places, and walked him to Iris's. She remembered the soup and the bread and how she couldn't stomach any of it. She remembered how Anna held tight to Boy's arm and how Jack never left his side. She remembered the hushed tones and lowered voices and William's face. And she remembered her bed and how her soft sheets felt like lead.

CHAPTER 38

UNITEA

Violet walked up past the school where a zombie had just finished cleaning the yard. She was getting used to seeing the creatures around now. Most people had one in their homes to help with odd jobs, but the Browns hadn't got a zombie yet – all three felt it was just a little too creepy.

She carried a bunch of flowers. The evenings were getting shorter now and there was a bite in the air, but the sun still warmed her back like one of her dad's hugs. She pushed open the graveyard gate.

He was sitting in his usual place, easy to spot as she walked down the wood-chipped path and plonked on the bench nearest the grave. She waited, not wanting to disturb him.

After a few minutes he walked over and sat beside her.

"It's nice here, isn't it?"

She nodded. An easy silence spread out between them.

"I suppose if you have to be buried somewhere, I'd like here," Violet replied after a while, watching the last of the butterflies and bees swarm round the flowers that hugged the walls of Town's graveyard.

"Are they for Mam?" He gestured at her flowers.

"Yeah." She smiled. "Grown specially. My mam said Macula loved wildflowers!"

"I wish I knew more about her." He lowered his head, picking at some loose skin on his finger. "I wish I knew how she thought or the things she appreciated."

"But you did." Violet's voice was soft. "You knew how much she loved you. That's all you ever need to know about mams. Oh and whether they can cook or not. Mine can't so I always pretend to eat and wait for Dad to cook something good when she's not looking. He doesn't tell Mam she's a bad cook, but she burns everything, even after all her classes. Dad says she should stick to the numbers!"

"Violet, you're very funny for a girl." Her friend smiled.

"Hey, what's that supposed to mean?" She elbowed him hard.

He laughed and silence surrounded them again. She watched the orange evening light seep across the sky.

"I saw her, you know." He broke the quiet. "When I was really sick."

"Saw who?" she asked.

"Mam."

"Oh…"

"I haven't told anyone else. She said she loved me and that I was a good son. She said she could take care of herself and that I should return to Dad and Boy, who needed me, and that she'd see us all again when it was our time. She seemed very happy, Violet. She said she was the happiest she'd ever been because her family had found each other."

"Was that when you were in a coma? Teresa said you might have strange dreams as your body came round. You were so lucky she's was one of the best toxi…tocic… whatever you call them in the world!"

Violet remembered that night – she'd probably never forget it. Her dad knew what each of Arnold's old Hegel friends specialized in and sought out Teresa straight away. It turned out black-widow venom had an antidote, but it was a long and scary wait to see if Tom woke up.

"Toxicologists, Violet!" He smiled. "And it wasn't a dream, it was real, it was magic."

"Do you believe in magic?" she asked, thinking about

William and Eugene and all the scientists she knew.

"Yes, it's everywhere," he replied, as though the answer were obvious. "Otherwise how do you explain life?"

Violet could think of a million ways her dad and the others would answer that question. They'd fill it with facts and numbers and weird equations and theories. But she also thought about what her mam or Macula might say, and about the feelings deep in her stomach and the wildflowers in her hand. She knew Tom was right. Magic was everywhere.

A large black bird swooped down from the skies and landed on the wall behind them. Boy's twin turned round to rub its glossy head.

Violet's eyes watered – happy tears. She looked away.

"It's okay," Tom laughed.

"What is?"

"Crying. I know you mask it from Boy at times, but I followed you, remember? I know you cry!"

"You stalked me, more like!" Violet joked, rubbing her eyes. "Anyway I wasn't hiding it! Mam said crying is a strength not a weakness. She wishes Dad cried more when he's sad. It's good for you, you know!"

"Hey, crybabies!" Boy laughed, pushing onto the bench, almost knocking Violet off. "Dad wants us, Tom – he's almost finished dismantling the Brain but he needs our help now linking the plants in the dungeons to the smaller control centre in the Committee room!"

"Oh, I'm meant to be helping with the eye plants too," Violet remembered, standing. "They're shipping them away to that hospital soon. Those things are disgusting – I'll be happy when they're gone!"

"They showed the world how crazy Arnold was though, didn't they? They helped catch Edward and George more than once too. And now they're being put all around the Town Hall dungeons, making sure Powick, Arnold, Edward, George and the Watchers never get out! If it wasn't for Eugene's plants, we might be living in Perfect again or, even worse, Zombie Town!" Boy joked.

"If it wasn't for me, you mean!" Violet teased.

"Anyway, think of all the people those eye plants will help to see again," Boy replied, ignoring her. "Your dad's transplants are going to be world famous!"

"One of the greatest minds alive according to Grandmother. She told me Joseph Bohr's informing everyone about Eugene! And he's all over the cover of *Eye Spy* magazine, they're calling him a *vision*ary!" Boy's twin added.

"Yeah, he's embarrassed – Dad said he can't take all the glory when William helped too!" Violet replied.

"Oh no." The twins laughed in unison – they were doing that sort of thing a lot lately.

"Our dad said Eugene can have all the praise! Archers have a bad track record with science." Boy snorted. "He said from now on, he's going to stick to making tea. It brings people together!"

THE END.

A LETTER FROM THE AUTHOR

Dear Boy and Violet,

I'm sitting here in the semi-dark having just finished the very last edits of your story. It's a weird time, happy and sad and strange all at once.

I won't see you both again, at least not in the same way. I mean we'll probably meet briefly in a classroom or a bookshop; maybe we'll even stumble into each other somewhere random like on a train or a bus – wouldn't that be nice? But we won't be together again, not really. I won't go to bed dreaming of how your day went, or reluctantly bring you to work or on holidays or to my yoga class (you always managed to disturb me even when I was desperately trying to be zen). I'll miss your random whispers in my ear, forever pulling me towards adventure.

You've been there for all my greatest memories, made me happier than you'll ever really know and dragged my aching heart through some of its toughest times.

And so in many ways I wish I didn't have to write this letter, but I know it's time to set you free.

You see I've planned another adventure and I really hope you'll take it up.

Will you go into the world for me, make new friends, ones more your age, and tell them something?

Will you tell them that they are special, that children are the most special people on this planet. Tell them that whether they are an orphan or a doctor's daughter, they can do anything. Make them believe that they are brave, braver and wiser than even they know, and that they should never hope to be normal – normal is boring. Make them understand the power of their imagination so they don't let anyone steal it – not even an Archer brother – as it will bring them everywhere.

And most importantly, Boy and Violet, please remember this bit the best… Tell them that no matter the situation or the size of the problem – whether it's a thousand zombies or a bad day at work – that they, our children, save us adults every single time. If you can tell them just that, you've done me proud.

I'll miss you two, so much.

Your loving friend,

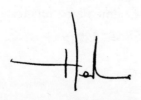

VIOLET NEVER WANTED TO MOVE
TO PERFECT. FIND OUT HOW ALL THE
TROUBLE BEGAN IN:

Winner of the 2018 Crimefest Book Awards
Best Crime Novel for Children (8-12)
Shortlisted for the Waterstones Children's Book Prize
and the Bord Gáis Irish Book Awards

BOY'S NOT BAD – IS HE?
LOOK OUT FOR VIOLET AND BOY'S SECOND
PERFECTLY CREEPY ADVENTURE:

Shortlisted for the An Post Irish Book Awards

"Wonderfully weird."
Sunday Express' S Magazine

IF YOU LOVE MYSTERY AND
ADVENTURE STORIES
GO TO:
USBORNE.COM/FICTION

🐦 @USBORNE
📷 @USBORNE_BOOKS
📘 FACEBOOK.COM/USBORNEPUBLISHING